Waterfront Rats

Peter H. Zindler

David Bauer Press
Las Vegas, Nevada

Waterfront Rats

For information, contact

David Bauer Press
826 E. Charleston Blvd.
Las Vegas, Nevada 89104

Cover art by Jeff Bedrick, San Rafael, California
Cover design and layout by Dunn and Associates, Hayward, Wisconsin
Text design and layout by Robert Goodman, Silvercat™, San Diego, California

ISBN 978-0-9797119-2-3

printed in the United States of America

To Him

For Him

With Him

There are many people that help an author in the process of writing a book. I would like to thank Ramona and Latrice for initially looking at the rough manuscript. My writer's critique group, Sharon, Gail, Edna, and Byron-you're the best and invaluable to the process.

Rick and Don, thanks for expertise in weaponry, tactics, and your skillful command of the English language.

Audrey thanks for your editing. Thanks Kathi for your expert help and your continued encouragement.

Vic, Dan, Corey, Rich, Jim, and Mike thanks for the critical reviews.

Merci, Johanna!

Lisa and Danielle your insight to life aboard a ship was invaluable.

Terance, I'm proud of you son!

Adrielle—you're Daddy's little precious!

Sweet, the love of my life—thanks for your faithful and skillful guidance in this book and life.

Author's Note

Now Sarai, Abram's wife, had borne him no children. But she had an Egyptian maidservant named Hagar; so she said to Abram, "The Lord has kept me from having children. Go sleep with my maidservant; perhaps I can build a family through her."

When Abram was ninety-years old, the Lord appeared to him and said, "I am God Almighty, walk before me and be blameless. I will confirm my covenant between me and you and will greatly increase your numbers.... No longer will you be called Abram; your name will be Abraham for I have made you the father of many nations.... As for Sarai your wife, you are no longer to call her Sarai; her name will be Sarah. I will bless her and will surely give you a son by her."

So Abraham had two sons, Ishmael and Isaac. One by the slave woman, Hagar, and one by his wife, Sarah. After the birth of Ishmael and before Isaac, Sarah became jealous of the slave woman, Hagar, and cast her into the desert of Beersheba.

God said to her, "Lift up the boy and take him by the hand, for I will bless him and make him fruitful and will greatly increase his numbers. He will be the father of twelve rulers and I will make him into a great nation."

Ishmael lived a hundred and thirty-seven years. He breathed his last and died. His descendants settled in an area from Havilah to Shur, near the border of Egypt, as you go to Asshur. And they lived in hostility toward all their brothers (excerpts from Genesis 16, 17, 21, 25).

These things may be taken figuratively, for the two women represent two covenants, two great nations that even today are at odds with each other.

Prologue

From the deep-sea fishing boat they watched the fiery launch of missiles. Their untended nets, dropped earlier in the day, hadn't caught anything. On the stern, hidden under a tarp, was a high-speed "Go Fast." Inside the forward cabin were two huge screens, with lights and figures flashing. Numbers changed as the frequency finder honed in on the transmissions broadcasted from the USS Sheboygan. Utilizing surface radar they plotted the course of the US Naval ship and its unmanned waterborne surveillance craft, Sea Flyer.

At dusk ten men went aft to the stern of the fishing boat and removed the tarp. Three of them climbed aboard the Go Fast as another operated the winch. Every defining line on the high-speed craft was modified so it was invisible to the Sheboygan's surface radar. In the boat were automatic weapons with thousands of rounds of ammunition and high-tech signal-jamming equipment.

After the boat was lowered into the water, the other men climbed aboard. The vessel swiftly took off and slipped in between Sea Flyer and Sheboygan and began jamming signals. Using a remote control they redirected Sea Flyer to the fishing boat. Once alongside the men boarded the unmanned reconnaissance vessel and quickly loaded it with the AK-47's, 9 mm Sig Sauer machine pistols, grenades, and plenty of ammunition. The transfer took less than fifteen minutes, and then the black clad terrorists climbed aboard. Working methodically they constructed a false bulkhead in the cabin, then directed the boat back toward the Sheboygan and stopped jamming the frequency so the ship could retrieve its recon craft.

1

Pacific Ocean off the coast
of southern California

"Pull the slack out of that line, you monkey!" the crusty old bosun yelled at the top of his lungs as the ship cut through the water at seven knots. Crow's feet etched the weathered skin around his cobalt blue eyes and left no mistake that he was "old school." Bosun "Boats" Browder didn't care for the newer, kinder, politically correct Navy, but the fresh ocean air and sea spray on his face was tonic to his bones. It quietly reminded him why he loved his job. He'd been in the Navy for thirty-five years and wasn't about to clean up his vocabulary for anybody. Strangely, nobody complained to the captain about him, because he knew his job and treated everyone fairly. "What are you ladies waiting for? Tighten that line up!"

Blue-gray dolphins surfed the ship's bow wave, darting back and forth. Suddenly two jumped out of the water and dove deep into the ocean and under the belly of the warship USS Sheboygan. The sea sparkled like dancing diamonds under the bright sun, while puffy white clouds traversed the sky like sheep heading to pasture.

"Put a turn on that bit!"

The seamen on the port side manned the steadying lines for the new eleven-meter life boat. They put their backs into the line and pulled it tight around a Sampson post. Farther aft a sailor put a lazy "s" around a two-horned bit as the ship's ready lifeboat was automatically being lowered into the water. This was the second time the new lifeboat davit was being used. The weight and operational tests had been executed flawlessly in the shipyard, but now the USS Sheboygan was at sea, and this was a training exercise for the crew. Ship's force hadn't been to sea for five months, and the day couldn't have been any better for the long-awaited venture.

Without warning the forward winch drum screamed, unexpectedly paying out its wire cable at high speed.

"Shut it down! Shut it down!" the bosun yelled.

In seconds the bow of the small lifeboat crashed fifteen feet into the choppy waves below, dumping the four sailors into the water. The last sailor's orange life vest caught a boat cleat as he hung momentarily before it was torn from his body. His head slammed into the steel sides of the ship and he went limp, plunging into the water.

"Man overboard! Man overboard!" Browder yelled into the radio mike, then kicked off his boots and dove into the water.

꙳

The ship's whistle droned six times.

"Full speed ahead! Hard left rudder!" Captain Davey ordered from the bridge wing fifty feet above the main deck. He grabbed the handrail and leaned out as far as possible, looking for any sign that his sailors had made it past the two screws chopping through the water. The ship hadn't taken on much ballast, so the propellers were slightly exposed.

"Man overboard, port side," the Boatswain Mate of the Watch announced over the 1-MC, which broadcast to every space on USS Sheboygan. "This is not a drill. This will be a shipboard recovery. Submit muster reports to the Executive Officer on the bridge. The men have been in the water fifteen seconds."

Sailors spilled into the passageways, skipping over the knee knockers and running to their divisional quarters mustering stations. Two Search and Rescue (SAR) swimmers raced to the swim locker, stripped down, and slipped into wetsuits.

⌒

Browder plunged beneath the surface of the water, the cold water instantly snapping his skin. Immediately he opened his eyes to look for the unconscious sailor. Precious seconds raced by, and still he hadn't spotted him. He kept swimming underwater alongside the ship.

Thump, thump, thump came the rumbling rhythm of the twin propellers, steadily sucking the unconscious sailor toward the vortex of the churning blades waiting with mechanical coldness to chop him into shark bait.

Bosun kicked with his feet and pulled water for all he was worth. His years of ocean swimming and conditioning paid off as he saw the sailor, unmoving, drifting back to certain death. Again he kicked with all his might as he saw the man slip beneath the curve of the hull, being drawn by the suction of the propeller blades in the water.

Thump, thump, thump. The reverberation of the propellers sounded much louder as he pulled closer to the keel with each pulse of the massive bronze blades. Time was running out, and certain death awaited them.

Undeterred he lunged forward and reached for the motionless sailor suspended over seventy fathoms of water with blank button eyes staring out at the gray hull. Hooking an underwater padeye with one foot, he missed the sailor's collar by inches. Diving under the belly of the ship was suicide, but the only other choice was to let his crewmember be disemboweled and scattered across Davey Jones' locker. Boats could not let the young sailor be turned into chum for seagulls. Panic grabbed his lungs as the air expired and burned to be refreshed. Committed, Bosun swam further down the curve of the stern toward the keel, knowing that it was a chance in a million they would clear the rotating propeller blades. He reached again and finally grabbed him by the collar, but it was too late. The swirling vortex to the underwater meat grinder had them firmly in its grasp.

No matter how hard he swam, they kept getting sucked into the eye of the port propeller. If he could just hit the side of the propeller housing, they might be able to drift on by, but the water's pull was too great. He turned as the shiny blades got bigger and bigger, louder and louder. *Thump. Thump. Thump.*

Just as Boats saw his life pass before him, the blades stopped. The engineers must have secured the shafts, but they might start them up at any time to execute the Williamson Turn to return the ship to the spot where the sailors went into the water. Swimming quickly, Boats and his unconscious companion passed the propeller blades. When the bosun looked up, he saw sunlight through the ocean water, but if the propellers began rotating in reverse pitch, they'd get sucked back down. He was completely out of breath. Just as he was about to break the surface, the ship's screws began turning again, and he felt the pull of the propellers. With lungs afire, he used his last bit of energy to kick and pull himself and the unconscious man to the surface. Finally he broke the watery plane and gulped a huge breath of air.

How he'd survived the screws he didn't know, but God had spared him again. He looked at the unconscious sailor and knew what had to be done. Grabbing the man by the stomach, he gave a quick thrust to his belly to clear the water from his lungs. Foamy water spilled from his lips with partially digested remnants of his breakfast. Boats wiped the young sailor's mouth and began breathing into it, while barely holding the man's nose shut and treading water to keep afloat.

⌒

"Have you spotted them?" the captain asked over the sound-powered phone to the lookout.

"No, Sir. The wind is kicking up and there's a big swell."

"Are the swimmers ready?" the captain asked the First Lieutenant.

"Yes, Captain, but with the davit out of commission, how do you want to launch and retrieve? You do know the bosun dove over the side?"

"What?" Davey exclaimed. "That's against regulations. Why did he do that?"

"One of the guys lost his lifejacket and hit the side of the ship pretty hard."

"I'll deal with him later. Rig the J-bar davit for a forecastle recovery, and when we complete the maneuver we'll be close to the spot where they went into the water."

"Aye, aye, Captain. Let's hope they made it."

"I see something! Three orange dots off the starboard bow," the excited lookout radioed from the signal bridge.

"Maggie, take the conn," the captain ordered to his executive officer (XO) as he left the bridge and hurried down to the forecastle. "Make a hole," the captain yelled to the sailors who had gathered on the starboard side as he ran to the forward-most part of the ship. Three bright orange dots bobbed up and down, disappearing and then reappearing between the ocean swells in the distance. A surge of relief filled his heart, but where were the other two?

"First, get the SAR swimmers lowered into the water. Make sure Doc and the corpsmen are standing by."

"Aye, aye, Captain," the First Lieutenant replied, as he grabbed his wireless side phone from its belt holder and quickly punched in the number for the ship's doctor. "Doc, get your medical team to the forecastle ASAP."

With binoculars raised to his eyes, Captain Davey slowly and carefully scanned the open water. Where were the bosun and the other sailor? He didn't want to go aft and see if there was blood in the water.

"Captain, we've completed the turn, and I think we should reverse the engines and stop the ship's headway," Maggie suggested over the radio.

The captain knew it would take over a quarter of a mile for the ship to come to a complete stop. "Very well. Make it so."

"All engines back one-third," Maggie ordered to the lee helmsman. The sailor behind the ship's wheel repeated the order and immediately pulled back the shiny chrome levers on the engine order telegraph (EOT), ringing up one-third astern. Down below in main control, the engineers watched, as the temperatures and firing pressures of the engines automatically increased as the diesels sped up. Engine alarms went off momentarily, as operating parameters changed dramatically.

"All back two-thirds!" Captain Davey ordered from the forecastle while looking through his binoculars. The engines immediately responded and the ship began going astern.

⌐

"There's the bosun!" one of the sailors yelled jubilantly, having spotted the two bobbing up and down on the port side of the ship.

"Make the lines up and get the swimmers in the water, First," the captain ordered.

The Chief and the others quickly secured the lowering lines for the harness to the cleat on the bow's deck that looked like a pair of steel bullhorns welded to the deck.

The swimmers attached themselves to the lowering harness, walked to the ship's edge, and jumped.

"Ease the line out, lads, and put another turn around that cleat," the chief ordered. "Move behind the elephant toes as you lower the swimmers."

"Take your time! Careful!" the First thundered, as the first SAR swimmer was lowered twenty-five feet into the water, using the J-Bar davit and pulley. The swimmer released himself and with powerful strokes began moving toward the bosun and the sailor in the water. The crew lowered the other swimmer to the waterline, and everyone on deck manned the rails, watching the rescue. The ship drifted closer and closer, as the swimmers reached their fellow crewmen.

The First looked over the side. "Lower the retrieving apparatus." A vertical type stretcher was lowered to the water line. The injured sailor was harnessed and brought up the side of the ship.

"Heave to!" he called out, as a line of sailors, pulling in unison, raised the injured sailor to the forecastle. The Corpsmen grasped the stretcher and pulled him aboard. They quickly gave him oxygen and helped him out of the stretcher's restraints.

"Son, are you all right?" the captain asked. He got no response, but the sailor's clouded eyes stared forward into the space between life and death. "Take him to medical."

The ship's company lowered the retrieving apparatus four more times, bringing up the bosun and the others who had fallen into the water. Finally the deck crew brought the SAR swimmers back aboard.

Bosun stood barefoot in a growing puddle of water. "Was he breathing?"

"Yes, but that's not the way we retrieve a man who's gone overboard."

"Yes, Sir, Captain. Sorry, Sir."

"Doc, take the others to medical and check them out," the captain ordered, looking at each of them as if they were his own children and then turning to the bosun. The doc and his team carefully escorted the rescued sailors to the medical ward to treat any injury they might have sustained when they went over the side.

"What went wrong with that davit? And what in the world were you doing? You more than anyone know the procedure for shipboard recovery."

"Yes, Sir, I do, but he hit the side of the ship so hard it knocked him out, and I knew the propellers would get him if he went under the water."

The captain looked at him for a long moment.

"That's right, sir," the chief added. "And he lost his life vest."

"I'll address that later; now what happened to the davit?"

"I don't know. We had the wires rigged correctly, but suddenly that forward winch let loose and paid out its cable in a hurry. We better call the port engineer and have him take a look at it when we're pier-side. I've heard on the East Coast they've had a lot of problems with this new-fangled davit."

"Boats, I don't know whether to cuss you for violating procedures or write you up for a Navy Cross."

"Captain, I was just doing my job."

"I want a full report of this incident on my desk by 1500, and retrieve the lifeboat using the davit's hand crank," the captain ordered. Turning to the SAR swimmers and the deck department, he said, "Great job! You all pulled together, even after a five-month shipyard period."

Then he looked directly at the two SAR swimmers. "I wish I could swim like the two of you, but I float like a rock."

2

32nd Street Naval Station San Diego, Pier 6

The cool crisp morning beckoned the port engineer to the foggy waterfront pier where he knew she'd be. The pungent smell of salt air brought back fond memories of time spent together. Her smooth curves were inviting to his eyes, and he never tired of looking at her. They'd been together for eighteen years and seen many changes. Although age had taken its toll, she hadn't lost a step; in fact, with the new automated bridge controls installed in the shipyard overhaul, she had even picked up an extra knot.

Hungry seagulls barked their morning calls as the USS Sheboygan's port engineer, Jake Markey, walked down the pier, dodging moving forklifts, oil drums, and boxes. A high-reach crane plucked the loaded wooden pallets from the pier and deposited them on the boat deck of the ship. At the bow, amidships, and stern, heavy Kevlar lines tied the USS Sheboygan to the pier. It had been three thousand years since the Phoenicians had sailed, yet the world over, sea-going vessels still used heavy mooring lines. Attached around each three-inch diameter line was a large round aluminum rat-guard that defended the ship against hungry rodents. Similar three-foot diameter metal guards were used by fleets around the globe to keep the rats from climbing up mooring lines, devouring ship's stores, and bringing deadly diseases aboard.

Barely awake, a forklift driver with reddened eyes slammed into a pallet loaded with boxes, causing them to spill onto the pier. Bosun Browder noticed the man's forks hadn't been low enough, and he figured the clumsy operator was probably hung over from a night of heavy drinking. "Open your bloodshot eyes, ya lazy buzzard, and watch what you're doing!"

The unshaven man wearing a dirty Hooters t-shirt slammed his tow-motor in park and shut off the propane-powered engine. With his big belly sagging over a wide leather belt, he eased off his machine, scowling from ear to ear and muttering obscenities. With angry eyes trained on Browder he approached.

Just as he was about to cuss him out, Browder pointed his finger in his face. "Get your fat butt back on that forklift and keep your mouth shut! Open your eyes and watch what you're doing. You see that man with the white hardhat over there? That's the port engineer, and one word from him to your foreman and you'll be toast by noon."

The forklift operator glared at Browder for a long moment, turned, again cursed under his breath, and grudgingly walked back to his tow-motor as Jake Markey, the port engineer, joined the bosun.

"What was all that about?" Jake asked.

Browder smiled brightly. "Oh, nothing. I just had me a little 'come to Jesus' talk with the clumsy oaf."

"Really? Did you get a convert?"

"Oh, you can count on that!"

Jake laughed and changed the subject. "I heard you had trouble with the new davit. What happened yesterday?"

"A little trouble!" the bosun repeated, glaring at Jake. "That fancy French davit ya'll installed in the yards let loose on the forward winch and dumped four of my sailors into the drink, that's what happened."

"Was anybody hurt?"

"No, thank God."

Jake raised his eyebrows. "I didn't know you were a believer."

"I became one fast when my lads tumbled into the water. I don't know how we missed getting sucked up in the props and being chopped to pieces. It was a miracle the blades stopped turning."

"Miracles do happen, Boats."

The bosun grunted, and the port engineer followed him up the gangway to the main deck and then went to Captain Davey's cabin and knocked on the open doorframe. He was hunched over his computer, reading his morning message traffic. He was a tall man, with wide shoulders and a thick, weightlifter's chest. He'd played starting linebacker for the University of Wisconsin football team before joining the Navy, and he still looked like he could strap it on.

The "old man" looked up. "Bosun, Jake, come in. Thanks for coming so early." The captain was only forty, but every Commanding Officer was called the "old man," regardless of age.

The two men walked into the CO's office, which had an adjoining stateroom.

"Have a seat, guys. You want some coffee?"

"Sure, Captain," Jake replied.

The CO reached over and pushed a button. Twenty seconds later a neatly dressed messman came in with a silver coffee pot and four china cups on a highly polished silver tray. Before leaving the office he poured a cup of coffee for everyone, and the strong smell of navy coffee filled the air.

"Jake, I've filed a casualty report on this new davit. Good thing no one was hurt or we'd have a full JAG investigation on our hands. When do you think you can get the manufacturer's rep out here to take a look at it?"

"I don't know, Captain. As you recall, after the weight test in the shipyard the tech rep quickly headed back to France."

"I can see why," Boats interjected. "This davit is way too complicated for us. Shoot, why do I need a computer equipped with an air conditioner hooked up to the davit?"

"I know what you mean," Jake agreed. "The old davit had only one motor, a counterweight, and a controller. Simple. Now we've got seven motors, four hydraulic pumps, yards of high-pressure piping, electronics, air-conditioning, and a computer. Whoever sold this to the Navy must not have gone to sea. This is over-designed, and it's going be a maintenance nightmare. I wonder what the big elephants in Crystal City were thinking."

"Jake, those designers need to take a trip to sea once in awhile. Look where they've installed the electrical controller. It's right aft of the house outboard so the sea spray whipping around the superstructure blankets it with salt. How absurd."

"Maybe that's why the davit failed," the bosun said, venting his own frustrations. "I need a tech rep out here right away to tell me why that winch failed and what to do to fix it. We've started an intense training cycle with workups before deployment, so I need my davit operational. I don't have time to waste."

"I'll get right on it, but those tech reps are almost impossible to get on a moment's notice."

Boats nodded. "Thanks. Let me know what you find."

Captain Davey bore down on Jake. "Are we getting any more repair funds this quarter?"

"Are you kidding, Captain? The budgeteers reduced our maintenance money because of these new Shipview metrics. Their mantra is, 'We can do more with less.' We had a brief yesterday, and they're cutting all the budgets. I don't know how we're going to keep this ship operating if they keep reducing the maintenance dollars. I remember some bright young lieutenant telling us about all the money we'd save by using Shipview, but I hear the money for next year is even leaner. I've been a port engineer for twenty years, and I don't know why they're spending millions on these new accounting tools to help me do my job. I sure wish we could have that money for repairs. I have to brief these fancy metrics once a month, but I still haven't seen what these tools do to improve the readiness of our ship. I spend more and more time at my computer answering emails and inputting Maintenance Figures of Merit so a computer can tell me which job is more important. I wish one of those admirals would ride the deck plates to see what's really happening. In fact, I believe the readiness of the fleet is steadily declining. I just don't get it."

"You're not supposed to, Jake. That's just a way they can check up on you to see if you're doing your job."

"Don't start with me, Boats. Last week I bailed you out by repairing one of your winches, and you didn't even have a job in the system. Do you realize what the electronic police would do if they caught me improving the readiness of the ship by going around their new computer systems?"

"The Navy's changing, and you two better get aboard," the CO said sternly.

"But, Sir," Jake pleaded, "the shore-side infrastructure is being dramatically cut. There's a move to do away with all shore-side maintenance shops. The new teaming arrangement with the shipyards is driving repair costs through the overhead because there's no competition anymore. We're paying pass-through costs to two shipyards before the subcontractor even gets the job. The prime contractors are making millions without ever turning a wrench."

"We've got to do more with less," the captain said.

"Oh, come on, Captain! Big Navy is cutting crew sizes, training, shore-side shops, and decreasing budgets. The brass thinks by using private contractors it'll be cheaper, but in the long run it's going to cost more, not less. I'm telling you, there's a train wreck coming with ship repair and readiness."

"All right, Jake, quit bashing the admiral's Shipview's initiatives and get to work," the captain ordered.

Both men got up to leave, though the bosun knew the old man wasn't quite sold on the "new Navy" as he let on.

"Oh, one other thing, Jake," the captain said. "The chief engineer wanted to see you about a leaking valve. He said the supply system won't make any more for another six months, so you're going to have to use your connections on the waterfront to see if anybody has it on the back shelf."

"I can't do that, Captain; that's not in the new Shipview rules. I'm supposed to check the MFOM to see if this is a job that has a high enough priority. Then I put the job in for an estimate, and of course they have to write the specifications for repair. Then the shipyard proposes the job. Three weeks later, if we're lucky, we'll have a cost proposal, and then the contractor will tell me if there's a valve available."

"Cut the sarcasm!" the captain ordered. "Get the valve and we'll put it in ourselves."

"Roger that, Captain. I'll call around to the boiler shops on the waterfront and the salvage yards in Long Beach and see if anybody has one."

"Thanks. One last repair issue—if you get a chance, my chair on the bridge is a little wobbly. Some of the hardware wasn't put back after they replaced the deck covering."

﹏

Walking out of the captain's office, the port engineer headed to the chief engineer's stateroom. He too was busy looking at his computer, reading his morning message traffic.

"Hey, Larry, how're you doing?" Jake asked the CHENG.

"Boy, am I glad to see you," he replied, looking up at Jake. "I need a level-one valve in a hurry, and the Navy stock system said it wouldn't have any available for six months. I'm not sure they even make them anymore."

"That doesn't surprise me. When I sailed in the Merchant Marine, we carried all our spares onboard, but that's too logical for the Navy. So, what's wrong with the one in place?"

"It's blowing steam at the bonnet."

"I'll make some calls. What size is it?"

"It's a six-inch, high-pressure angle globe valve, and if we don't replace it we can't use the aft boiler next week. That could make it tight drinking water because the forward evaporator keeps tripping off line. I don't want to go on water hours. By the way, are you going to sea with us this time?"

"Are you kidding me? I can't wait to hot-bunk again."

"Jake, I promise that won't happen this time. We had a full complement of Marines and a bunch of midshipmen on the way back from Pearl Harbor. It couldn't be helped."

"The company that designed the davit isn't too cooperative either. We've paid over two million for the unit and its installation, and you'd think we get better service. I hear a ship on the East Coast has had the new davit for an entire year, and it's only been operational for three months."

"The politically correct brass in Washington need to stop purchasing equipment built overseas. What's wrong with built in the good old USA?"

"I hear ya, Jake. Don't forget, I need that valve. If you can locate one, I can have my guys go over and pick it up."

"I wish they'd make me Admiral for a day. I'd straighten out a thing or two with the supply system," Jake said walking away.

3

The White House, Washington D.C.

Vince Ryland, short in stature but fiery in personality, rose early in the morning and went to his desk in the Oval Office. He put on his reading glasses, and before he read the messages marked "Most Urgent" pulled out a well-worn leather book and began reading the Holy Scriptures. He knew he didn't have the wisdom to deal with all the different people and situations that were happening throughout the world without help from above. He finished his reading and said a prayer to help him through the day. Then he opened a top-secret message that had arrived while he was sleeping. His night secretary had put it on the top of the pile.

"Oh, my God," he whispered, as the impact of the printed words hit him. Immediately he snatched the phone from its cradle. "I want the Director of National Intelligence and the Chief of Naval Operations in my office immediately!"

Thirty minutes later a tall man in a dark business suit, along with the CNO, appeared in the Oval Office. President Ryland scarcely allowed time for greetings before drilling his minions.

"Are you telling me that we have somehow lost ten nuclear equipped Tomahawk missiles? How in the world is that possible? This isn't the Soviet Union!"

"Mr. President, I've initiated a full-scale investigation into the matter," William Stevens, the Director of National Intelligence, replied, as the sweat slid down the edge of his face even though it was the cool of the morning in America's capital. In 2004 his position had been created to coordinate all the intelligence agencies, and now he was being called on to earn his keep.

"Do you realize what this could mean?" the President questioned, the tension building in his voice. "Those missiles have nuclear warheads. They must be found immediately!"

"Yes, Sir. We're doing all we can. Military intelligence is cooperating with the National Joint Terrorism Task Force," the CNO added quickly, while standing at attention for the Commander-in-Chief of the world's foremost military.

"They'd better be, and they'd better be cooperating with each other or heads will roll. Do I make myself clear?"

"Perfectly, Sir," the CNO replied.

"Mr. President, we do have another preliminary report," Stevens interjected.

"Well, out with it."

The four-star admiral, seemingly jockeying for verbal position, cut in. "Three weeks ago we discovered a discrepancy in our accounting of the experimental Tomahawks. I had my aide fly out to Seal Beach, California, and check the accuracy of the figures."

"How long were they missing?" the President asked, turning his gaze from Stevens to the admiral and then pulling out a hanky so he could clear his sinuses. Years ago his nose had been permanently reshaped by a sharp right cross in a Marine Corp boxing ring, and every spring it caused him trouble.

"We don't know right now, but whoever did this knew how to move our warheads around without anyone else knowing about it."

"That's impossible! Marines guard those missiles when they're moved. This has to be an inside job."

"Exactly what we were thinking, Mr. President," the admiral continued. "Because of base closures and military downsizing, we riffed two old employees from Seal Beach Naval Weapons Station about a month ago. We investigated them both and found them missing."

"What do you mean, missing? I thought you said they were let go."

"Sir," Stevens quickly interjected, "we eventually found one of them at the morgue in Long Beach, and the other had flown to Rio de Janeiro. We checked his hotel in Rio, but he's disappeared. We have no further report of him, but we're still looking."

"What makes you suspect these two?"

"Both had over five hundred thousand dollars deposited in their bank accounts four weeks ago, just before their final day on the job."

"Sounds like a payoff. Have you talked to their families?"

"Can't. Neither one had any close relatives in the area."

"So I should suspect the worst?"

"Perhaps. We got a report from the Border Patrol. They caught what we believe is an al-Qaeda operative."

"This gets better all the time. Stevens, when were you going to tell me about this?

"This morning, Sir."

"I should hope so. Well, at least our efforts to keep terrorists from coming into our country is working."

"Not quite, Sir. The border patrol caught an al-Qaeda operative trying to sneak out of the country, and he had various photographs of military bases with him, especially the Naval Base in San Diego."

"Do you think the two are related?"

"I don't know. We haven't got much out of him. The Border Patrol is going to turn him over to us."

"Interrogate him and see if you can find out what his plans were," the President ordered, getting up abruptly and fixing his steel gray eyes on each of his subordinates. "Find those nuclear warheads! I don't care what it takes. I don't need to remind either of you that we're at war with these terrorists."

4

San Diego, California

"Abdullah, are you sure they're activating us?" Haviv asked his lifelong friend as they drove down Harbor Drive after working all day in the San Diego Shipyard. The two Arabs had grown up together in the Sinai desert and had helped in the overthrow of Yemen. Abdullah had a smudge of dirt on his face, and though his hands were clean, his fingernails had dirt under them from fitting the steel plate together before welding the seams. Heavy black eyebrows crouched against a hooknose gave him a terrifying countenance, especially when his quick temper raged.

"It's been twenty-six years since we've been in battle," Haviv continued. "I thought they must have forgotten about us. They didn't use us when they attacked the first time, and America has given us so much." He slammed on the brakes after being cut off by a young driver, automatically cursing him in Farsi.

"Haviv! Is that the way you want our parents to be remembered? Have you forgotten how the American dogs bombed our homes and killed our brothers and sisters? Have you forgotten how they support the Jews? Have you forgotten that our homeland is now under Jewish law?"

"No, no, Abdullah, I've not forgotten. But maybe Mohammed's way is wrong."

"Haviv!" Abdullah's face contorted with rage. "If you don't stop that kind of talk, I'll be forced to slit your throat and make a martyr of you."

31

"And who would guard your back, Abdullah? Who would you trust? I've bailed you out of jail twice, saved your job in the shipyard, and helped you with your son. If our leaders found out about your trouble, you'd be useless to the *jihad*."

"Could I stand by idly and let them call us ragheads? I've prayed for many years that the call would come and we would strike a mighty blow of vengeance. Finally, the time has come. *Hamdulillah,* may Allah be praised."

"It's been a long time," Haviv countered. "We have families now—families that don't even know who we really are or what we are. Over the years I've read the Koran, and the early writings of Mohammed tell of kindness. I have reservations about our militant movement to force others to become Muslims."

"You disgust me! Don't you remember when we fought alongside Osama bin Laden in Afghanistan? Living in America has made you soft, like a young boy. The great Satan, who gave the Jews planes and tanks to kill our children, must be destroyed! We will have our revenge after all these years to settle the score, to finally do our part in this *jihad*!"

"Look what America has done for us," Haviv said, as he pulled up into Abdullah's driveway in Carlsbad. "And what of our sons? Why must they be involved?"

"It's all part of the Light of Allah's plan. They must do their part in eliminating all infidels. Have you seen how many were killed when we attacked their towers of commerce in New York and their military complex in Washington? That plan was brilliant! This one is too. Only Allah himself could have inspired the new *Mujadid,* our Renewer. Again, I must warn you, old friend, if I hadn't fought with you many times, I'd slit your throat."

"Spare me," Haviv rebuked. "I know you are a true believer and a man of action, but I was only testing you."

For a moment Abdullah stared at Haviv, then he laughed and got out of the car. "Testing me? Testing me? Oh, that's rich, Haviv."

⌒

As Haviv drove away, he thought of the relationship he had shared with Abdullah. Twenty-six years ago the two of them had dodged the rolling sagebrush and darted past the roving spotlights that chased their shadows across the border between California and Mexico as they followed their *coyote* guide. Their long trek had started with their escape from the refugee camps of Lebanon, and then gone on to a remote desert camp in Saudi Arabia, where they met bin Laden as he was forming his organization. They fought at his side in Afghanistan against the Russians and were sent by ship to Costa Rica. Journeying up the Central American coast to Mexico City, they acquired new identities. With their Mediterranean features they could pass as being from Italy, France, or Spain. Both chose France as their European country of origin because they had learned French as part of their cover.

With their dark good looks, it wasn't difficult for them to acquire blue-eyed blondes for wives. Both had sons a year apart, and they had pushed them to get top grades. During the summer they took their boys to secret "wilderness camps" in Oregon. Upon graduation from high school, one boy entered the Naval Academy, the other West Point.

Abdullah and Haviv acquired trades in the apprentice program at the Long Beach Naval shipyard. Haviv, an expert in mathematics and simulations, could easily have become a systems engineer, but chose to work in a trade and eventually ended up as a computer programmer. Abdullah, a strong, physical man, liked to work with his hands and became a ship fitter. Both worked for the shipyard for ten years, and as part of the plan, moved to San Diego where there were more naval ships home-based. Quickly they both acquired jobs in new ship construction. Other than an occasional detonation of Abdullah's temper in the defense of his heritage, they had kept their noses clean—until now. Haviv could only wonder how life as they knew it was about to change...

5

USS Sheboygan, Pier 6, Naval Base San Diego

"Bosun, can you have a secure phone line set up for midnight tonight?" Jake asked as he opened his trusty notebook with numerous phone numbers in it. To be good at his job, he had to know whom to call to get something fixed at a moment's notice.

"Sure, but why?"

"The tech reps are flying in, and they want to download a new program from the factory in France to the lifeboat davit."

Boats stopped what he was doing and focused on the port engineer. "You mean to tell me we're going to tie up the International Maritime Satellite during the night to reprogram the lifeboat computer controls?"

"It appears that way. It's proprietary information, so the company won't give us the codes."

"Are you saying a United States Navy warship is going to be under the control of some Frog company?" The bosun's obvious shock and disapproval registered on his face, as well as in his words. "Aren't you concerned that the computer systems on the ship could be compromised? You know the French never supported us in the Iraqi war!"

"I know that. This global parts acquisition is part of a big plan to help our NATO allies, so they won't forget us when we need help."

Boats shook his head. "Since when has France been our ally? They opposed us going into Iraq."

"They did, but for now that's what we have to do."

"How much did we pay for this davit?"

"Two million. Why?"

"Seems to me they ought to be the ones getting up at midnight to reprogram this screwed-up davit. And I suppose they want us to pay them to fix their mistakes."

"Naturally, it's a cost-plus contract. Any mistakes or extra repairs and we pay the bill. Unfortunately the designers at Crystal City released the davit to the fleet before the final testing was done."

"Wait until the captain hears we're using maintenance dollars for Washington's science project. You, of all people, know how much money we need to keep this old girl running."

"I've argued with the shipyard about a warranty, but there isn't any. It seems we told the lifeboat company how to design this davit in the first place, so they're off the hook. Used to be a company stood behind their product, but now they just have their hand out."

"What kind of outfit are we running here, Jake?"

"One that has very little accountability. New construction yards are even worse."

⤿

When Captain Davey walked out of the ship's superstructure and onto the boat deck, the sailors stopped what they were doing and saluted him. He always took time to encourage and chat with a few of them because he genuinely cared about his crew. Life aboard USS Sheboygan was demanding, and the old man appreciated their dedication and hard work.

Petty Officer Booker, who had just walked up the truck tunnel to the boat deck, approached the captain with a look that made the CO think he wanted to talk to him about something. But before either of them could speak, Chief Barnes intervened. From the corner of Captain Davey's eye, he noticed a visibly disappointed Booker quickly change course and return below. But Chief Barnes was already talking to him, and there was no time to wonder what had been on the petty officer's mind.

"Captain, the CHENG would like to light off the forward auxiliary boiler and check to make sure the valve Jake got us doesn't leak."

"That's fine, Chief, but tell him to light off tomorrow at 0700. I know the engineers have been putting in some long hours in the last month, and I want them well rested when we head out to sea."

"No disrespect, Captain, but it may leak, and then we'll have to take the plant down again."

"Do we have any other problems down there?"

"No, Sir."

"Then tell CHENG to come see me. I don't want to miss our underway time tomorrow. We're going out because I want to test the lifeboat davit and do a full-power run. You and I both know your gang will be in early."

"Yes, Sir, Captain. I'll tell him right away."

"Thank you, Chief."

The captain turned away from Barnes and looked at the bosun and port engineer. "I don't like to see the two of you staring at the lifeboat davit. What have we got here?"

"Captain, Jake here wants a secure phone line set up for midnight so the tech reps can download a program from their home office in France."

The captain fixed his eyes on Jake. "All right, but who in Washington made the decision to buy a foreign lifeboat davit anyway? I'm glad it's only the lifeboat they're going to have control over and not my engines. By the way, thanks for the valve. How'd you get it?"

Jake grinned. "You don't want to know."

Captain Davey raised his eyebrows. "Okay. We should be ready to go tomorrow. You coming?"

"Captain, I've got plenty of sea time, but if the CHENG is going to run the engines at full power, I'll come, plus I want to see how this lifeboat davit works, so I'll pack a small bag tonight."

"You're always welcome."

"Thanks, Captain," Jake said and then pointed at a small red "W" pin on the CO's jacket. "I hear the Badgers have a great running back. They could be pretty tough this year."

The captain smiled at the memory of those glorious fall days when the University of Wisconsin was competing for a national championship and only Michigan stood in their way. He looked the port engineer square in the eyes and nodded. "You'd better bet Wisconsin's going to be tough. Michigan's going to take another beating from the Badgers. That kid they recruited from Texas is big, and he can 'flat fly.' And you know they always have a great line."

"Yes, Sir, Captain, but if Ohio State were on their schedule, they'd pick up another loss."

"Not likely, Jake," the captain said, smiling, and then asked, "So, are you ready to test all the new equipment tomorrow?"

Jake shrugged. "Are you going to test the retractable flight deck and fire off one of those dummy missiles?"

"Absolutely. Has the shipyard finished its work?"

"I raised holy hell with the shipyard superintendent yesterday. He wanted another week, but I told him to go round the clock. We'll pay overtime for that, but I think they're ready for operational testing. They completed a simulated launch, but it would be good to put that system through its paces and see what we've got."

"Boats, see the XO and have her put it in the plan of the day. The Commodore from the Expeditionary Strike Group has been a big proponent of this new vertical launch system from a modified well-deck. As you know, with fewer ships in the Navy, they're trying to make these platforms more capable. We'll be able to launch Tomahawk missiles. The new retractable flight deck gives greater capabilities to the aging amphibious fleet. The taxpayers will love the fact that fewer ships will be needed if this works out."

"We better get more capability out of these old ships, because construction on the new ships is way behind schedule and is costing three times what the government agreed to. If the big boys in the Navy really wanted to save money, they'd put a penalty on late delivery of a ship. They do that in the Merchant Marine and it works. By the way, are you going to test the new twenty-five millimeter gun? I hear it's got a remote-control firing system."

"We've got to have everything ready for the training cycle, so all the new installations must be tested."

"I'll have test coordinators come to sea with us, Sir."

"Good. Make sure the XO has a list of the sea riders. I'll see you in morning."

The bosun nudged Jake and, with a twinkle in his eyes, said, "I'll see you tonight at the Lion's Lair."

The captain shook his head and then pointed his finger at his two subordinates and warned, "The two of you better not get into any trouble!"

"Captain, we wouldn't dream of it," Jake answered, his tone sincere but the grin on his face saying otherwise.

Lion's Lair, Imperial Beach

The parking lot behind the Lion's Lair was filled with motorcycles, trucks, and a few cars. The weary building with a sagging roofline could use a coat of paint, but nobody seemed to notice. The overpowering smell of stale sweat permeated the establishment. Like spies in an Amsterdam café, people surreptitiously checked each other out, glancing quickly in the mirrors along the walls. Some really tough-looking men hung around the entrance, drinking a cold one or two, while a couple of attractive women lingered in one of the corners. Jake and the bosun made their way to the center of the room to check out the action.

"My, my, look at those sheilas over there," Bosun exclaimed, thoroughly impressed with their athletic ability but also noticing their shapeliness.

"Settle down, big fella. Those two seem out of place, especially with their pretty outfits and makeup. I bet they're here to check out the men."

Bowing to them, the bosun blurted out, "Well, here I am, ladies."

A tall black man with a chiseled physique and thick arms walked over to them. His prominent forehead magnified his disjointed nose. Sweat dripped down his forehead and face.

"Gunny, what are you doing here?" the bosun asked the Marine Corps Gunnery Sergeant assigned to the Sheboygan as the combat cargo officer.

"What's it look like? I've been lookin' for a place like this since I reported aboard your ship," he answered.

Boats grinned. "Gunny, this is our Port Engineer, Jake."

"Call me Deek," the gunnery sergeant said, extending a big hand that enveloped Jake's. "This place looks like it's got all the right equipment."

"You can say that again," the bosun agreed. "Gunny, you see those two sheilas in the corner? I haven't seen such fine looking women since I pulled into Sydney after five months of turning donuts in the Persian Gulf."

"Mind your manners around them," Gunny cautioned. "That blonde-haired beauty will kick the ever-lovin' tar out of you. Watch her pound that power bag. Can I get a witness?"

As if on cue she began hammering away on the big black bag suspended from the ceiling with a heavy chain. Every time she threw a hard round kick, the bag jumped with a loud resounding thud. Heads quickly turned, and men watched in amazement as she ripped into the heavy bag. Meanwhile the brunette began tattooing the speed-bag with a high, uninterrupted cadence that few men could match.

"Deek, I just fell in love with that blonde sheila over there."

"Please," Deek said with a smirk, "you said that when you walked ashore in Australia. I like a sista with a little bounce to her booty. Shoot, you can keep them two. They way too skinny for me."

"I'll admit you do like big women."

"Shapely, in all the right places. Can I get a witness?" Deek asked with a big grin. "Try five months on a supply convoy in Iraq, dodgin' sandstorms, roadside bombs, and snipers. Shoot, dawg, we had to sleep on the hard ground most nights."

"This last deployment was pretty tough, but I remember the nine months we spent off the coast of Somalia."

Deek laughed in deep voice. "Ya, buddy. That was my second float in two years, and when we went ashore, it was like a wild-west town. After spendin' seven months on the Ogden, we had only two liberty ports, and we cut loose once the ships pulled into Mombassa. There's some fine looking sistas in the motherland."

"Excuse me, guys, but I thought we came here to train," Jake interjected as he stretched his calves and thighs. "Besides, Boats, you work with a crew that's fifty percent women onboard Sheboygan."

"Big difference. I never mix business with pleasure—and believe me, I've had plenty of opportunity. Now the way I look at it, them two in the corner are free agents."

"One of you man enough to climb into the ring with me?" Deek asked, with a hard look on his face that would stop most men in their tracks.

Boats laughed. "You may look bad, but you don't fool me."

"Bring it, squid."

"I swear, if I didn't like you, Deek, I'd clean your clock six ways to hell and back again."

"In your dreams, dawg. In your dreams."

Boats climbed into the ring and began sparring with the Marine Corps gunnery sergeant. The taut canvas was stretched like a pro ring, and the two men with sixteen-ounce gloves began throwing jabs. In the other corner of the Lion's Lair was a wrestling mat with a couple of guys practicing submission holds. Beyond the mirrored room were a bunch of free weights. There wasn't any music and only one locker room in the place. The training was very serious, and people with the wrong attitudes or loud and obnoxious voices didn't last. They weren't asked to leave; they were literally thrown into the street, never to return.

The light heavyweight and heavyweight champions of Ultimate Fighting Championship trained here.

Jake coached the Ramona High School Wrestling team and when they went up against Patrick Henry High School he met their coach, Roberto Tito—the former world heavyweight UFC champion. Tito's son attended Patrick Henry High School, so he helped the coaching staff by volunteering and giving back to the community. At the meet Jake recognized the former world champion and introduced himself. Roberto was very gracious, and the two became good friends by the end of the season. Tito invited him to train at the Lion's Lair, free of cost. The first day the USS Sheboygan was back in town, Jake invited Boats to come along. The two had been training there ever since.

"You want to work some submission holds tonight?" Deek asked as he and the bosun took a breather.

"Sure," Jake answered. "Where's Roberto been lately?"

"Ever since the television networks picked up ultimate fighting, he's started training again," Deek explained. "They're going to have a round robin tournament next month in Las Vegas. The winner walks away with a million Benjamin's."

"That's some serious bucks," Jake admitted.

"You bet it is," Boats said climbing into the ring.

"Cut the chatter," Deek ordered. "Boats, give me ten scissor kicks, but only go about one-third speed."

As Boats and Jake moved to comply, Jake asked, "So, Deek, where did you get your black belt?"

"Marine Corps."

"What? I thought you had to go to some dojo and qualify. Don't tell me the Marines are now qualifying their own people."

Boats was also surprised at Deek's revelation. "Yeah, what's up with that, Gunny?"

"About six years ago the Marines initiated the Marine Corps Martial Arts Program (MCMAP). We began pullin' in the different disciplines, such as boxin', Kung Fu, wrestlin', judo, kickboxin', and submission holds. We're teachin' our recruits to make them superior hand-to-hand fighters."

"I would have thought they'd been doing that all along."

"Now that I look back, I agree, but with the ultimate fighting championships on TV, MCMAP training is growing rapidly."

"So how did you get to be the MCMAP's Champion?" Jake asked. "Did they have a big national event?"

Deek shook his head. "No. It was on the down low. At the start of the program they invited all the instructors that held black belts to a big conference where we set up MCMAP and decided how to introduce it into the Corps. It was pretty intense. We walked around showin' moves and puttin' the program together for the Corps, all the time sizin' each other up. Colonel Davis was cool and could sense the tension building. On the last day of the conference, he held an unofficial Marine Corps fight championship. I happened to come out on top, but the colonel got in some hot water for holding the tournament, so they haven't officially held it for a while. I hear they're gonna put one together soon, though."

Jake grinned. "So you're the baddest of the Marines?"

"You might say. I've trained a lot of Marines over the last five years, so I'm sure there's someone out there who's every bit as tough as me. Just haven't met him," Deek said coolly with a quiet air of confidence.

"What are the three red stripes on your black belt?" Boats asked.

"That's the degree I hold. Now get practicin', or I'll come in and kick the tar out of you both."

The two men began circling each other, waiting for the other to throw a kick. The bosun landed a solid kick to Jake's thigh.

"Easy there, Boats. I thought we were supposed to go one-third speed," Jake complained, as a tear ran from his eye.

"Sorry. I got a little carried away."

At that moment Boats made the mistake of sneaking a glance at the blonde, and Jake delivered a punishing shot to the bosun's ribs.

"Whoo, solid." Deek nodded approvingly.

"Dang," Boats grunted, the air whistling from his lungs. "You knew I wasn't looking."

"And your point is?" Jake asked, smiling.

Boats shrugged and shook his head slightly. "To be honest, I sure wouldn't want to meet that blonde in a dark alley."

The men looked over at the two women who had broken into a light sweat while sparring with each other. Although both were quite pretty, it was obvious they knew what they were doing.

After thirty minutes of ring work, Bosun slipped through the ropes and went right over to the women.

"Don't even think of starting," the blonde said icily with a serious attitude, not missing a beat with her scissor kicks. "My sister and I came to train, and that's it. So unless you're going to use that bag, you need to move on, cowboy, or you might get hurt."

Rejected, Boats didn't need any further prompting and began pummeling the bag. Like a rooster strutting his stuff, the bosun's kicks landed crisply, with more power than hers, and he was pleased to see the bag snap and jump. It wasn't long before the sweat was rolling off his forehead, his workout shirt drenched. In the meantime, Deek and Jake went to the wrestling mats, practicing takedowns for the next thirty minutes. Finally they all took a water break and wandered over to the girls.

"You gals come here often?" the bosun asked the brunette who was sipping her bottled water. He couldn't help but notice the inviting smile on her face, as if she were laughing at him.

"You don't give up easy, do you?" she replied. "I thought my sister shut you down pretty good."

The blonde ignored the exchange, though Boats knew she was taking it all in.

"Naw," he said, "I've learned to take a punch or two. Where did you learn how to train?"

"A couple of different places, but mostly in Brazil. That's where we met Roberto."

"Really? You know Tito? You Brazilian?"

"Not originally. We're French by birth," she explained.

"Tito's not around this week. He's getting ready for a fight," Jake interjected as he and Deek joined the Bosun.

"We saw him fight the Brazilians. He's pretty rugged," the woman added.

"They don't call him 'The Animal' because he's tame," Boats said. "How long have you been in San Diego?"

"A couple of months."

"Do you like jazz?"

"Maybe." Her voice was cool, but Boats caught an encouraging glint in her eyes.

"I don't think so!" the blonde said shooting her sister a hard look. "Come on, Liz, we've got to be going."

"Look, if you're not busy later we could meet you downtown," Boats offered. "They've got great food, and the music is tops."

"I'm sorry, but we've got other plans," Liz said softly as the other woman steered her toward the door. "Perhaps some other time," she called over her shoulder, turning back to offer a quick smile.

"Jazz! You don't know nothin' about music," Deek said, laughing.

Boats was still eyeing the door that had just shut behind the two women. "Don't you start on me," he warned. "With two classy babes like that, you can't invite them to the Red Rooster for shooters."

As the bosun continued to stare at the door, he noticed a large, powerful-looking, black sweat-shirted man drop the rope he'd been skipping and exit the room, his head down but glancing out of the corner of his eyes. Boats frowned as he watched him. He didn't like the looks of what he'd just seen, even though he had no real reason for feeling that way.

"Now that you mentioned the Red Rooster," Deek said, interrupting the bosun's thoughts, "let's go knock down a couple of beers. You comin', Jake?"

"Sure, but I don't drink alcohol."

Deek shrugged. "I'm cool with that."

Boats dismissed his concerns about the man in the black sweatshirt, and the three friends walked out of the gym. He had just walked over to his dirty blue Jeep when he spotted the two women they'd been talking to minutes earlier. In the evening light the brunette looked prettier than the blonde, so Boats stole a second glance at her just as a black-bearded man came up, grabbed her arm, and twisted her around. Pain and fear instantly filled her face. Obviously frightened at what was happening to her sister, the blonde backed off.

Boats had five sisters and had defended each of them at one time or another in his life, so he didn't think twice before hustling over to them before it got ugly.

"What's going on here?" he demanded, looking at the bearded man.

"None of your concern!"

Boats looked him square in the eyes, his face firm, his body tensed and ready to strike. "I'm making it my concern. Let go of her arm!"

The man's scowl deepened. "Didn't you hear me? This is none of your concern. Now get in your truck and get out of here. This isn't your business!"

"I'm making it my business," Boats countered raising his fists.

But the bearded man was quicker. A crushing blow from his left hand slammed into Boats' right cheek. The calloused knuckles smashed the soft cheek against Boats molars, ripping a gash inside his mouth. Salty warm blood coated his tongue as stars cascaded in front of his face. Instinctively Boats defended himself, covering his face as the man threw another punch. Boats swung a wide hook in the man's direction, not really seeing him, and he heard the snap of his opponent's nose.

Boats spit blood. The bearded man circled, then threw a right cross. Boats ducked and delivered a powerful round kick to his stomach, knocking the wind out of him. Straightening up, Boats sent a thundering uppercut to his chin. Landing squarely, it knocked the man backwards, but he rolled to the right and got up.

Quickly reaching behind his back, the man pulled out a long curved knife. Thrusting off balance, Bosun easily deflected the blow and grabbed his wrist and pulled it behind the man's back. Boats squeezed as hard as he could and stomped on his opponent's instep. The knife dropped to the asphalt and both men grabbed each other's throat. With all their might they tried to squeeze the life out of each other.

Suddenly rounded cold steel dug into the bearded man's temple.

"Let 'im go!" Deek roared.

The two men released their grips on each other.

"Now get in your car and don't ever make the mistake of comin' back here."

"You talk big, surrounded by your friends," the man replied in an obvious attempt to save face. "If it was just you and me, I'll bet it would be different."

"Someday you may get your chance," Deek said as he turned and nodded at the two women. "You gals take off. It seems your friend here wants to test his manhood against my forty-four, and I'd be more than happy to oblige him."

The girls jumped at the chance and got in their car and drove off. Deek moved closer to the bearded man's face, the big Desert Eagle inches from his nose.

"You want a taste of me?" the bearded man challenged. "Discard your weapon, and let's do this man to man, if you've got the guts."

"Deek, he's not worth it," Jake pleaded. "The captain will be furious if he has to bail you out of jail."

Deek's eyes never left the bearded man's face. "You want some of me? I'll whip the snot out of you."

The man hesitated, but it was obvious he realized the wisdom of leaving while he could. He eased over to his car and climbed inside.

"Oh, by the way," Boats called as the man started the engine, "the next time I see her, there better not be a mark on her."

The three men watched the man's car pull away as Boats mused aloud, "I wonder what that was all about."

No one had an answer. As the car turned the corner, Deek said, "He came close to meeting his maker." They climbed in their cars and headed for the Red Rooster.

7

Murphy Canyon—defense contractor building

Amused, Abdullah sped away. He was late for his rendezvous because of the confrontation, but he was surprised at how the bosun had reacted. The information they had received about Browder was quite limited. However, it had gone much better than he expected. Pulling into the parking lot at the coffee shop, he spotted Haviv.

"You're late, Abdullah. What took you so long?"

"Keep your shirt on, Haviv. I didn't want to rush it."

"Our window of opportunity for tonight is closing, and we need to pick up Liz."

Abdullah began putting lampblack to his face. "Just drive, Haviv, and let me worry about the timeline. I hate relying on women for anything."

Haviv ignored Abdullah's remark and pointed at Liz in her parked car, then pulled up. Dressed in all black, she got out of her car and jumped into the backseat of Haviv's car.

They took off and drove North on the I-5. Taking the Ocean Beach exit they pulled off into a dark alley next to a modern, two-story building complex. The lighted office buildings were surrounded by razor wire interwoven on the top of a cyclone fence. A gate guard manned a booth at the entrance to the complex. Haviv stayed in the car as Abdullah and Liz dashed into the shadows along the fence line. They dropped to one knee and waited.

"Quiet!" Abdullah said as the watchman began his trek around the grounds. "Don't even breathe until I tell you."

⤸

Liz, more than a little frightened, looked up at Abdullah's blackened face. She didn't know what to expect from him. She'd known about his temper and how he could be quite violent. While waiting for them to arrive, she had changed her clothes and wasn't surprised to notice a large red handprint on her arm where Abdullah had grabbed her. The resonating pain assured her that a huge purple bruise would be there in the morning. Liz understood that this sort of thing went with the territory, but it didn't give her much sense of security to know her life was under this man's control.

As the watchman disappeared, Abdullah's powerful hands gripped the pliers and snipped the heavy-gauge steel wire fence straight up for three feet. He lifted one edge of the cyclone fencing, and they slipped under it.

"Stay down until he gets to the edge of the building, and then we'll run for that door at the rear of the last building." Though he spoke in a whisper, there was no mistaking the tone of authority in his words. "Do you understand?"

"Yes, Abdullah. It will be my pleasure to serve Allah." Liz had a degree from a French school in computer science, and she knew that was the only reason Abdullah tolerated her presence on this mission.

They quickly ran to the building where Abdullah masterfully picked the door lock, but the Sentry Alert System instantly began blinking red.

"Give me a boost," Liz suggested. "I'll disarm it."

Like a father lifting a small child, Abdullah hoisted Liz up. Racing against seconds before the audible alarm sounded, she quickly opened the cover of the motion sensor and cut the white wire, then the yellow. The security status went from red to green, and she heard Abdullah's sigh of relief as he lowered her.

"We don't have much time to penetrate their computers and get out of here. You've got thirty minutes."

"With thirty minutes I'll just have time to set up the feed and break the passwords. We'll still need to penetrate the computer system and find the personnel information for the Sheboygan."

"Work quickly. We must have the ship's information."

"Don't worry, Abdullah; we won't have to come back." Liz opened her black bag, which held screwdrivers, a soldering iron, small gage wire, tie clasps, and a lamp attached to a headband. She slipped the headlamp on her head and turned on the light, then opened up the front of a hard drive and pulled out a small transmitter. She attached the tiny microcircuit to the drive, giving her access to the Navy Marine Corps Internet. Soldering the transmitter onto the drive-in series with the main boards would allow her to ghost the system. She could then access secure information available on the web when someone else logged in. The Navy would never know she was even on their system because it would all come back to this terminal.

Next Liz replaced the cover for the hard drive and sprayed some neutralizing scent into the air so no one would smell the soldered wiring. Abdullah didn't have a clue what she was doing, and she knew it infuriated him that a woman knew more than he did.

"Twenty-one minutes to go," he announced. "Did you get the passwords?"

"Not yet."

"Hurry up!" he snapped.

Ten minutes passed, and they heard a dog bark outside.

Abdullah ran to the window and peered out, just as the dog barked again.

"We've got to get out of here!" Abdullah whispered, his voice frantic as he looked back at Liz. "Why aren't you finished?"

Frustrated at his constant demands but holding her temper in check, Liz replied calmly, "Just a few more seconds and I'll have the password set up so we won't have to come back."

"How could they have known we were here?" Abdullah asked, pulling out his P6 Makarov with silencer attached. He eased his head over the windowsill. "They're on the fence line," he announced. "They've picked up our scent. Aren't you through yet?"

"Quiet!" Liz demanded, too focused on her job to be concerned with the effect her words had on Abdullah. "I've almost got it."

"I'm going to let them get closer," he said. "Get behind the desk, and shut up!"

She broke her concentration long enough to glance at Abdullah just as he reached over to the window blinds and cut the pull cords with his knife. He quickly looped them over the doorknob and slightly opened the door. Then he slid behind a steel desk and steadied his shooting hand on the top of a chair. Still watching him, Liz obeyed Abdullah's order and crouched down behind the desk.

Patiently he waited for the guard and dogs to reach the door. Liz heard the guard fumbling with his keys as the dogs barked. With what she knew was powerful resolve, Abdullah waited a few more seconds and then, with his left hand, pulled the rope. The door flew open, slamming against the wall and catching the handler off guard. The dogs exploded into the room, escaping their leashes. Four rapid-fire shots caught both dogs in the head. The lead dog's momentum carried him across the room, with teeth bared. He died at Liz's feet. Abdullah fired one more shot, and the surprised guard fell to the ground.

Liz didn't even realize she was screaming until, with the gun still smoking, Abdullah looked at her with clenched teeth, pointed the pistol at her forehead, and said, "Shut up, or I'll shoot you right here."

Liz had no doubt that he would do exactly that, and she immediately closed her mouth.

"Let's go!" Abdullah said, and she quickly followed him out the door. They ran to the fence, slipped under the wire, and got into the waiting car.

8

Imperial Beach—Red Rooster

Deek, Boats, and Jake pulled up in front of the Red Rooster and got out of their vehicles. They were all in their forties, but you couldn't tell by looking at them. Their conditioned physiques made them look at least five years younger. Deek leaned his chromed-out midnight black Harley Dyna Guild against the kickstand and took off his helmet. The Screaming Eagle pipes on his One Hundredth Anniversary model sparkled brightly in the early twilight. With little fanfare Boats parked his dilapidated open-air jeep. Jake pulled up behind them in a big silver pickup truck. They walked in and, like conspirators, strolled over to a corner table to sit down while the sound system played the Temptations' song "My Girl." The Red Rooster catered to an older crowd but kept their barmaids young and sassy.

"I'm thinking you boys want a round of beers," announced the red-haired barmaid whose plunging neckline easily caught the men's undivided attention.

"That's not all we want," Deek replied with a big smile, drinking in her loveliness from the top of her head down to her knees.

"Slow down there, big fella," she cooed, patting him on the shoulder. "I'll get your beers."

"Could you please bring me a diet Coke with a twist of lime?" Jake added.

"Sure thing, honey," she said with a lingering smile.

The bosun could see why the woman's tips were always the highest at the Rooster.

"Hey, dawg, you almost got your head blown clean off back there. That clown wasn't playin'. I don't know if you noticed, but he wasn't pullin' a banana out of his back pocket. What were you thinkin'?"

"What about you, Deek? You're not supposed to leave base with a weapon. Do you have a permit for that thing?"

"Shoot, I've been packin' since I was fourteen. Don't need no permit in South Central. You either survive or die. What I want to know is, what were you gonna do if he pulled a gun?"

"I don't know, but I've faced men before."

"And you think you're that fast?"

"I didn't think, but I knew you had my back."

Deek pulled out his forty-four. "Yeah, me and the Eagle go way back. He delivered me several times in life. Alleluia," Deek said fondly

"Put that away before somebody sees it," Boats exclaimed. "You're crazy, man."

Deek pulled the hammer back and then, with his thumb, eased it down. He quickly slipped the big gun under his shirt. "Were you gonna back down if that fool pulled a pistol?"

"Not even maybe. I hate it when someone tries to hurt a woman. Usually they're nothing but bullies that don't measure up in a man's world. If no one opposes them, they have their way. I've found that nine times out of ten all you have to do is stand up against them. I don't even care if the man was her husband; twisting her arm was uncalled for."

"What if he'd blown your head off? Then what?"

"Hey, I'm just passing through this world."

"Yeah, well it's a good thing me and the Eagle kept an eye on you."

"By the way, Jake," Boats said, quickly changing the subject, "I heard you talk about the Lord the other day, but I saw you checking out the barmaid."

Jake's face reddened. "You got me there, Boats. I'm not going to lie. Sometimes I struggle with the flesh."

"So you're not perfect."

"Never said I was. Truth is, I believe in Jesus as my Savior, and I'm constantly repenting of my sins."

"Yeah, well, you must have to do a lot of repenting," Boats said with a big laugh.

"You're right. My flesh is weak."

"Whoa," Deek interrupted, "is this some sort of Bible study or somethin'?" When Boats and Jake laughed and assured him it wasn't, he said, "Somethin' tells me that guy was a raghead, and you know how they treat their women."

"Yeah, like dogs," Boats agreed. "But enough about him. Are you bouncing at Déjà Vu tonight?"

"Naw, they gave me the night off. Why? You want to go there later?"

"Not tonight; we're getting underway tomorrow."

"You gettin' old, dawg. I remember the time when we could party all night and work the next day."

"Those were the good old days," Boats reminisced.

"By the way, the Colonel of the Expeditionary Strike Group heard you had a little problem with your davit," Deek said.

"A little problem!" the bosun shot back. "We almost killed a boat crew when the forward winch let go."

"How'd that happen?"

"The forward winch paid out its cable all at once, and the bow of the boat slammed into the ocean, dropping my crew into the water."

"Anybody hurt?"

"Thank God, nobody."

"What are they doin' about it?"

"Ask the port engineer."

Their eyes shifted to Jake. "We're bringing in a troubleshooting team from France to look at the controls, and then they're going to reprogram it."

"France?" Deek said. "What's up with that? Why in the world would we buy anythin' from them?"

"Because we contracted the Frenchies to design and build the davit in the first place," Boats explained.

"You've got to be kiddin'. That's like a bank recruitin' a thief while he's still in prison."

Jake nodded. "That's right. And now it doesn't work. What will the people in the Ivory Towers think of next?"

"You haven't heard the best part," Boats said. "When the Frenchies get here, they're going to download a new program into the davit's computer by tying up the ship's satellite communication system for eight hours."

"Good thing this download is for the davit only. Heck, they might be able to control the whole ship the way we're putting electronics and minicomputers on just about every piece of equipment we have. I'm involved in the building of a new amphibious ship class that'll have a computer system that runs throughout the ship, and every system is controlled by it. They call it Ship Wide Intelligence Systems." Jake shook his head. "Just think. If the wrong person somehow got control of the ship's computers from shoreside, they might be able to take control of an entire ship."

"Lord Almighty," Deek exclaimed. "That sounds better than science fiction."

"I know," Jake countered. "We've got those unmanned aerial vehicles, flying in combat zones and gathering Intel, cruise missiles with cameras on them, and a torpedo that'll circle and hunt down an enemy submarine."

"I'm sure there's a firewall in the computer systems onboard," Deek said.

"There are, but they're only as good as the people that invent them."

"That's why I'm getting out, boys," Boats said. "We've entered the computer age, and pretty soon they'll have some officer sitting behind a desk in Washington issuing orders from a Dick Tracy watch."

Smiling, the barmaid arrived with the drinks. They lifted their bottles and drank.

"So, Deek, tell me more about Iraq."

"Iraq's no fun, Boats, but I'm glad we're there. We've got to take the war on terrorism to the terrorists. If we aren't actively huntin' down their operations and puttin' them on the defensive, we'll never stop 'em."

"It's pretty tough to stop an attack from terrorists unless you're actively pursuing them and their cell groups," Boats added. "Look how Libya's leader changed his tune about America after a few bombs smoked his palace bedroom."

"The world's a different place now. I remember goin' overseas, spendin' a week in port, doing anythin' and never havin' to worry. Last float we cancelled two liberty ports because the command was worried we'd be targets for some terrorists."

Jake took a long pull of his diet soda and got up to go. "Deek, if you've got time, I'd like to learn some of those throws you teach the Marines. I might be able to teach them to my wrestlers."

"Snap, be happy to, Jake."

"Hey, listen guys, I've got to get going," Jake said, turning to leave. "My wife's waiting for me."

Just then a tall sultry woman with a golden honey hue glided into the bar. People openly stared at the exquisite beauty as she slowly turned her head, surveying the room, her lush figure captivating their attention. High cheekbones accented her smooth satin skin as her oval walnut eyes painfully searched until she zeroed in on him. Instantly she threw back her woven tresses, her beautiful eyes smoking like a cat focused on her prey. Heels resounding throughout the bar she marched up to Deek with a serious attitude.

"Where you bin?" she demanded with a hand on her hip. A soft sensuous bouquet of fresh flowers subtly floated past the table. "I 'spect my man home on time. Not hangin' around some honky tonk."

"Whoa, baby, slow down now," Deek offered in obvious hopes of quieting her verbal thrust. "I was just fixin' to go."

"Say what? It's nine-thirty and you got a full bottle. Now how you gonna tell me you was fixin' to leave?"

"Baby, we had a tough day. I was just chillin'…"

Interrupting him with a raised upturned palm she snapped her fingers, "Chilling! Don't you baby me, Deek Matthews! You better git home in a hurry."

With that she threw her head back and marched straight for the door.

"I gotta go, guys," Deek said, grabbing his beer and finishing it in one shallow.

Boats laughed and said to Jake, "I ain't seen nobody ever back Deek down. You be careful on the way home, Jake, and be sure to repent of your sins. Hey, sweetheart," he called to the waitress, "bring me another beer."

9

National City strip mall off Broadway Avenue

The last storefront on the strip mall had brown paper covering taped to the inside of the windows and a big "No Solicitors" sign on the door. Liz was sitting in front of a computer monitor, tracking the chip she had installed in the contractor's computer to see if she could hack into the system.

"When will you have the information?" Abdullah demanded after they had returned to their makeshift office.

"It might take some time because we've got to wait until the contractors log onto their computers in the morning, but I doubt if they'll use their computers right away." She knew she was walking on thin ice, but she couldn't help adding in a cool tone, "They've got to deal with the dead guard and the dogs."

Thankfully Abdullah didn't take the bait. "We need to be hacking into their system now!"

"We could, but we better wait until they're already online. Otherwise it'll leave a trail."

"I don't care. I need information on the Sheboygan's crew. We've got to target another sailor and begin our operation. We're already behind schedule."

Haviv sensed Abdullah's growing frustration and realized if they stayed there, Liz couldn't do her work. "Come on, Abdullah. Let her work. Let's go to the massage parlor."

Liz was well aware of Abdullah's contempt for her, and she didn't doubt for a moment that he'd be happy to snuff the life right out of her if given half the chance, but apparently Haviv's suggestion of a visit to the massage parlor had diverted Abdullah's attention. She'd heard that the two men frequented such an establishment in the nearby town of Lemon Grove, and it looked as if the parlor was about to receive another visit from the them because within minutes of Haviv's suggestion, Liz had the room to herself. At last she could work in peace.

⌐

"I've got to call Elena. Her part of the mission starts soon," Haviv said, as he pulled out his cell phone and dialed her number.

Abdullah frowned. "What are you talking about? Who gave you instructions without going through me?"

"Khalif did. He's in town and wants to see us."

"And you didn't bother to tell me!" he exploded just as his cell phone rang. "Yes," he answered harshly, but quickly changed his tone when he recognized the caller. "Of course. We'll meet you there in fifteen minutes."

They drove in silence down University Avenue. Arriving at their destination, they parked the car and then solemnly walked into the shop and ordered a couple of cups of "joe." They walked over to the bespectacled man wearing an expensive business suit sitting in the corner. With his glasses on and reading a newspaper, he looked like a university professor as he sipped his coffee.

"*Salaam alaikum*; peace be with you," Abdullah said, bowing slightly to the Light of Allah's messenger.

Khalif looked up from his Arabic paper and stared into Abdullah's eyes, letting him feel the harsh intensity of his controlled emotions. Finally he spoke. "*Alaikum salaam.*" Then, as if Abdullah were a bad dog, he issued a one-word order: "Sit!"

Abdullah and Haviv obeyed.

"What in Allah's name were you doing twisting Elizabeth's arm?" Khalif demanded. "You bruised her."

"The confrontation had to look real."

"And that required grabbing and twisting her arm?"

"She's a woman. What does it matter? You know if we were in our country I would have beaten her."

"Abdullah, Abdullah, you're in America. You've done well to be here so long without being detected, but now I want you to control yourself. Your thirst for violence will soon be satiated, but first we need all the information we can get on the Sheboygan. That is our primary mission, and it's much greater than a woman. I need both Elizabeth and Elena." He paused, his eyes fixed on Abdullah. "Your son is being assigned to the Sheboygan."

"What?" Abdullah's words were heavy with surprise and concern for his only offspring. "When did he transfer?"

"It's been arranged. *Hamdulillah*. Elena will be meeting him when he comes out here. Do not interfere with her mission. Is that understood?"

Abdullah clenched his fists. "Yes, Khalif. I understand. I've heard nothing from Jim about his assignment. When were these orders given?"

"Do not concern yourself with my business. The rest of the team will be crossing over the Mexican border tomorrow night. One more thing. I don't want you to be seen with Elena. She's working directly for me. If you see her with your son, you're to act like you don't know her. Understood?" Khalif asked, his eyes narrowed, focused. After a long, intense moment, during which Abdullah briefly nodded his answer, Khalif turned to Haviv. "When will we have the Sheboygan's schedule?"

"Very soon. Either Elena will get it through Abdullah's son, or Liz will hack into the ship's next up-line."

"Good. I want as much information about that ship and its people as we can get—and I want it yesterday. I need to know who's in financial trouble."

"We'll have their records soon," Haviv assured him. "Liz is the best there is at hacking into their systems."

Abdullah seethed, as he thought of his son's transfer being made without his knowing about it, and now Liz being praised for her work. Struggling with his inner thoughts, he kept his mouth shut as Khalif continued to speak to Haviv.

"I'll be going back across the border," Khalif said, "and flying out to meet with our leader. He has enlarged the scope of our attack. The Light of Allah has envisioned a way to shut down most of San Diego, but we must get our computers set up and running immediately."

"Khalif," Haviv said softly, "I've got an idea, if you're kind enough to listen."

"Speak."

"Instead of the operatives crossing the border, maybe we could set up the computers in Mexico. It would be easier to get people in and out, and it would be harder for the U.S. authorities to find our base. We could also pay the Mexican police to leave us alone."

Now Abdullah had a third component to add to his list of slights. Haviv would receive the glory and the credit if Khalif accepted his suggestion. From the pondering look on Khalif's face, that's exactly what was about to happen.

"Maybe," Khalif said. "I'll consider your idea, Haviv. With the enlargement of the Light of Allah's plan, you may be right."

"Thank you, Khalif. It will also be harder for the U.S. authorities to raid."

"Yes, I see what you mean. *Hamdulillah*. He has inspired you again."

Haviv smiled. Abdullah forced himself to do the same. For the Messenger to reward Haviv with words like this was not a small matter.

"Abdullah," Khalif said, finally directing his focus away from Haviv, "make sure all is ready for my return. Elena already has her instructions."

"Yes, Khalif. I understand."

"Now go, enjoy your massage. Very soon we will bring the great Satan to his knees like we did on that holy day in September. *Salaam alaikum.*"

"*Alaikum salaam,*" Abdullah responded, as he and Haviv got up and left the coffee shop.

10

USS Sheboygan, Naval Station
San Diego Pier 10

The next morning Jake came on board the Sheboygan early to meet with the captain and the CHENG. To do his job effectively as a port engineer, he always went aboard the ship when it was pier-side. He walked up the gangway and presented his Common Access Card (CAC) to the quarterdeck watch, even though he knew the officer of the deck.

"You going to see the captain, Jake?" asked the signalman third class, who was at the quarterdeck checking ID's. Most of the sailors on the ship knew the port engineer by his first name because he spent a lot of time in all the spaces checking out the various repairs to the ship. After overhauls and on special inspections, he would go out on sea trials with them and take notes for future repairs.

"You know it," Jake answered.

"Do you know the way, or shall I send my escort?" the young man kidded.

"I was a port engineer on this ship when you were the gleam in your daddy's eye," Jake responded. "After twenty years, I think I know the way."

The engineman laughed. "I'm sure you do. When do you think they'll balance the electrical load on the generators? That number three generator doesn't want to play with the others."

Jake frowned. "I hadn't heard about that. When did that start happening?"

"Just the other day. I think the CHENG was trying to fix it."

"Hey, thanks. I'll look into it," Jake said, appreciating the heads-up.

"No, thank *you*. I don't know what this ship would do without you."

"Oh, you might be surprised," Jake said, pleased and only slightly embarrassed by the compliment. "This old girl would still make it from point A to point B. Thanks for the kind words, though. Have a nice day."

Jake made his way up to the captain's office, greeting almost everyone he met along the way. He had learned a long time ago that the sailors on the deck plates were his eyes and ears, and most of them knew their plant quite well.

He arrived at the captain's office and knocked on the door.

"Where's the bosun?" the old man growled, as he looked up from his morning message traffic on the computer screen.

"I don't know, Sir."

"Go get him, and then come back," the captain ordered. His usual lighthearted attitude had been replaced by a no-nonsense look, and Jake knew he meant business.

The port engineer found the bosun in the wardroom, pouring himself a cup of coffee. Boats greeted him with a smile. "Hey, Jake, fresh pot," he said. "You want a cup?"

"Not now. The captain wants to see us."

"Oh, boy. He must have found out about last night. Well let's get this butt-chewing over," Boats said, putting down his cup and heading out the door. The two men hurried up to the captain's office and knocked on the door.

Captain Davey motioned them in with a wave of his hand and a look that could stop a dump truck. "Boats, I overheard you and Gunny talking about your exploits last night when I was on the 06 level getting some fresh air." He turned to Jake. "And how old are you?"

Jake had a feeling where this was going. "I'll be fifty next month," he answered.

"Did the thought ever occur to you that you might not make it to fifty?"

"No, Sir," Jake replied weakly. He knew the captain was going to chew him out, and the best thing to do was keep quiet and take it.

The captain shut off his computer and hit the button under his desk. Seconds later the messman appeared with a pot of coffee and four cups. He set the silver tray down on the captain's desk, poured a couple of cups of coffee, and left the office.

"Have some coffee," the CO ordered.

"Thanks, captain," the two men answered in unison.

"What were the two of you thinking last night? As I understand it, the man you confronted was quite a bit bigger than you, and he looked pretty tough. Deek said he was reaching for a weapon before he stepped in to help you. Don't you think you're a little old to be picking a fight?"

"Captain, I wasn't picking a fight," Boats countered. "The guy was manhandling a woman, and I wasn't about to stand around and do nothing."

"What would have happened if he'd shot or knifed you?"

"Captain, I've been training in no-holds-barred fighting for years," Boats offered in his defense. "I probably shouldn't tell you this, but I've already had two fights."

"Where was this?"

"Mexico."

"Mexico?"

"Sure. They'll put anybody in the ring."

"How'd you do?"

"Knocked 'em both out."

"That may be, but if Deek hadn't been there last night, we might be having this conversation by your hospital bedside—or worse. Now I could order the two of you to stay away from the Lion's Lair, but I won't—for now. But I don't want to hear about any more incidents."

"I appreciate your concern, Captain, but trust me, I saw him reach behind his back, and I was just about to subdue him when Deek pulled his weapon."

The captain shook his head before he took a long sip of coffee. "I know you're a Christian, Jake. Can you tell the bosun what the Good Book says about this?"

"Yes, Sir. It says to turn the other cheek. This country was founded on God's principles, but it was also bought with the price of many men's lives."

"Captain, if somebody wants to wail on me, I'll turn the other cheek," Boats interjected, "but I won't stand idle when someone is bullying a woman. My blood runs hot when I see that happen, but let's cut to the chase, Captain. What would you have done in my place?"

Captain Davey paused for a moment, and Boats knew he was searching for a good comeback. Apparently he didn't have one because he just looked Boats in the eye, took another long drink of his coffee, and changed the subject.

"Jake, tell me something about this new generator control system we've installed in this yard period."

With the butt chewing over, Jake jumped right in with enthusiasm. "Basically, we've installed a system that can put all four generators on the line and feed excess power shore-side into the electrical grid here in San Diego."

"Now why would we want to do that?"

"If San Diego lost its electrical load, like in that brown-out last summer, we could actually supply power to the city. It might not be much, but it would keep emergency circuits alive."

"How's that possible?"

"We have an automatic buss synchronizer and a paralleling control module integrated into our shore-power breaker. With all the natural disasters happening around the globe, we could pull into a port and supply electrical power to a small city. Some of the big decks have this feature as well. Remember when San Francisco had that devastating earthquake a few years back? Well, the USS Tarawa steamed into port and supplied power to the Bay Area from their generators."

"We ought to get a rebate check from San Diego Gas and Electric if we did that."

"You'd think so, Captain, but it doesn't work that way. The way I see it, everyone should have photovoltaic panels on their roofs here in Southern California to turn the power of the sun into electricity. Then we wouldn't have to worry about oil from the Persian Gulf."

"I'll bet a lot of mothers would agree with you. How much does it cost for solar panels on a home?"

"Too much—about forty grand. But if big government was smart they'd give bigger rebates, and more people would take advantage of it. In the long run this would be an inexhaustible source of power. If they'd invest larger rebates in a bunch of homes, making the process affordable, a lot of people would jump at the opportunity not to have an electric bill. The electrical grid here in Southern California really gets taxed during the hot summer days, but we just keep building more and more houses. The grid demand keeps going up, but nobody wants a power plant installed in their backyard. The situation is a disaster waiting to happen."

"I suppose oil lobbies would probably prevent the governor from pushing that sort of legislation through," the captain commented.

"It's all about the money. British Petroleum has bought up many of the photovoltaic factories that build the solar panels. I was in Palm Springs last weekend, and they have hundreds of windmills built in a canyon just outside the city. Now if they'd add solar panels, they'd have a real energy farm."

"You've really thought this out."

"My dad and I talk about it all the time. He's a genius, and he's designed a new kind of windmill that gets four times the power of the existing ones."

"Good for him. I couldn't agree with you more. Solar power is the way to go." He paused, and a grin crept over his face. "Now you know Wisconsin is going to tear up Michigan this weekend, don't you?"

"You got some money to back that up?" Jake countered.

The captain pulled out his wallet and slapped a five-dollar bill on his desk. "Can you handle that?"

"Sure thing, Captain. In fact, I'll even give you two points. That's how confident I am."

"I don't need your points. Now both of you, get out of here, and do something good for Sheboygan."

"I'll see you later, Captain," Jake said, smiling as he and Boats got up to exit the office. "Next week I'll be five dollars richer."

11

Planning Offices of San Diego Shipyard

Haviv was at work at the shipyard, sitting at his desk and holding the phone to his ear as Khalif issued orders. "I need you to set up the new computers that just arrived."

Beads of sweat broke out on Haviv's forehead. "Khalif, I can't just leave in the middle of the day."

"I've got fourteen men ready to use the computers, and we need your expert help. Liz is busy hacking into the government's system."

Haviv took a deep breath. It was useless to argue. "Let me call you right back."

"Abdullah is right," Khalif added. "You've gone soft."

"Abdullah said that? I'll call you back in thirty minutes." He hung up without waiting for a reply, wondering why his countrymen had to be so ignorant of the modern world. They wanted to show strength by brute force, but Haviv had a more intelligent way, a much better plan, and the Messenger had been impressed. His plan would bring the great Satan to their knees.

He got up from his desk and was about to leave the shipyard when his boss, the program manager for amphibious ships, called to him.

"Haviv," Mr. Thorson said, "I just got a call from the captain of the San Diego Regional Maintenance Center. He wants to know what we're doing about the lifeboat repairs on Sheboygan. I guess there are a lot of people concerned about this new installation."

"Tell him I have a computer specialist from Stanford that I'm trying to hire for the shipyard. She's trained in programming and speaks French, so it might be easier for her to communicate with the French company."

"That's great. When's she due to begin work?"

"I'm on my way to meet with her and present an offer. I hope she accepts. Perhaps you could forward her recommendation up the ladder."

"Sure. What's her name?"

Haviv paused. He didn't know Liz's last name, and the only thing that came to his mind was a European car. "Elizabeth Ferrari," he blurted out.

"I'll tell the Captain at SDRMC that we're hiring our own specialist. Make sure she accepts the offer."

"I'll do my best. She's quite good, so I may have to pay her a little more."

"Use your judgment, Haviv. I need her on the deck plates ASAP. This lifeboat issue is getting ugly for us, and I want to be proactive in trying to solve the problem."

"Sure thing, Mr. Thorson."

Without another word Haviv hurried from the office, climbed into his car, and drove down to the building they had leased to set up their computers now that the ghost circuit was activated.

12

Murphy Canyon office building

Pulling up in black unmarked cars, two Naval Criminal Investigative Service (NCIS) agents dressed in conservative business suits got out of their cars. The young light-skinned black woman carried a soft black leather briefcase under her arm, but it did little to hide her concealed shoulder strap and weapon.

"How did this happen?" John Silvas, the agent in charge, asked. The National Joint Terrorism Task Force had ultimate oversight, but because this was a defense contractor for the Navy, NCIS had initially responded to the call.

The nervous gate guard lifted his shoulders, looked to the right and left, and shrugged. "I don't know. I called Roy on his cell phone a couple of times, but he didn't answer. I got concerned, so I called in back-up. Then I found him with the dogs. I immediately called 9-1-1. I hope that was right."

"You did exactly what you were supposed to do," the slender crew-cut man with glasses said. "But didn't you see or hear anything?" Silvas had been an investigator with NCIS for eighteen years and had just rotated back to San Diego from the Far East, where he had been doing advance intelligence work for Navy ships before they entered port, checking to see if there were any terrorist threats to American sailors there.

"No, Sir. My post is on the other side of these buildings. I doubt if the sound could have traveled through them."

"They must have used silencers," John said to no one in particular, as he glanced around the room, looking for anything unusual.

"Sir, look over here," the female agent said.

John turned his attention to his associate. "Well done, Laticia." He leaned down and used the tip of his pen to pick up a shell casing from the floor. Laticia stood ready with an open baggy as John dropped it into a bag and rolled it over in his hand.

"Unless I miss my guess, this is a forty-four caliber casing from a Markov P-4. Take a good look around. They were after something in this room."

As Laticia began checking the desks to see if anyone had left their CAC cards in their computer, John turned to the guard. "What do the people in this room do?"

Before the guard could answer, an older man, who had entered behind them while John and Laticia were examining the shell casing, said, "They're off-base analysts for the new Shipview Process the Navy has adopted."

John turned and raised his eyebrows questioningly. "Who are you?"

"I'm Tim Benton, with the Rivers Consulting Group. We're part of the Shipview process for the Navy."

"And just what are you analyzing?"

"We've been hired by the Navy to help them in their business practices and to make their advance planning more cost-effective and timely. We've made up metrics to analyze data for cost analysis and to help the repair community do a better job planning their work. So we have access to the Navy Marine Corp Information Computer System."

"I was afraid you were going to say something like that. They must have been hacking into our system."

"You may be right. There's nothing else of value here."

John nodded. "Excuse me. I've got to make a phone call." He stepped outside to get a little privacy and called his boss. "Sir, we'd better go to Cyber Threat Con Zebra. I think the NMCI system has been compromised."

By going to Cyber Threat Condition Zebra, all off-base computer links in San Diego would be denied access to NMCI. With that accomplished, Silva reentered the room and approached Laticia. "I'm going back to the office. I'll probably be up all night explaining this to Washington. Let me know what else you find, and meet me back at Thirty-Second Street later today."

"Yes, Sir."

"Laticia, how many times do I have to tell you to call me John?"

"Yes, Sir, John. I won't forget."

John shook his head and walked to his car, wondering who was trying to compromise government computers and why. Computer hacking was one of the biggest threats to national security; so much information was tied to the Internet, and many foreign nations, especially China, were trying to hack into the government systems where this secret information was stored. John Silva was determined to do whatever he could to keep that from happening—at least on his watch.

13

Oval Office, the White House

Director Stevens waited for the President in the outer Oval Office, having called earlier to meet with him as soon as possible. He had a new DVD in his hand. How it appeared in the interoffice mail pouch was a mystery he'd solve later. Stevens wondered if the message was a hoax, but he wasn't going to take any chances. The fact that the DVD made it to his desk was cause enough to consider it authentic. William Stevens was the second Director of National Security since '04. He was tenacious in finding things out, and used any resource possible. Sometimes his abrupt attitude made instant enemies, but he didn't want to waste time, and rarely overlooked small details.

"The President will see you now, Mr. Stevens," Jennifer, the President's executive secretary, announced.

Vince Ryland sat at his desk, going through a file, as Stevens walked in. The Republican incumbent lifted his head in greeting. "Bill, what's so important that you made me put off the vice-president this morning?"

"I'm not sure, Mr. President, but I think there's a new militant threat rising from the Muslim world. Somehow this disk made it into our interoffice pouch and up to my desk, and that troubles me."

"Pop it in the player, and let's see what we have."

Stevens walked over to the screen, inserted the disk into the receiver, and hit the play button. The screen was blank, and then it briefly showed the Al-Jazeera news station. There was some talk in Arabic, and then a news clip came on, showing a man dressed in a full-length white *khamis* and wearing a white *emamat* embossed in gold on his head. His high cheekbones, dark eyebrows, perfect teeth, and olive skin made him appear quite handsome on the screen. The television camera moved in closer as he began to speak.

"*Salaam alaikum*, Mr. President. Unless all of the holy Islamic warriors now being held in Guantanamo Naval Prison are released, we'll strike a mighty blow in the name of Allah on one of your largest cities. You have convicted six of Allah's holy warriors using your secret military court and had them murdered. Be forewarned if you murder one more prisoner fire will rain down from the sky on one of your cities. However, if you release our prisoners of war, I will call off the attack. I truly wish there were another way. When my people are released, we will again be at peace. Please consider my proposal, Mr. President. I realize that you do not negotiate with terrorists, but I assure you that I am not a terrorist, but rather a man seeking peace. Doesn't your Bible say, 'Blessed are the peacemakers'? So please consider my first request as a peace offering for both sides. I trust that you have been given this disk on the twenty-fourth of March." The man appeared calm and confident, as if he knew beyond a doubt that the President would be playing the recording.

The monitor went blank, and the President looked at Stevens.

"When was this recorded?" he asked.

"We scanned all Al-Jazeera broadcasts and found this one being broadcast yesterday morning. I don't know how it got into the interagency pouch, but I received it this morning and knew you needed to see it immediately."

"Check all your contacts to see if we know who this guy is."

"We have, Sir. His identity and voice modulations don't match anyone we have on file."

"That's good; maybe it's a ruse."

"My gut feeling is that it's not. How real, though, I don't know."

"Well, you'd better find out. What has the media said about this so-called peace offering?"

"I haven't heard a word. I don't think they know about it, or else they're not paying it any attention. Nobody seems to be able to identify this man, but we've received reports that one of Osama bin Laden's people is trying to unify the militant Muslims worldwide."

"If that happens we could be in some serious trouble."

"Are you going to respond, Mr. President?"

"Not yet. He's right, whoever he is, that I don't negotiate with terrorists. Do all you can to find out who he is, and what did he mean by very soon?"

"I don't know, Sir, but maybe I can get an informal response to this. If I can get something from you, then we might be able to buy more time to figure out who he is."

"I see where you're headed with that and the answer's no!" The President paused, and then asked, "Is that all?"

"Yes, Sir."

The President nodded. "Let me know what you find."

Stevens got up and retrieved the disc, and then walked to the door, wondering about the wisdom of the President's plan. After all, it was obvious that whoever this new terrorist was, he was very well connected.

14

USS SHEBOYGAN—Pier 6, San Diego Naval Base, 32nd Street

"Hey, aren't you the guy that helped me out last night?"

The bosun frowned at the attractive young woman, sporting a white hardhat, dark safety sunglasses, and a San Diego Shipyard badge that hung around her neck on a small chain. "Do I know you?"

"You sure do," she said, removing her hardhat and glasses, "and I want to thank you for standing up for me last night."

Boats couldn't believe his eyes. "Well, I'll be...I never thought I'd see you on my ship. You look much different in work clothes, but...what are you doing here?"

"I'm here to look at the lifeboat davit," she replied putting her prescription safety glasses back on.

"What? Nobody told me anyone was coming." He paused and studied her for a moment. She was every bit as beautiful in the sunlight as she'd been at the Lion's Lair the night before. He realized he was staring and decided he should say something. "So, how's your arm?"

"A little bruised."

"Whoever he was, he'd better hope he never crosses my path again." When she didn't offer an explanation, he changed the subject. "So do you work for this French company?"

"No, I'm from the shipyard. We've been tasked to provide an on-site rep for this monstrosity."

"You can say that again. This thing never has worked correctly. Well, there it is, but I'm getting ready to do an operational test on the retractable flight deck panels. I think you'd better come back a little later."

"I wish I could, but my ride back to the shipyard already left, and he won't be back for another six hours. Look, Bosun, I'm here to look at computer programming for the davit, so if you don't mind, I'll just power it up and check the automatic features," she said, pulling out her multi-tester from her tool bag.

"Do you know how to use that?"

"They wouldn't have hired me if I didn't. Now I'll need to get to work."

"Suit yourself. I'll send one of my guys to assist you."

"Thanks. And thanks again for last night," she said, her smile bright as her eyes lingered on his, warming Boats clear down to his toes.

About an hour later the bosun walked over to Liz, who was looking at a tech manual by the controls for the davit.

"Must have been twenty tons of steel uncovering the well-deck," Liz commented. "How'd it go?"

Boats smiled. "It went fine."

"Why would you want to fold the flight deck up?"

"It's a new system the Navy came up with," he said, and then quickly changed the conversation. "Let's operate the davit."

He put the controls in manual and did a test-run, lowering a boat from the davit. As usual it worked perfectly in port, when the conditions were perfectly calm. As he worked, Liz's slight scent of perfume reached his nose, and he turned to face her.

"What's your last name?" he asked.

"Ferrari."

"Like the car?"

"You got it."

"Well, come over here, Miss Ferrari. I want to show you how we've got to operate this davit."

Liz watched while the bosun shifted the control lever from automatic to manual as the boat was lowered with two hoist wires, one on the bow and the other on the stern.

"So why do you do that?" she asked.

"If I don't, when the boat hits the waterline, the automatic tensioners on each hoist begin to fight each other once the boat touches into the water."

"How does it work when you're out on the ocean?"

"It doesn't. All that money the government spent on automation and we have to use this in a modified operation."

"Sounds like a computer problem to me. When you get done with your test, I'd like to get into the panel."

"Sure, but I'll need the electricians to tag out the system."

"I'm an electrician." She smiled, and that warm feeling poured over Boats again. "You don't need somebody else."

Ignoring his feelings, the bosun answered, "You don't understand. I need a ship's electrician to put power on the computer so you can work on it. Nobody knew you were coming, and I've got to talk to the CHENG." He pulled out his side phone and made a quick call. When he replaced it in the holster, he noticed Liz checking him out.

She quickly recovered and asked, "Can you operate this davit from somewhere else on the ship?"

"We haven't tried it, but there's a computer on the bridge that allows us to lower the lifeboat from there."

"Really? Why haven't you tried it from another location?"

"Are you kidding? We've got enough problems with the local operation without trying to go to remote on the bridge."

"That could be the source of some of your problems. I'll have to check that out, too," she said, pulling out her notepad and writing something down.

"Miss Ferrari..."

"Call me Liz."

"Liz, if you can fix this thing, I'll give you all the access you need," the bosun offered, only too glad to see someone working to fix the davit. He'd heard from a bosun on the East Coast that this same davit had little or no support from the parent company that designed and manufactured it.

"Hey, Bosun, what's that boat used for?" Liz asked, as she pointed to the starboard side of the boat deck.

"That's the latest and greatest technology for unmanned waterborne surveillance."

"What's it called?"

"Sea Flyer."

"How's it launched?"

"With the ship's crane."

"Very unusual. Does it work?"

"Sometimes, but I've seen it get off-course a few times."

With that he decided the question-and-answer session had ended. Liz Ferrari was a gorgeous, but she sure asked a lot of unusual questions.

15

San Diego Airport

Sitting in an obscure corner near the payphones in the baggage section of Terminal One at Lindberg field in San Diego, Elena quietly observed all that was going on around her. Hidden behind dark sunglasses, she watched as travelers of all ages hugged and kissed their loved ones, as they waited for the stainless steel chute to dump their precious bags onto the carousel. Elena knew that Abdullah would be here, but she wanted to observe the interaction between Jim and his mother without Abdullah's knowledge.

The only thing Elena knew about the young lieutenant was that he was tall and had dark hair. His flight was to arrive at 11:00 A.M., and she watched as the people a deck above her rode the escalator down. A glass partition served as a wall so that the people down below could begin to make eye contact with the arriving passengers before they transited to the lower floor. A pang of jealousy erupted in Elena's heart, as she saw a young lady wave to her father above. To know a father's love was something Elena's heart painfully craved. Elizabeth and she had started life in a Romanian orphanage and never knew a family's love. Khalif met the orphans barely surviving in the sewers of Bucharest and brought them to a desert camp in Sudan for training. In the past Elena had been able to suppress any emotions. For some reason, as she watched the people meeting, greeting, hugging, and kissing, she wished she were one of them. Like an L.A. street gang, the al-Qaeda network had provided her with a sense of belonging. They were always there for her, but at a great personal expense. When she initially entered the training camps as a young girl, the price of membership didn't matter. Now, as she completed the transition from girl to woman, she questioned the life she had been living. In the quietness of her heart, she even did the unthinkable: She questioned the killing of innocent women and children by the militant Islamic extremists.

Khalif had given Elena the assignment of getting Abdullah's son to fall for her, an assignment no different than many of the others. With her stunning good looks and sensuous curves, she never doubted for a moment that she would succeed. Elena couldn't think of a time when men weren't constantly looking at her, trying to make eye contact. All she had to do was add a little sweetness to their lives, and they were like putty in her fingers.

Elena had been trained to study people, especially men, and she watched as the steady flow continued to arrive at the baggage claim area. All the kissing and hugging was compromising her emotions, and she knew it, so she began a game to discover Jim before his family claimed him.

⌒

Lieutenant Jim Sherock walked off the jet-way with mixed emotions. Coming home was bittersweet. He loved his mom with all his heart, but his dad was a malicious, overbearing tyrant. Jim reflected on the times when he was younger, when he had lived in fear of his father, especially when Abdullah came home drunk in the early morning. Jim still bore scars from eleven years ago when, at fourteen, he had stood up to his dad. He would never forget that day as long as he lived. When he heard his mother's flesh being pounded, he rushed into their bedroom with a baseball bat in his hands. With uncontrollable rage, he swung it with all his might. He didn't care what happened to him; he just wanted the beating to stop.

Jim's father staggered to his knees after the first blow, but quickly regained his footing and came at his son like a hungry wolf, ready to devour its young. Abdullah took the bat away from Jim and beat him unconscious. When the boy awoke, his head was in his mother's lap, and his blood had dripped down on her. From that day forward they shared an everlasting bond that could never be broken. Jim missed her and looked forward to seeing her again.

He had one week of leave before he reported to the USS Sheboygan, and he planned to have some fun now that he was home in San Diego. It had been raining in Norfolk, but when the plane flew over the desert, carrying him home, the clouds had parted and the sun shone brightly. In addition to visiting with his mother, Jim looked forward to hanging ten in the Pacific.

After deplaning he walked down the long, sterile corridor that led to the baggage claim area. From his vantage point he looked through the glass partition and scanned the area. Immediately he saw his parents, looking around, wondering when and where he would show up. Jim noticed a little more gray in his mother's hair, and he hoped the last couple of years had been kind to her. He knew he didn't have the courage to tell Abdullah what had happened to him a year ago that had changed his life.

Jim put on a warm smile for his mom as he rode down the escalator. As soon as she spotted him she waved, but stood back and allowed Abdullah to greet him first.

"Son, it's so good to see you," Abdullah said, as he kissed the boy on both cheeks.

Respectful of her place in this marriage, his mother waited as they embraced, smiling warmly at her only child. Finally, leaving his father and dropping his bag, Jim eagerly embraced his mother. Their hug was deep and tender.

"Mom, I've missed you," he said, kissing her on the cheek.

"Oh, my little Jimmy, I've missed you, too" she replied, her tear-filled eyes sparkling.

"Come on. Come on, you two," Abdullah snapped, grabbing his wife by the arm and pulling her away from Jim.

She scarcely seemed to notice, her eyes fixed on her son. "How much time off do you have?"

"I hope a week. I'm supposed to report to my command tomorrow."

"Oh, that's wonderful! Maybe we can take a trip somewhere."

"Cynthia, the boy probably wants to rest," Abdullah said. "He's been working hard in the Navy."

"Sure, Mom, whatever you want," Jim said, daring to contradict his dad. "But I also want to get some surfing in. The East Coast has nothing on the waves and beaches out here."

"And to look upon the shameless, naked girls," his father accused with harsh disapproval.

〜

Still hidden behind her sunglasses but near enough to hear, Elena watched the interchange between the family. She was especially attuned to the interaction of mother and son, and she checked out what Cynthia was wearing. It was conservative, low-key. Elena quickly buttoned her sweater all the way to the top but didn't put on her coat. She wanted to appear modest but didn't want to hide her hourglass figure. Then she made her move.

Strolling up to the baggage turnstile, she nonchalantly dropped her claim ticket in front of Jim and then looked the other way. It was an old claim ticket she had used on her return trip from India.

"Excuse me, miss," Jim said, bending down to retrieve the ticket. "I believe you dropped this."

"Oh, *mon Dieu*," she replied, accepting the ticket from him and allowing her fingers to rest on his for a long moment as she pulled off her sunglasses, allowing him to see her eyes. "*Merci. Quesque c'est*... Is this the right baggage claim?" she said, watching his reaction while still holding his hand.

With raised eyes and surprise on his face, Abdullah watched, as Elena smiled sweetly to his son.

"You're welcome," Jim said, obviously flustered as he observed her womanly beauty from head to toe. "I think your flight must have come in at the International Terminal, which, as I recall, is Terminal Two."

"Oh, *excuzez-moi*," she replied, her French accent thick and sweet.

"How did you get so lost?"

"It must have been your San Diego sunshine. Paris is so dark and gloomy. I went outside just to bask in the sun a little, and I must have turned the wrong way."

"There's a shuttle out there. I'm sure it will take you to the International Terminal. Let me get my bag, and I'll show you."

"*Merci beaucoup*. You are a true gentleman. You have a wonderful son," she said, turning to Cynthia and flashing a friendly smile.

Jim spotted his bag on the turnstile. "Just a minute and I'll walk you to the shuttle." He squeezed between two people, reached down, and snatched his suitcase off the conveyor, quickly returning.

"*Merci*, but no. You have been kind enough. Just point the way. I don't want to bother you with your family."

"It's no trouble. Besides I'm home for a while. Follow me," he said, and then turned to his parents. "I'll be right back."

Elena stole a quick look at Abdullah's smoldering eyes. Defiantly, she quickly turned her head and nodded to Cynthia, as she followed Jim out the doors and to the curb.

"There's a shuttle here every five minutes. It'll take you to Terminal Two. I think you'll find your bags there."

"*Merci*," she purred warmly. "You've been very kind. Here's my card. I'll be staying at the Harbor Marriott. Give me a call, and I'll buy you a drink."

Jim looked at the embossed card and read it aloud: "'Elena Dubois, diamond dealer.' Wow."

"Oh, I'm just starting in the business. I'm going to gemology school in Carlsbad, wherever that is."

"Carlsbad! That's where I live. My name's Jim."

"*Je suis* Elena," she said with a dazzling smile.

A shuttle bus pulled up to the curb and opened its doors. Jim again took Elena's hand and helped her on the bus. She let him hold on just a little longer than normal and then slid her hand from his palm.

"Maybe, if you're not too tired, we could have that drink tonight," he offered.

Climbing into the bus she turned around and smiled. "I'd like that."

↩

Jim returned to his parents. Abdullah had that stern look on his face that Jim had seen too many times before, but his mom was smiling warmly.

"She's a pretty girl. Did you get her name?"

"What do you think?" he replied with a grin, showing her Elena's card.

"A diamond dealer. I'll bet she's interesting."

Abdullah shook his head but said nothing, and that sealed it for Jim. He'd call Elena in the afternoon and meet with her that evening. Later, he'd tell his mom how it went.

16

Rosarita Beach, Mexico

Khalif's men had obtained the names of the custom agents employed in Ensenada, Mexico, and then they shadowed some of them to find the right one. One man, Horate Ruiz, was married and had two children, but he enjoyed the "finer" things in life, away from his wife. Often he would drive up the coast and stay at the famous Rosarita Beach Hotel and Spa. It was there the two men made contact with him and arranged a meeting for Khalif. They ordered Margaritas and were enjoying the night air when Khalif quietly joined them.

"I hear you're a shipping agent in Ensenada."

"*Si,*" Horate replied, pleased by the attention and free drinks he was receiving. "It's a good job, and it pays the bills."

Khalif's lips offered only a thin smile in response. "I have need of your services," he said, his voice as cool and businesslike as his smile. "A ship is coming in, and I need the right agent to help me clear my cargo. Can you arrange this for me?"

"Oh, *Senor,* I don't know. I don't schedule who's on duty when a specific ship comes into port and unloads."

"I understand, but I need someone who can handle my custom matters rather delicately. I will make it worth your while."

"Delicately can mean a lot of things, *Senor.*"

"Perhaps quietly is a better word."

"I'm sorry, *amigo,* but you have the wrong man. I would never break the law."

"I'm not asking you to break the law. I fully intend to pay the tariff for my shipment of farm equipment. It's just…" Khalif's voice drifted off, and his thin smile returned, doing little to dispel Ruiz's sudden but growing discomfort. "I would feel better if I knew that the man inspecting my equipment was someone I trusted."

"*Si,* all of us inspect cargo the same way and charge the correct amount of tariff. You are not trying to smuggle drugs into our country?" Ruiz asked. The last thing he wanted was to upset the local drug cartel.

"Of course not. But I can see you have a taste for the finer things in life here in Rosarita…away from your wife and children."

"What are you talking about?" the shipping agent demanded, rising from his seat and nervously eyeing the exit, as Khalif's men moved to block it.

"Sit down, Horate," Khalif ordered, all pretense of civility gone. "We've been investigating you, and it wasn't hard to see that you like a little action on the wild side."

"Investigating?" Horate asked, his heart racing, as he felt beads of perspiration break out on his forehead. "Who are you?"

Disregarding his question and calmly motioning Horate to sit down, Khalif continued. "I understand your concern. I truly do. I'm a man like you, and I think we can come to a mutual agreement that will enrich both of our families."

"If I do any business with you," Horate declared, hoping his voice sounded more confident than he felt, "my wife and children are not part of it."

"I didn't want to imply anything in particular," Khalif suggested in a low conspiratorial tone, his dark eyes unwavering, controlling the situation. Then in a commanding tone he stated, "Of course, if you do as I say, there won't be any trouble. Now sit down, and I'll explain what I need."

His legs shaking, Horate did as ordered, and Khalif pulled out a fat white envelope. From that point the one-way transaction took about twenty minutes. The Light of Allah's Messenger made it perfectly clear to the shipping agent what the implied consequences would be if he were betrayed. Having concluded the arrangement, Khalif got up and walked away.

⌐

Confident that he had Ruiz right where he wanted him, Khalif boarded the plane and returned to Mexico City for the next leg of his journey. Once there he took his time with his makeup and grayish-black wig before leaving his hotel room and going to the airport for the next flight. The body padding he wore added a little weight and gave him a matronly figure. Years ago he used too much body padding in the right areas and was constantly being approached by men. But with less padding, glasses, and the gray wig, he could hide behind a book and not have to worry about men while traveling. Clearing security, customs, and immigration, he finally made it to his gate. When they called his flight number, he boarded an Air Mexico plane with connections at Charles de Gaulle Airport in Paris before proceeding to the Seychelles Islands. In his luggage he packed the front money he would need for the arms dealer. Hiding currency in his luggage was risky, but the bills were packed in vacuum-sealed bags and sewn into the lining of his suitcase. The only way it could be detected was by an x-ray.

Khalif breezed through customs and immigration without a problem. The forgers they used in Paris were the best. No one would suspect that The Light of Allah's Messenger traveled inconspicuously throughout the world as an old woman, particularly after shaving. Before meeting with his comrades, Khalif made sure all information was transferred through a children's Internet chat room. The secret code that Allah had inspired the Light of Allah with had never been broken, even after ten years.

When an older flight attendant came around with drinks, Khalif allowed himself two Johnny Walker Blacks from the free cart they served in first class as a reward for once again fooling immigration. He insisted on flying in first class because most of the terrorists had flown coach. In first class he was usually left alone. His slender body and delicate face had undergone a remarkable transformation, and as long as he talked softly, no one suspected he wasn't a woman. His ability to transform himself got him out of many tight places when people were looking for a man. The only time he got into trouble was when a woman confronted him in a *loo* in Paris when he was applying his makeup. He wondered if they ever found her body. Some curious women, like the aging flight attendant who seemed to be studying him each time she passed by, were simply eliminated.

The preparations to bring San Diego to its knees were going well, and Allah would be pleased. Khalif knew he would have an honored place in paradise when his time came.

The dull roar of the jet engines lulled him to sleep, as the Airbus 303 soared over the Caribbean and across the Atlantic Ocean. Khalif dreamed of a Swedish stewardess he would meet in the islands.

Someone bumped him, jolting him from his erotic dreams.

"Oh, excuse me, ma'am," the attendant said. "I didn't know you were sleeping."

Khalif was furious, but he held his temper. If they were on the ground, she would have paid dearly for her mistake.

"Bring me two Johnny Walkers, and be quick about it," he snapped with a little too much authority in his voice. The attendant did a double-take, but before she could think about it, he quickly added in a sweet tone, "Please, darling." The rest of the flight was unremarkable, but every once in awhile that same attendant cast him a long, questioning look, and Khalif knew he couldn't allow her to compromise his identity.

After fourteen hours the plane landed in Paris, where he changed carriers before heading to the Seychelles. Finally the plane touched down amid swaying palm trees in the humid island breeze. Khalif looked forward to his business with the Russian and getting out of the dress.

Retrieving his bag and clearing customs, he walked out of the terminal building and hailed a taxi. The warm island air enveloped his body as he walked to the vehicle.

"Le Meridien Fisherman's Cove," he softly told the driver, inviting no further conversation.

They drove along a lush tropical coast for thirty minutes and arrived at an older beachfront hotel. Though not modern, the hotel boasted a superb view of the bay. Khalif paid the driver but wouldn't let the bellboy take his bag. He walked up to the ebony receptionist with the big bright eyes and gleaming white teeth and pulled out his French passport and a credit card.

"Do you have a room for Mr. and Mrs. Forquet?" he asked.

"Let me see," the dark haired island beauty replied with a charming smile. "Here it is, ma'am. Please sign here."

Khalif signed the voucher.

"Your suite is ready. When will Mr. Forquet arrive?"

"Later. I'll need two keys."

"Of course," she said handing him two plastic key cards.

Khalif picked them up but went straight to the bar, Lo Cocoloba, which had a spectacular view of the azure seas just below the hotel. A jazz band was playing a smooth number to the few customers enjoying their sundowners. Khalif waited to see who showed up and how many bodyguards the arms dealer brought with him this time. One time in Cairo he avoided disaster, as he watched a Turkish agent show up with the Egyptian secret police. He had a traveling companion, another woman, and the two of them continued drinking, as one of the policemen tried to hit on them. Hoping to trap Khalif, the police waited for an hour and finally gave up, leaving the bar.

While in Paris, Khalif had studied theater and makeup at a special school, where he quickly became a master of disguise, providing him with an array of transformations that he could produce at a moment's notice. The ability to go undetected was a huge asset to him after America had declared war on the terrorists.

The Light of Allah's messenger watched as the Russian made his way into the bar. While the arms dealer ordered vodka, Khalif noted the perimeter position of his three steroid-enhanced Slavic bodyguards. The waitress arrived, and the Russian took in her dark slender loveliness before she left his table with a sizable tip.

Khalif quickly left the bar and went to his room. He tore off his clothes and wiped the makeup from his face. Changing outfits, he grabbed a silk tie he'd purchased in Stanley Market on the other side of Hong Kong. He put on a silk, wool, and cashmere business suit that he'd had made by his favorite tailor on Scott Street in Singapore earlier in the year when he had delivered the Light of Allah's invitation to Jemaah Islamiah. He then traveled to Iraq and met separately with the leaders of the Sunni and the Shiite Muslims. He talked with them, but they were reluctant to join The Light of Allah. As always they were at war with one another over control of Iraq. Separately they listened to the plan that would bring the Muslim world together and the infidels to their knees, worshipping Allah or having their heads chopped off.

Never before had such a thing happened. The Arab world was filled with mistrust and country-specific agendas. Each of the

Islamic terrorist leaders had their own ideas on how to attack the infidel's strongholds, and The Light of Allah had been smart enough to help finance some of their attacks. He'd also set up secret training camps in their own countries and financed them. He rarely traveled, but often made the trip to Mecca as a true believer of Islam. The Light of Allah had proved his *jihad*, like many of the older soldiers in the hills of Afghanistan. Inspired by a divine vision, he broke away from Osama bin Laden and formed his own movement.

Entering the bar carrying his briefcase Khalif saw the arms dealer ordering another drink. He looked around and smiled as he approached him.

"Sergio, how good to see you."

The big Russian bear got to his feet and embraced Khalif, kissing him on both cheeks before he sat back down. "Khalif, you're always late to our meetings. Why is that?"

The Messenger smiled. "Is my money ever late, Sergio, my old friend?"

"No, never. That's why I tolerate your tardiness. What would you like to drink?" Sergio asked, turning his gaze toward the beautiful, exotic waitress who had just strolled up to their table. She flashed an inviting smile.

"Tea would be nice," Khalif said, not wanting his mind impaired by alcohol. Later, when he was alone, he would imbibe of the forbidden drink.

"How was your flight over?" Sergio asked.

"How do you know I flew?"

"Take it easy, old friend. I was just making small talk. What do you need from me this time?" the former Soviet colonel asked. Since the Cold War had ended, a stockpile of Russian military supplies had become available. The Ukrainian government struggled to pay their army, so some of the officers had taken payment in their own hands. They confiscated weapons and delivered them to the highest bidder. Sergio had a bright mind and the aggressiveness to eliminate his competition and his commanding officer. He and his men now moved tanks, trucks, and guns to their own warehouses and dumped them on the global black market at ridiculously low prices. As a result, Sergio had armed the Light of Allah's growing army with many weapons.

"I need a transport plane, eight short-range missiles, and their launchers."

"Khalif, I don't have any airplanes, missiles, or launchers."

"I know, but you must find them. I will pay handsomely. You have two weeks to acquire them and ship them to Ensenada, Mexico."

"Two weeks! That's not a lot of time."

"Maybe I've got the wrong man?" Khalif rose, as the bodyguards quickly moved forward.

"Easy, easy, my friend," Sergio said, flashing a look at his men and then at Khalif. "Let's not be hasty. Please, sit down. This will cost extra, you know."

"Of course."

"But how will we clear customs in Mexico?"

"It's been arranged. When we meet in two weeks, I will complete the payment and give you shipping instructions."

"This will cost much more than you've given me in the past."

"Take my briefcase from under the table. It's filled with more than enough for your purchases. Do you have any questions?"

"No. But let's meet again tomorrow."

In the distance Khalif spotted the aging flight attendant who had been suspicious of him, sitting at a table by herself. He made a mental note to find her later and take care of unfinished business.

"Yes, that would be fine," Khalif said, though he had no intentions of meeting Sergio again. He always changed his plans once business was concluded so that he wouldn't be predictable. "I will contact you with the shipping company's name."

17

Marriot Hotel, San Diego

Elena fussed with her hair while waiting for the phone to ring. Then, scanning the clothes in the closet, she quickly decided there was nothing that expressed a conservative image. She remembered a small boutique in the hotel lobby and decided she would have to go down there later and buy a new outfit. She wanted to establish a meaningful relationship with Jim, not scare him off with seductive clothing. She also knew that Khalif would be pressuring her for immediate results.

Awaiting Jim's call she turned on the TV. It was Sunday, and the first image that flickered onto the screen was an enthusiastic, yet humorous, black man, who preached in a way that made Elena feel he was hollering at her. Sweat formed on his bald head, and he wiped it off with a black handkerchief. She tried to change the channel, but the remote wasn't working, so she left it on. Her day had been long, and the TV provided just enough background noise that she quickly fell asleep.

The ringing of the phone jarred her awake.

"*Da*," she blurted out sleepily in her native Romanian dialect.

"Da? I must have the wrong number. Is this Elena?"

"*Oui, c'est* Elena," she answered sweetly, recovering from her slipup and hoping Jim would buy her cover-up.

"What's with Da? I thought you were French."

"*Mais, oui, je suis Francaise.* I fell asleep and was dreaming about my grandfather. I called him Da-Da."

"That's cute. Are you tired from your flight?"

"*Oui*, I'm still a little ah…ah, how you say…fuzzy? But I feel rested."

"Your card says you're a diamond dealer. That's pretty interesting. Do you go to Africa to purchase your diamonds?"

"Actually, no."

She could hear the surprise in Jim's voice. "I thought that's where all the diamonds came from."

"It's true; most originate from Africa, but that's before they're cut."

"Fascinating. I'd like to hear more about what you do. Are you up for buying me that drink?"

"Oh, I don't know," Elena responded hesitantly. She didn't want to seem like a loose woman, and she knew that if she wanted to capture Jim's heart, she would have to dance a bit.

"I'd love to show you San Diego. Have you eaten anything today?"

"Just a petite snack on the plane."

"Well, San Diego has great seafood and a beautiful waterfront. If you'd like, I can pick you up and we can drive downtown."

"Well, maybe. I suppose I will be hungry a little later."

"How about seven? I know a place on the bay that would be wonderful for dinner."

"*Oui*, Jim, *au revoir*," Elena said, hanging up the phone and knowing she'd better find another dress to wear. She dashed from her room and took the elevator down to the lobby, hoping the boutique was still open. Relieved to discover that it was, she hurried inside and searched to find a conservative, yet sexy, dress for her dinner date. She didn't want to appear underdressed, but she did want to leave him wanting more. After trying on a few outfits, Elena settled on a black sleeveless shift that accented her blonde hair but wasn't too revealing. It was overpriced, but when she looked approvingly at herself in the mirror she thought, *How can he resist?*

⌐

Jim hung up and pumped his fist in the air. "Yes!" He had two hours to get ready, and he couldn't wait.

"I need to talk to you," Abdullah demanded roughly.

Startled, Jim turned, wondering how long his father had been standing outside his old bedroom door. All the excitement of a date with a beautiful French woman suddenly rushed out of his body, like a dam bursting its floodgates. The last thing he wanted was another Islamic sermon from his dad. While at the academy he'd been quietly questioning the Muslim faith. He began attending a Christian church with one of his classmates and soon found a way that was filled with love, kindness, and gentleness. It was like discovering a fresh water oasis after being trapped in the Sahara for many years. He couldn't wait to tell Haviv about it. Haviv was always much warmer than Abdullah, and over the years Jim had confided in him, rather than his dad.

"Can't this wait till tomorrow? I have a date tonight."

"No, it can't," Abdullah countered stubbornly.

Jim decided to give it one more try. "Please, Dad, I don't want to get into it with you. You and I just don't agree on politics. Can't we leave it at that?"

Abdullah frowned and spoke in heavy-handed notes of confirmation. "When you're ready, Son, come to the living room." Then, without waiting for a reply, he turned and walked away.

Jim pounded the air with his fists and said to the wall. "Why? Why do I have to talk with him? What's he going to do to wreck my life this time? Why can't he be normal, like all the other fathers?"

Although difficult, life at the Naval Academy had been great. For the first four months they restricted the plebes to the grounds. Away from his dad the academy quickly became Jim's sanctuary. He excelled at everything he did, applying himself to his schoolwork and graduating near the top of his class. The language classes came easily, and he floored his professors with his natural inclination for languages, especially Farsi, though they never suspected where he had learned it. Jim attracted the attention of the intelligence communities and was recruited his senior year by a new military intelligence organization run by a Navy captain who had spent his career in military intelligence. They wanted Jim because he could go into many areas, using his Navy commission as cover. San Diego, the largest West Coast Naval port, was a prime terrorist target, and the captain got Jim assigned to one of the ships on the waterfront. He was to keep an eye out for any unusual activity and be available for special operations.

Reluctantly Jim went down to the living room where his dad sat waiting. He knew from past lectures that the best way to handle this was to agree with everything Abdullah said and end the meeting as quickly as possible. He didn't want to be late for his date with Elena.

"Have you enjoyed your time with the Navy?"

"It's a job. It's got its good points and bad points. Is Mom here?"

"I sent her to the store."

Jim cringed inside when he heard his mother was away. The seriousness of his father's tone was not a good sign.

"Do you remember the summers we spent up in Oregon?"

"Sure," Jim said, his sense of dread growing. "The 'wilderness' camps. Why?"

"Your people may need you in the near future."

Jim struggled with his father's words. He had heard them before but could never understand how the people in the Arab countries were his people. His mother was American. The United States had been good to him, especially the academy. He couldn't understand the hatred of America that was preached in the secret camps.

"What do you mean?" Jim asked, struggling with his emotions as he always did with his father. Just being around Abdullah made him uneasy.

"I'll let you know more later. Are you going out with that girl you met at the airport?"

Jim perked up. This was highly unusual! Abdullah had never been the least bit interested in the girls Jim dated.

Abdullah pulled out his wallet and handed Jim a couple of crisp one-hundred-dollar bills. When he held them out in an obvious gesture of offering, Jim was shocked. "What's this for?"

"I want you to have a good time tonight," Abdullah said as he handed him the money. "You've earned it. Here, take it."

Jim sat there, stunned. His father had never given him money for a date. Finally he found his voice. "That's okay, Dad. I've got enough money. But thanks anyway." It was true he could have used the extra cash, but he was leery of accepting anything from his father. He didn't want to be indebted to him.

"I know I've been difficult to live with and made a lot of mistakes raising you, but I want you to enjoy yourself tonight. Besides, that girl was very pretty, and I want you to make a good impression on her. Take the money, and enjoy yourself."

Jim couldn't believe what he was hearing. His dad never admitted any mistakes, but always blamed others. Jim stared at the money.

"Please, Jim," he pleaded, "let's start a new chapter in our relationship."

Jim was floored. If that could be possible, he didn't want to blow the chance, so he reached out and took the money.

"Thanks, Dad," he said, wanting all this to be true. Deep down in his heart something wasn't right. Still, he couldn't wait to tell Mom about Dad's change of attitude. He quickly exited the house before Abdullah changed his mind and started another long boring lecture.

⌐

Free from his father, Jim raced down the freeway in his silver steed. The old 911 Porsche Carrera galloped down the highway, and his excitement rose the more he thought of the enchanting Elena. She had captivated his thoughts by her striking good looks and quaint French accent. Something about the tone of her voice melted his heart. He only hoped she was at least moderately interested in him and not just going out on an obligatory date with him out of a sense of gratitude for his help at the airport.

Noticing his speed reaching eighty, he slowed down but still arrived at the hotel a half-hour early. He went to the bar and ordered a Heineken. The cool green bottles reminded him of Department Head School in Newport, Rhode Island. After a long day of naval classes he would kick back on his balcony with a couple of cold ones and watch the ocean waves roll up on the shore.

Jim looked up at the bar clock and noticed that it was five after seven. The thought never occurred to him that Elena would stand him up. He took another swallow of beer and looked around at the lobby, but he didn't spot her. *Maybe she was just being nice to me on the phone to get rid of me,* he thought. But no, he wasn't going to accept that—at least not without a fight. He reached back into his pocket and pulled out her business card again, reading it for the umpteenth time. He downed the beer and ordered another one.

"*Bonjour,* Jim," a soft, sweet voice purred from behind him, reminding him of the siren's call of the Greek coastline that he'd heard so much about, beckoning the windblown sailor to shore. The rolling lilt of her voice as she pronounced the "J" in his name sounded musical.

His heart leapt as he turned around and took in a vision of loveliness that he had only seen in magazines. Her flowing blonde hair was flipped to one side, complimenting her sleeveless black dress, which quietly accented the muscle tone in her arms. Jim liked a woman who was athletic and was surprised he hadn't noticed that feature at the airport. Shimmering diamonds around her neck shot colorful sparks of fire throughout the dimly lit bar.

"Elena, you look absolutely stunning." He was glad he had taken his father's money because after seeing the way she was dressed, he was changing dinner plans. An Ocean Beach nightclub was not going to cut it.

"*Merci pour le compliment,* Jim," she said, gazing into his eyes for a moment before looking around the lobby. "Are you going to make me stand here, or are you going to let me buy you that drink?"

"Actually I was thinking we'd drive along the coast and go to La Jolla for dinner."

"*Tres bien,* Jim. That sounds nice. La Jolla. What kind of place is that?"

"It's pretty upscale, and it has some fashionable restaurants with great views of the water. We could do a little dancing if you'd like."

"*Ou mais oui,*" she said, with what looked like a combination of excitement and curiosity shining in her eyes.

"Let's go then," Jim said, as he left a twenty on the bar and eagerly took her hand, guiding her out the door and straight to his car.

*

Elena was pleasantly surprised when Jim opened the car door for her. When on assignment with Arab men, she was treated like a second-class citizen and expected to walk behind them, even when they were on the same mission together. That always made her angry, especially since she had gotten many of them out of some tough situations.

On the drive she could sense a genuine difference between Jim and the other men she had been with. He was a little reserved, and she didn't know if he was shy or a true gentleman. Elena had heard that some of the American men could be quite nice, but in the past she hadn't seen much of that. In some of her earlier assignments, she was used as a probe or a decoy. The targets were all womanizers.

They pulled up into a tight little one-way street and parked the car. Expectantly, she waited for Jim to come around and open her door.

"Thanks," she said, genuinely impressed when he did.

They began a slow stroll down the street, looking in the various shop windows.

Jim interrupted her reverie. "I was planning on going to the beach, but you look like a beautiful, elegant princess from a faraway kingdom."

Deeply touched, Elena said softly, "I've never been called a princess before."

"The rest of the world must be blind. You look like you just stepped out of a castle." He smiled, and it was as if he had introduced a new language to her heart. Before she could respond he said, "I hope we don't have to wait too long before we can get a table. Normally you book reservations before coming to some of these restaurants."

"I don't mind, *mon cheri*," Elena said, reaching out and laying her hand on his arm to reassure him. They stopped at a jewelry store, and she pulled out a pen and paper and wrote down the name of the store. "I've got to come back and visit this La Jolla. I can see they sell a lot of high-end diamonds."

"I'm sure they do. La Jolla's a rich place." Jim smiled again. "Let's walk a little further. I think I see another jewelry store up ahead, and then a restaurant just past it. Maybe they have a table open."

They strolled down the block, and Elena stopped at another jewelry store and wrote down its name, while Jim checked out the adjacent restaurant. When she was finished writing, they walked another block. Elena's exquisite beauty captured an admiring glance from both men and women. Quickly she reached over and put her arm through Jim's, as a spark of static electricity bolted between them.

"My, Jim, I didn't know you could have such an electrifying effect on a woman."

The color in his face reddened, and Elena smiled. She had never been with a man whose inner feelings were so transparent. In the Arab world the men treated women like cattle and rarely shared any emotion with them. This was new to her, and it gave her an inner glow.

They walked into a fashionable, yet elegant restaurant, where the maitre d'greeted them.

"I don't suppose there's any chance we could get a table?" Jim asked.

"Did you make a reservation?"

"No, this is my first night home from Norfolk."

"I'm sorry, Sir, but we're booked two days in advance."

"There's no way I could have known that I'd be here tonight. I've just been transferred to a ship, and I wanted to show my date the nicer part of town."

"What's your rank?"

"Lieutenant."

The man smiled, and with a twinkle in his eye said, "If you give me ten minutes, I think an old chief can take care of you. Why don't you just wait at the bar, and tell Bernie this drink's on me."

"Wow! Thanks. I really appreciate that."

"It won't be long, Sir. I'll come and get you when I have a table ready. I wouldn't want to keep you and your lovely date waiting."

Jim and Elena walked into the lounge area, where a thin black man was delicately massaging the black and white bones, while singing softly in a deep, bass voice. The melodious sound was rich and soothing, and Elena felt herself relaxing and hoping Jim was doing the same.

"So, how did you get into the diamond business?" he asked, as a waiter arrived and took their drink orders.

For the first time in her life Elena regretted having to lie about what she did. "My father was a diamond dealer who wanted a boy to follow in his footsteps. I guess he wasn't too disappointed when I was born instead because during the summer months he took me on his buying trips. So I received a firsthand education in precious gems. I recently returned from a buying trip," she added, carefully omitting the part about smuggling diamonds into the United States and selling them in the back rooms of the jewelry district in downtown LA on Sixth Street to pay for the operation.

"To Africa?"

"No, India. We always bought in India."

"I thought you said most of the diamonds come from Africa."

"They do, but the really good cutters are in India."

"Don't they have cutters in Africa?"

"Some, but India and Thailand are where most diamonds are cut. The workmanship is much better, and labor is still quite cheap. So the diamonds are mined in Africa and sent to India to be cut. Then they're sold to dealers."

"Interesting. I've never heard that before."

The maitre d' arrived shortly and moved them to a prime table overlooking the bay.

"Wow, Chief, thanks!"

"My pleasure, Lieutenant—and take your time."

The night sky was vibrant, as a full moon splashed its golden rays across the rolling waves that slapped the sandy beach. Smooth music and soft lights bathed their bodies in soothing tranquility. Moonlight gently caressed Elena's face highlighting her beauty. She knew Jim was studying her every feature.

The dinner wine warmed Elena's heart, and the easy flow of conversation made her feel as if she had known Jim for years. He talked freely of his naval career, and Elena responded with her cover story, complete with details drawn from her own life. Often, throughout the evening, they looked deeply into each other's eyes, and Elena found herself desperately wanting to compromise her mission and tell Jim the truth. She felt as if she were drowning in the deep waters of his heart, but knew there was something very good about that.

"Would you like to go for a walk?" he asked, as they finished dessert.

"Sure, but let's sit for a while first," Elena said, wanting to hold the warmth of this moment for as long as she could.

Jim ordered Turkish coffee and drank it slowly. After paying the bill, they ventured outside. This time he put his arm in hers, as if it were the most natural thing to do. She welcomed his affectionate touch, and they silently strolled toward the ocean's edge, enjoying the gentle warm breeze that swept over them. Elena took off her high heels so she could walk in the sand, which was still warm from the day. They found some weathered boulders near the water's edge and sat down. Jim withdrew his arm and put it around her shoulders, drawing her close to him.

Elena could feel the beat of his heart and wondered if he would try and kiss her like the other men who had taken advantage of her. This time, however, she would welcome it. But as they sat there together, she realized that if they were going to kiss, she would have to initiate it.

They continued to talk late into the night, as the moon chased the blackened sea, slipping away unnoticed. As if on cue, a cool wind kicked up, stealing the warm embrace of emotions.

"Elena, I really hate to say this, but we've got to be going," Jim whispered. "I'm due to report to the Sheboygan tomorrow to meet the captain."

The ship's name snapped Elena back to reality, and she couldn't believe that for one long moment in her life she had somehow let go of that intense reality, escaping her past and present. She knew her job and did it well, but there was something totally different this time. She had never met a man who respected her as a person and treated her so nicely.

"I've got a big day too. It's my first day at the Carlsbad Diamond School," she said, suddenly excited about her cover, knowing that Jim was very interested.

Hand in hand they slowly strolled to his car. Jim again opened her door and then drove her back to her hotel. Pulling up to the entrance, he shut down the engine and sat there for a moment. Elena didn't move, hoping this euphoric feeling wouldn't disappear the moment he opened her door.

"I had a nice time."

"So did I, Jim. So did I," Elena replied lightly but meaning it with all her heart.

"When can I see you again?"

"*Ca depent.*"

"What did you say?"

"It depends."

"On what?"

"If you call me."

"How about tomorrow?"

"*Demain?*" she asked with a frown. "Did you want to wait that long?"

"No, not at all. I'll call you as soon as I can," he said, dragging himself out of the car. He walked around to the passenger side and opened Elena's door, offering his hand. She took it, and they walked into the hotel and to the elevators. Pushing the call button, the doors opened quietly, and Elena got in—perhaps a little too quickly, she thought—but Jim reached out and stopped the door from closing, then got in with her. Gazing down into her eyes, he put his arms around her and kissed her softly. The moment was quick but exhilarating, and for the first time in Elena's life she thought she might be able to experience true love. She didn't want to open her eyes or leave the warmth and security of his embrace. Hugging him tightly she savored the moment for a long time, and then the doors opened and an older couple got in.

"I'll call you later today."

"I'd like that. Now you've got to go. A girl's got to get her beauty sleep," she said, pushing him out of the elevator while trying to catch her breath, all the time not wanting him to go. She reached out to him, but the elevator doors closed, while the older couple just smiled at them.

18

San Diego Naval Base

The next morning, as Jim made his way down the I-5 freeway, all he could think of was the lovely Elena. Her priceless smile, her slender, supple body, and the inner beauty of her soul dominated his thoughts. He felt so blessed to meet her and thanked the Lord as he pulled up to the entrance to the San Diego Naval Base. A long line of cars and trucks moved slowly into the base, as Threat Condition Alpha had been upgraded to Bravo. Sentries were checking every single CAC card before allowing base access. Dogs stood by while a guard checked underneath the vehicle frames with a mirror. Jim waited patiently, as his thoughts returned to last night. He was so preoccupied with thoughts of Elena that when he reached the gate he mistakenly showed the guard his driver's license instead of his ID.

"Sir, I need to see your CAC card before I can let you on the base," the helmeted guard said, a tinge of irritation in his voice. He was wearing a green camouflaged flack jacket with a nine-millimeter Beretta strapped to his waist. An imposing Humvee overlooked Gate Five. The new-style jeep had a manned fifty-caliber machine gun in its turret, fully loaded and ready for action.

"Sorry," Jim said, quickly recovering and pulling his CAC card from his shirt pocket. The sentry looked at the picture on his computerized military ID, checked the expiration date, and then scanned it on a remote handheld scanner.

"Good morning, Sir," he said, obviously satisfied that all was in order, "and welcome to San Diego Naval Base." The guard saluted Jim with one hand, while returning his ID with the other. Then he waved him through under the watchful gaze of the machine gunner in the Humvee. Jim put on his game face and drove to Pier Six to meet the commanding officer of the USS Sheboygan.

Walking up to the pier sentry, Jim again showed his CAC card. The military guard quickly saluted Jim and allowed him access to the pier, where Jim got a good look at the Sheboygan and admired her paint job. Instead of going up the gangway, he walked forward toward the bow, where he noticed a warrant officer talking to a young sailor, who stood next to the mooring lines that were tied to a bollard on the pier. Though Jim was within earshot of their conversation, he hung back until they were finished.

"Now, Son," the warrant officer explained, "I don't know how to make this any clearer to you, but you do see that rat-guard dangling from the mooring line? Can you tell me what good it's doing?"

The duty seaman, who couldn't have been more than nineteen or twenty, answered, "It's not doing any good, Bosun, Sir."

"That's right," the bosun continued, his voice raising a notch. "It's not doing a doggone thing. Do you realize that an improperly attached rat-guard is a personal reflection of your performance of duty?"

"Ah, no, Sir. I mean, yes, Sir, Bosun."

"Not only is it a reflection of your poor performance of duty," the bosun shouted, his voice in full-bloom by now, "but it reflects on me and on the captain of the Sheboygan. Do you have any idea how that makes me feel?"

"Ah, yes, Sir, Bosun. I believe I feel your pain, Sir."

"You feel my pain!" the Bosun exploded. "Don't get smart with me, Sailor, because the next time I see a rat-guard hanging upside down, you'll feel my pain at captain's mast. Someday your life may depend on the proper securing of those rat-guards."

The seaman recruit looked totally bewildered. Jim knew the young man was wondering how his life depended on the proper placement of a rat-guard, but it was obvious he was too scared to ask.

"Now get up on the bow and straighten out that rat-guard," the bosun thundered. "Move it!"

The young sailor didn't waste a moment and quickly ran up the gangway, as Jim strolled up to the bosun, noticing the man's small brass anchors on his collar.

"Boats, my name is Jim Sherock," he said, introducing himself.

"Good to meet you, Sir. We've been expecting you."

Jim smiled. "I hope I didn't interrupt your discussion with that young sailor."

"Oh, not at all, Sir. With some careful guidance I believe we can make a sailor out of that young whippersnapper."

"So he has possibilities?"

"Oh, yes, Sir, or his mama and daddy wouldn't have sent him to me. I think we can save that boy from his wretched ways, but I can see I'm going to have to do me a little follow-up with him in the near future to make sure he straightens up. Now, if you'll follow me, Sir, I'll take you to meet the old man."

Jim followed the bosun up the gangway. Just before stepping onto the quarterdeck, Boats stopped, faced aft, and crisply saluted the flag with precise military bearing, even though he couldn't see the ensign, which was flying from the jack stand on the flight deck and wasn't visible from the quarterdeck. Boats, however, obviously knew exactly where it was on the ship. He then turned to the officer of the deck and held his salute. "I'm reporting my return."

"Aye, aye, Sir," the OOD replied, returning the salute.

Jim followed the bosun and saluted, but not with the same level of sharpness. Then he asked permission to come aboard.

With permission granted, they walked up the steel stairway that was located twenty feet from the quarterdeck, through a horizontal hatch to the boat deck above. Like honeybees sucking the nectar out of orange blossoms, shipyard workers and tech reps surrounded the new lifeboat davit on the port side of the boat deck.

"There's your biggest headache," the bosun said, pointing to the davit. "It's never worked right since we installed it two months ago."

"Didn't you do a weight test and op test?"

"Yes, and like a fool I signed off on it as complete while we were in the calm waters of the shipyard basin, but ever since we started trying to launch boats here on the naval base, it's been messing up. It's never worked in automatic. In fact, every time we fix something on it, something else goes haywire. Now we've got some Frenchies here, re-computing the computer."

"So what's the biggest problem with it?"

"I don't know. All I know is that it's a Jonah, and if I had my way, I'd cut its foundations with a blow torch and throw it over the side."

"So what are they working on now?"

"The yard-birds are replacing two brand new hydraulic pumps. After we returned from sea, we ran another test, and the rotating elements seized."

"How could that have happened?"

"I think they had some metal grit on the bottom of the oil sump, and when we were at sea it got mixed up with the oil."

"Sounds like the factory should replace the pumps."

"You would think so, but the Frenchies claim the shipyard installed it and got dirt into the system."

"How did you get the ship alteration? Somebody must have approved it."

"Shipview assigns the alts, but you'd have to ask the Port Engineer for all the details. In short, somebody from Washington tasked a French company to design and build a boat davit that could carry any kind of boat in the Navy and make it fully computerized, but it hasn't worked since we left the yards."

"What happened when you tested it at sea?"

"We almost killed four sailors. The forward hook let go and dumped the bow of the boat into the drink. The captain's been expecting you, so I'll tell you more later. Right now we'd better head up to his cabin. We've got lots to do before we get underway."

Jim followed the bosun up the four outside ladder-ways, dubbed the "stairway to heaven," to the 05 level and the captain's cabin. The captain had a business office for his staff and one for himself just off his stateroom. He spent most of his time in the office connected to his stateroom.

The bosun knocked on the open door, and Captain Davey looked up.

"Come in, Boats. Who's that with you?"

"Captain, this is your new first lieutenant, Jim Sherock."

"Pleasure to meet you, Jim," the captain said, extending his hand. Jim reached out, and his hand disappeared in the captain's larger one.

Boats, exhibiting discreetness born of experience, said, "Captain, unless you need me, I've got a lot of work going on deck."

"Go ahead, Boats."

"Pleasure to meet you, Sir," Boats said to Jim, and then turned and left.

"Sit down, Jim. I'm sure you saw people working on the life-boat davit this morning. It's become a real concern for me. We almost lost four sailors due to its malfunctioning computer system. We're now hooked up to France via marine satellite, and they're reprogramming the hard drive. It scares the devil out of me that a French company has access to our computer system aboard my ship."

"I've never heard of that, Captain."

"Well, it's a first for me too. Do you realize that a nation that isn't exactly friendly with us, not to mention all the different terrorists they've hidden in their country, is programming a US Navy ship? I don't like the looks of that davit, and I wish I could get it off my ship."

"It does present some unusual problems for us, especially in light of the world situation."

The captain paused and looked past Jim to the open door. "Close the door, Lieutenant."

Jim got up and closed the captain's door, signaling the rest of the ship that the captain didn't want to be disturbed by anyone, except his XO.

"I've read your file. I see you've got intelligence training in your background. As Captain of the Sheboygan, I need to know if you're reporting to anyone off this ship."

Jim was shocked. They hadn't prepared him for this type of a confrontation with his new CO, and he didn't know what to say.

"That's what I thought," the wily skipper said. "Just so we have an understanding. I respect the work you do, but if you're going to be in my wardroom, I need to be able to count on you and trust you that the good of Sheboygan is always carried out. Do you understand?"

"Yes, Sir."

"If something is happening to this ship or my sailors, I need to know. You can report to your other chain of command, but you need to let me know if there's something not right aboard Sheboygan. I can't order you to violate your orders, but I'm asking as one professional to another. Sometimes on a need-to-know basis, I need to know. Do you understand?

"I understand, but..."

"Let me put it to you another way. You take the next week to see how things go around here and then give me your answer. By the way, this conversation never took place. I know there are terrorists out there, but my immediate concern is for Sheboygan and the people that man it. I don't need something happening here that I could've prevented."

"I understand, Captain. How did you know I was assigned to this newly formed task group?"

"You were deep-selected as an ensign, and your record doesn't have much in it. So I made a call to an old friend."

"The good-old-boy network?" Jim asked, hoping to gather a little Intel on how the captain discovered his dual role.

"Not the good-old-boy network, but a close trusted friend. Always remember one thing, Jim. Trust is something you earn in life, and my friend let me know you were coming. I have no disrespect for you or your job, but it's difficult to serve two masters. You may be loyal to one, but not the other."

"Captain, you've been upfront with me, so I'll do the same with you. I work for a newly formed counter-terrorist organization in Washington. My job is to serve you and do the best I can, but if I find any unusual activity aboard this vessel or out in town, I have to report it."

"I have no problem with that. All I'm saying is, let me know if it concerns my ship so I can do some damage control. I won't interfere with your job because, in reality, I'm glad you're here. My ship and I are here to fight the war on terrorism. I'm telling you right now that if someone talks to you about what we just discussed, then you slipped up somewhere because it didn't come from me. I'm not going to treat you any different than any of my department heads. If you screw up I'm going chew your butt off, and I really don't care whom you work for because when you're on my ship, you work for me. If you're smart, and I'm guessing you are, we can work together. By the way, you weren't due to arrive until next week. Did you ever wonder why they gapped your billet before you reported?"

"I was wondering why the bosun showed me around instead of the man I was relieving."

"That's because we have one of the finest bosuns in the Navy and I gapped the First Lieutenant's billet because of him. He may sound a little rough around the edges, but the crew respects and trusts him. So let him teach you."

"I will, Sir. And thank you," Jim said, exhaling a sigh of relief. "I wondered how I would have to explain this to you if something did come up."

"We're on the same team, fighting the same enemy. If you need time off to pursue something out of the ordinary, just let me know. Now get out of here and get that lifeboat davit working. We're getting underway next week."

Jim got up, and the captain stood. The two men were about the same height, but Captain Davey was forty pounds heavier, and it wasn't in his gut.

"Welcome aboard, shipmate," the captain said, extending his hand.

Jim again felt the strength of the captain's hand, and then left his office, heading for the boat deck.

19

Khartoum, Sudan

Khalif flew into Khartoum and stayed at the President's Hotel. It was a VIP establishment that few got to see, catering only to the dignitaries who visited Sudan. The Light of Allah had one of his men arrange for Khalif to unwind after his long trip to the United States, Mexico, and the Seychelles Islands. A bottle of whiskey and a beautiful Nubian woman materialized soon after he arrived in his room. He enjoyed them both, and in the morning headed out to an oasis where he would travel by camel to the underground bunker.

⌒

"Wow! Thirty-seven of the world's foremost Islamic terrorist leaders have arrived in Khartoum in the last week," the hunter said to his CIA counterpart. They were hidden in the top floor of a rundown apartment complex across the street from a nightclub. They had paid rent three months in advance and had given the manager another $200 so they wouldn't be bothered by anyone, especially the secret police. In the middle of the night, while their neighbors were sleeping, they hauled up Ziess telephoto lenses and Nikon cameras, using the dilapidated back staircase. If some of the tenants had known the expensive equipment that had been set up, they would have looted the place.

The hunter went out jogging early in the morning and always used the same route. He liked to gather Intel while he was running because after the first three weeks the secret police didn't pay him any attention during his exercise time.

"I can only imagine what's being planned, but we better up-link to Langley and send a report by satellite as soon as possible," the CIA operative said.

"We've been in and out of the Sudan for the past two years and haven't seen such a gathering of militant Islamic leaders. I could take a couple of headshots, and the world would be a much better place," the former Marine said, shouldering his sniper's rifle. He was deadly accurate at a thousand yards.

"You'd hit them, all right, but I don't think we'd get out of here alive."

"Maybe not, but I know innocent people will die because of these meetings."

"You're right. But at least this President is pursuing them, not like Clinton."

∾

Khalif departed Khartoum by Land Rover and arrived late in the afternoon at a nomadic camp near an oasis. From the sky it looked like an ordinary watering hole, but inside one of the larger tents was a trapdoor that led below. There were other oases in the area, and each of them had a corridor under the sand so the satellites overhead wouldn't see the same nomads at the same oasis all the time. One of the Bedouin tribesmen recognized Khalif from a previous meeting and lifted the door to the bunker.

Khalif walked down the tunnel and took the elevator to the main complex 200 feet below. He waited in an office outside the briefing room for the Light of Allah, as he was talking to the leaders of the other Islamic groups. Finally the leader of this new militant Islamic movement emerged and went to his office, where Khalif arose from his seat as he entered the room.

"*Salaam alaikum,*" Khalif said in reverential greeting.

"*Alaikum salaam.* Your trip was successful, Khalif?"

"Yes. We will have the planes and launchers delivered to our farm in Mexico."

"Good. How was the price?"

"A bit high. The Russian is getting a little greedy."

"I understand. The *jafka* will pay for his greed in the end, but for now we still need him. Is the cell ready in San Diego?"

"We're in full operation and gathering more information on the ship's crew. Abdullah's son has arrived on board the Sheboygan, and Elena is already working on him."

"Good. How is Abdullah behaving?"

"The same. He's still bloodthirsty after all these years."

"As he should be! Tell him his dedication hasn't been forgotten, and when this is over I have chosen to honor him with a new name—Avenger. Tell him his role is very important, and when he has completed his assignment, he is to return to me. I want his fire by my side for the days ahead. His unquestioned loyalty has not gone unnoticed."

"As you wish."

"We're already organizing a full-scale attack on Israel as soon as we have crippled America. We will win this war, and the world will be under Islamic dominion, for it is our destiny," the Light of Allah declared. "Stay a few days and learn the new code we are using on the Internet, and then quickly return to America and execute our revenge."

"As you wish," Khalif said, bowing and kissing the Light of Allah's hand.

20

USS Sheybogan

Walking the main deck with the bosun and concentrating on all he had to tell him was a difficult task. Jim's mind was elsewhere, as he contemplated what he had talked about with Captain Davey and considered his meeting with Military Intelligence later in the day. He tried to keep his mind focused on what Browder was saying about the retractable flight deck, but so many thoughts competed for his attention.

"NAVSEA tasked us to install these new Tomahawk missile launchers in the well deck. We're to go to Naval Weapons Base Seal Beach and load test missiles and then launch them at the range on San Clemente Island."

"When is the firing scheduled?" Jim asked, finally focusing his mind on the USS Sheboygan's tasking and schedule.

"I'm hearing next Tuesday, if we get underway on time. The engines have been giving us some problems, so I don't know if we'll make it out as scheduled."

"Why did the Navy want to install Tomahawks on an old amphib like the Sheboygan?" Jim asked regarding the surface-to-surface missiles.

"The big brass in the Navy wants to give the Expeditionary Strike Group greater capability to soften the landing areas for the Marines."

"How many landing craft are we taking on deployment?"

"With the new launchers and their control room taking up a lot of space in the welldeck, we'll only be able to carry one LCAC and still maintain our load-out. As usual they're having us do more with less, but you know the drill, Lieutenant."

"Only too well, Boats," Jim acknowledged, as he looked at the launcher hidden beneath the steel flight deck. Then his thoughts quickly shifted to Elena. He wondered when he'd be able to call her. He'd had such a great time with her last night, and he hoped they'd be able to get together again tonight. Refocusing, he noticed the bosun's lips moving and decided he'd better tune back in.

"Say again, Bosun," he said, trying to mask his daydreaming with a look of seriousness.

"I was wondering if you were going to the ship's party tonight. We were deployed in the Arabian Gulf during Christmas, so the captain has scheduled a dinner dance for the crew to make up for it."

"Sounds like a good time for me to see the crew in action."

"The captain wants everyone to go, with or without a date. You're new in town; maybe I could line you up with the new French tech rep. She's a knockout," the bosun said with a gleam in his eye and a growing smile on his face.

"Thanks, but I'll be fine. Fact is, I met somebody the other day, and she might be able to make it."

"That'd be good, Lieutenant. It's at the Sheraton on Shelter Island, and it costs forty bucks."

"Sign me up, and I'll pay tonight. I've got an appointment this afternoon, so I've got to get going, but let's continue this tomorrow. If I'm going to get a date and go to the party tonight, I've got to get moving."

"Understood, Sir. And we can start tomorrow with that crazy French davit over there."

Jim hustled off the flight deck and shot down the gangway. As soon as his foot hit the pier, warm images of Elena flooded his mind. He thought about her for a while before refocusing on his meeting with the Officer In Charge (OIC) of the new Intel detachment. He left the base, turning onto Harbor Drive, and then quickly drove through downtown and out to the airport. On the left-hand side was the Homeland Security Building, where the Coast Guard had housed their boats for several years. He showed his CAC card and was allowed on the base. He looked around and found building 17. It was right next to building 132, which made no sense at all. He had heard the numbering system wasn't in sequential order, but rather in the order they were built, which made finding a building without a map a real challenge. He walked into the building and again had to show his CAC card to the quarterdeck watch.

"I'm here to see Captain Fullerton," he said to the first class petty officer checking ID's at the front desk.

"Just a moment, Sir," she said, looking at his ID and giving it back to him.

She picked up a phone and punched in some digits. "Sir, a Lieutenant Sherock is here to see you. . . . Yes, Sir, I'll send him right in."

She hung up the phone. "Sir, you may proceed down the corridor to your left. The captain's office is the last door on the left."

Jim made his way down the hallway and knocked on the closed door.

"Enter," droned the voice from within.

A black man in a suit and tie stood up from behind his desk as Jim entered. "Lieutenant, I'm Captain Fuller. Please have a seat."

Jim took a seat in front of the captain's desk.

"Have you reported aboard the USS Sheboygan?"

"Yes, Sir. This morning."

"How'd it go?"

"Very well."

"Any reason you might not be able to carry out your work with us and your mission on the USS Sheboygan?"

"No, Sir," Jim said, his voice firm.

"Good, because we've been receiving Intel reports from the CIA that a major attack by Islamic terrorists is planned for San Diego."

"Isn't that true of any major city right now in America?"

"It is, but the border patrol picked up a man who only spoke Arabic, trying to sneak across the border. He had a map of the San Diego electrical power grid, with areas marked off."

"Electrical grid? Are you sure it doesn't pertain to bombing or drug smuggling?"

"Maybe. My contact in the Mexican Mafia would have known about him, and he didn't. Besides, he wasn't carrying drugs, and the tunnel he used had been demolished several years ago. It was just by chance that one of the border patrols was passing by when he noticed some movement. We're not sure who rebuilt it, since all the drug cartels know that we know about it."

"Did you capture anyone else?"

"No. But we found a shallow grave nearby, with thirty Mexicans in it, obviously the ones who rebuilt the tunnel. Normally the drug cartel operators don't kill their mules; their people know enough not to talk. I was wondering if you could talk to this guy first thing tomorrow morning, since you know the language."

"Sure. But do you want me to talk to him ... or interrogate him?"

"You know the rules, Jim."

"I doubt we'll find anything out about him or his plans. If he's an Islamic soldier, he'd consider it an honor to die for the cause."

"He's being held here and then we're supposed to ship him to Guantanamo Bay tomorrow night, so go and talk to him. I'll tell the brig to expect you tomorrow morning."

"I'll do my best, Sir, but I've never interrogated anyone before."

"Understood, but give it a try."

"Yes, Sir. You do you know the Sheboygan gets under way next week?"

"That's fine. Just call me, and let me know your schedule."

"Thank you, Sir. I will," Jim said leaving the office.

21

Abdullah's House in Carlsbad

Jim jumped in his car and headed up the I-5 to Carlsbad. He pulled out his cell phone and speed-dialed Elena's room, not really expecting her to answer but hoping she might.

"*Allo*," Elena answered sweetly.

"Elena," he said excitedly, the warmth in his heart conveyed through his voice. "I was wondering if you wanted to go out tonight. The ship is having a party near your hotel."

"Oh, Jim," she said, rolling her "J" like a snowball down a short hill, "that would be very nice, but I don't think I could take two late nights in a row."

His heart sank, but he wasn't ready to give up yet. "Elena, I have to show up at this dinner dance, but I don't have to stay till the end. We could leave early. I've got a big day tomorrow too."

He held his breath as Elena hesitated before answering. "*Oui*, Jim," she said finally, "I would love to see you again, but they've given me homework tonight."

Jim wished he could help her with her homework, but he knew next to nothing about diamonds and gems. Still, he wouldn't mind giving it his best shot. At least they'd be together, and maybe she'd get done in time to go to the party with him.

"I might be able to help you with your homework, even though I don't know much about diamonds."

Elena laughed slightly. "Maybe, but you're a naval officer, not a gemologist."

"True," he argued, "but I've taken a lot of courses, and I know how to study. I think I can help you."

"*On vas voir,*" she purred coyly.

"Does that mean we're on for tonight?" he asked, changing lanes near the Del Mar Race track.

"*Oui,* but we must make it an early night, *mon cheri.*"

Jim smiled. Sometimes Elena sounded so sexy that he would have gone out with her just to hear her speak. "I'll see you at six, if that's not too early."

"*Au revoir,*" Elena said and clicked off the line.

Jim exited the freeway and, in a matter of minutes, pulled into his parent's driveway. He shut off the car and rushed into the house.

Hi mother greeted him with a kiss. "Where are you going in such a rush?"

"To see Elena."

"I thought so. I think she's a lovely girl. I'm planning a barbeque this weekend; maybe you could bring her over. I'd love to sit and talk with her."

"Sure, Mom, but I don't know her schedule. She's in school for the next month and says the classes are pretty tough."

"Ask her anyway."

"Okay, but I can't talk right now. I'm in a hurry."

"Of course you are, darling. Don't forget to ask her."

Abdullah walked in then, and Jim tensed.

"I'd like a minute with you, if you have time" his father asked pleasantly.

"Okay, Dad," Jim answered, dreading the interrogation but remembering the gift of money from the night before. "Thanks again for last night."

Abdullah smiled. "So how was it, your hot date with the French woman?"

"It was great," Jim admitted, still uncomfortable with his father's uncharacteristic interest in his personal life. "Why do you ask?"

His father shrugged, still smiling. "You seem really excited about this girl. I was just curious."

"I do like her," Jim admitted.

"Good. Maybe she can come out this weekend. Your mother is having a barbeque, and we've invited some friends."

"Elena's pretty busy, but I'll check with her."

Something bothered him about his dad's remarks, but he just couldn't put his finger on it. Maybe it was the words that were so unnatural. In the past Abdullah had shown very little interest in anything that mattered to his son. The fact that he did now should have been encouraging to Jim, but somehow it just didn't add up.

22

Mexico City

Khalif landed in Mexico City and was met at the airport by Jamal Hassan, his primary operative setting up the launch site near the United States border.

"I have some bad news," Hassan announced.

Khalif narrowed his eyes as he drilled them into his associate. "What is it?"

"Mustafa has been captured."

"What? How could you let this happen?"

"We did a trial run through the tunnel, and he was spotted on the American side. I think someone tipped off the Border Patrol."

Khalif knew he needed to control his rage and concentrate on damage control. "We'll need to find another way to get our soldiers in."

"Perhaps by boat."

"Not in San Diego Harbor."

"No, but the California coastline is quite long. We could go a couple hundred miles up the coast and then use a go-boat to race towards the beach."

"And what if we're spotted on radar or satellite?"

"The "Go-fast" boat will outrun their ships."

"I don't like the idea. We're already going to attack by boat. All this might heighten their awareness that we're operating off their shores."

"We could always go further inland on the border and hire a *coyote* to get them across."

Khalif looked at him with raised eyebrows.

"The Mexicans that guide people and drugs across the border."

Khalif shook his head. "No, the border patrols have gotten tougher since our attack on their trade buildings. We must come up with a better idea."

"Perhaps we're too close to San Diego. Maybe we should go through another state, maybe through the country to the north. We could have someone meet them in Canada and drive them down here."

"Let me think about that. Do you think Mustafa will talk?'

"Not Mustafa. And not by the way the Americans interrogate. They're bound to follow the rules like they did in Iraq. Our people never gave them any information, and they were set free in a day."

"I hope you're right. Are the men ready to receive the farm machinery? It should be arriving by freighter next week."

"Yes, Khalif, all is ready. Every day we go out to till the ground, but it is hard work. We are not farmers."

"I know you're not, but all must appear that we are growing a crop. The Americans living in San Diego will never know what hit them. Let's go to the farm now. I want to see all that you've done."

Jamal drove Khalif to what looked like a rundown barn but was actually a very modern building with a beat-up façade to make it fit in with the other buildings in the area. The two men walked around the two-year-old building.

"Where's the shop the Chinese scientist will use to make the bomb?"

"Over there," Jamal said, pointing to a lone building. We've built the runway here, and when the missile is armed and ready, the plane will exit the barn and take off."

Khalif was satisfied with what he saw. He stayed the night before flying to Miami and then San Diego, keeping to his usual habit of never flying directly from Mexico to San Diego.

23

The Sudan, across from the President's Club

The hunter and CIA operative, keeping watch with high-powered telephoto cameras, began snapping pictures as a Chinese man arrived with two Arabs by his side. The doors to the nightclub opened, and the lively music spilled out into the street as the three went inside.

"I think I've seen that guy before," the hunter said, as he continued watching the front of the nightclub.

"Who is he?" the operative asked.

"I think I saw him in Iraq when we were trying to get Intel on Sadaam Hussein's weapons of mass destruction."

"We'd better up-line these pictures to Langley."

The two men downloaded the pictures onto their laptop and then sent them via satellite to CIA headquarters for verification. It took a long time, but the return message read, "*Continue surveillance and get better shots of the Asian. Inform ASAP if he leaves the country.*"

"I wonder what's so important about this guy," the hunter mused.

"I don't know, but it's going to be a long night. Do you want the first shift?"

"Yeah, I'm wired. I drank too many cups of Kenyan coffee, so I'll be up."

The agency's operative quickly fell asleep on the cot in their makeshift surveillance post, and the hunter began his watch. The night sizzled as time slowly passed. At 3:00 A.M. the hunter was relieved, as the operative took over. Soon after that the Oriental man and his escorts left the club.

"Let's go, John," the agent said, shaking the hunter from his sleep. "I think they're leaving." The two men rushed down the back stairway and hopped into their old junker. Keeping their lights off and hanging back at a discreet distance, they followed the car with its three passengers to the other side of town near the airport. There they watched as the trio got out of their vehicle and went to the hotel. The two agents slouched down in their car and waited.

Four hours later the trio re-emerged, and the surveillance team followed them to the airport. Being careful to avoid all eye contact, they checked the flight schedule, particularly the morning flights out of Khartoum. There was an Air France flight leaving at noon for Paris.

They grabbed newspapers and pretended to read them as they watched the three men book their flights. Lingering at the airport the hunter and the CIA operative completed their surveillance and observed the three men as they went to their boarding area. After the flight left the two agents rushed to the American Embassy and reported to the station chief, showing him the photos and asking if Langley had made any positive identification of the Chinese.

24

Torrey Pines State Beach

Khalif was waiting for Elena as she pulled up. She got out of the car and knew from the expression on Khalif's face that there was trouble.

"Are you making progress with the lieutenant?" he questioned.

"Of course. He's already falling in love with me. I'll be seeing him tonight."

"Do whatever it takes. You must make sure that his love for you is greater than his love for his country. Do you understand?"

"You know me, Khalif. Have I ever failed you before?"

"No, but our mission timeline has moved up."

"Moved up? But I need more time!" Elena knew her distress was obvious in her voice, but she couldn't help herself. "You just don't make someone fall madly in love you in two weeks. Besides, he's going on the ship for a few days."

Khalif's eyes narrowed, and he glared at Elena. "You're not telling me everything," he insisted. "What's wrong?"

Elena knew Khalif was very perceptive and it was difficult to hide anything from him. Turning away she said, "It's Abdullah. You've got to tell him to back off. At the airport he almost blew my cover. I can't have him interfering."

"I knew there was something," Khalif said, a triumphant note in his voice. "I'll speak to him again."

"Thank you, Khalif," Elena said, genuinely relieved. "Now I need to return to the hotel before Jim gets there."

"We'll meet again next week. Our plan will be in place by the end of the month, so work quickly."

"I'll be ready."

"You'd better be! Your life depends on it," he said, turning and walking back to his car.

Elena stared as his car sped off. Then she turned her head and watched the waves slowly rolling into the beach, reminding her of the warm dinner and soft moonlight she had enjoyed with Jim the night before. Could she pull this off? Elena questioned her heart. Yet she knew her very life hung in the balance. Her al-Qaeda masters were unforgiving. Her newly discovered life of love would die quickly if she didn't obey. Jim was so different than all the others, especially his father, Abdullah. Heavily burdened she got into her car and took one last look at the cascading waves before driving back to the hotel. She no sooner entered her room than her phone rang.

"Elena, I'm here," Jim said in a cheerful manner that made her troubled heart smile, soaring past the issues she faced.

"Come up, *mon cheri,*" she cooed, her heart bursting with expectation at the prospect of seeing him again. She hung up the phone and quickly changed into a casual but tight-fitting black tube-top and sweatpants that showed off her toned midriff.

Jim reached her room and knocked.

"Come in, *mon cheri,*" she said, opening the door. She caught the appreciative gleam of his eyes as he discreetly checked her out.

⌒

Without shoes she was a bit shorter than Jim remembered, but every bit as beautiful. His heart beat rapidly, and he forced his eyes to look out the window, but it didn't help. The image of her slender, voluptuous shape was etched into his mind.

"How's the studying going?" he asked, still gazing out the window at the swaying palm trees below.

"Okay, but I need a break. Sometimes I feel like my head is going to burst with all the information they've heaped upon us."

"I know the feeling. It seemed at the academy we had tests every day. I still don't know how I made it through," Jim said, turning around and taking her hand before leading her to the chairs by the window. They sat down, and he reached for her feet, placing them on his thighs.

"After a hard day on the ship in Phuket, Thailand, we'd go ashore and sit along the beach. For ten *Baht* the Thai women would massage our feet for an hour. I'll never forget that. It was so relaxing."

"Is that all you did with the Thai women?" she asked teasingly. "I hear they're quite beautiful."

"That's all I ever did, but some of the others went beyond that. Do you have any lotion?"

"Sure, I'll get it," Elena replied, as she got up and went into the bathroom.

"And bring a towel."

When she returned, Jim smiled. "Now sit down, and put your feet on my lap so I can get to work. Just sit back, close your eyes, and relax."

⤶

Within moments Elena was smiling, as Jim expertly massaged her feet. He was right; it did feel great. But then thoughts of her betrayal instantly tensed her muscles.

"Sorry. Did I squeeze too hard?" he asked. She relaxed again, marveling at how gentle his hands were and how nicely he treated her.

"My mother wanted to know if you'd like to come to our home for a cookout on Saturday."

Elena opened her eyes, wondering if Abdullah had set this up. "Will your whole family be there?"

"Sure. Why do you ask?"

"Well, you only mentioned your mother."

"Dad will be there, but he's never the one that sets up a social gathering."

Don't be too sure, thought Elena, as Jim added a little more lotion and continued to massage her feet.

25

Boat deck, USS Sheboygan

"Boats, we gonna get this ship out to sea?" Deek asked.

"We'll be ready, but I don't know about that lifeboat. Look at the techs over there. They've been working on it for days."

"Hey, is that the chick from the gym? What's she doin' here?"

"She's the tech rep," Browder explained, as he walked over to the boat davit where the computer panel was open.

"Liz," Boats said nodding toward his companion, "you remember Deek from the Lion's Lair, don't you?"

"How could I forget?" She smiled. "Thank you, Mr. Deek, for helping me out that night."

"What did that fool want?" Gunny asked.

"He was an old boyfriend."

"If you have any more trouble with him, just let me know."

"Oh, I don't think that will be necessary," Liz said, as she glanced at the bosun and smiled.

Deek grinned. "So that's how it is. Man, Boats, you don't waste time!"

Browder laughed at the Gunny and then turned his attention to Liz and put on his game-face. "Liz, is the davit going to be ready for tomorrow? We've got to go out to sea and begin our training cycle, and we're going to need the RHIB's."

"I hope so, Bosun. We've reprogrammed the computer, so it should work much better."

"When are you going to do an op test?"

"Later today, if you can support it."

"How about joinin' us for dinner after the test?" Deek asked. "I know a place not too far from here"

"It sounds tempting, Mr. Deek," Liz answered, smiling, "but I'm pretty tired. We've been working since midnight last night, and I haven't had much sleep. I don't think I'd be good company."

Boats didn't want this opportunity to slip away. "After all the hours you've put in, the least we could do is buy you dinner," he coaxed.

She looked at Boats, and her smile widened. "Maybe. But I've got to make sure this davit works. The shipyard superintendent is putting pressure on me. Do you think the captain would mind if my men and I went to sea?"

"Mind? He'd welcome it, especially the way this thing operates. We'd have to get some information from you, though."

"Let me know what information you need. We could do a little training for your crew on the davit while at sea," Liz offered.

"I'll need to go up and ask the captain. Meanwhile, I'll leave you in the good hands of 'Meester Deek.'" Boats smiled and headed up the steel stairway to the 05 level, the fifth deck up from main deck. He went to the captain's office and knocked.

"Come in," Captain Davey said, hesitating a moment before looking up. "Oh, Boats. What's on your mind?"

"Captain, the field tech for the davit wants to know if you want her to go to sea with us. She says she and her men could provide davit training to the crew while we're underway."

The captain paused, considering the request. "It can't hurt, and they could see how it operates at sea. If we have a problem they would be here to fix it."

"Yes, Sir, Captain. I'll get all their information."

"Please do. And I'll send it up my chain in case there are any issues. Be sure to tell Jake because he'll have to arrange it with the shipyard. We'll have other riders, so there shouldn't be a problem."

"Speaking of Jake, have you seen him?" Bosun asked.

"I just talked to him. He went to see CHENG. Call the quarterdeck in case he's headed off the ship."

The bosun left the captain's office and went to the CHENG's stateroom, but it was empty. Boats opened the door to the wardroom and found the CHENG getting a fresh cup of coffee.

"CHENG, where's the port engineer?"

"You just missed him. He's leaving the ship."

"Dang, I better call the quarterdeck and tell him to meet me in the captain's office," Boats said, pulling out his side phone.

Boats made the call and returned to the captain's office and knocked at the door.

"Come on in, Boats," the captain said. "The quarterdeck watch caught him before he stepped off the ship. He'll be here in a minute."

Moments later Jake knocked on the captain's door.

"Come in, Jake. I've got a question for you," the captain said. "I wonder if we can have the tech reps for the lifeboat go to sea with us. Is it too late in the day to make the arrangements?"

"Sure it is, but I've got everybody's home number, so I'll make some calls and have the project manager arrange funding. I don't think anybody'll squawk, but you know this isn't in accordance with Shipview's rules and procedures."

"Easy, Jake. Shipview is here to stay," the CO warned.

"Don't get me started, Captain. If Shipview is making the repair process easier and more economical, then why is Big Navy cutting our budgets? One thing Shipview will never be able to measure is how a man gets things done in a crunch when we don't have time or money."

"I hear you, Jake; now go work your magic. We'll only be out to sea for the day, and I think it would be beneficial if the techs came and observed the davit operation."

"Sure thing, Captain. I think I can make it happen."

"Thanks, Jake," Boats added.

"Just doing my job, Boats," Jake said, as he exited the captain's office.

⤳

When Jake got to the pier, he opened his cell phone and made the first call. "What do you mean, you can't cover the costs?" snapped Jake at his project manager, Leo Palmer.

"Jake, you know the Shipview rules. I don't have time to put the paperwork through. We can't just send them out. If our command finds out that I've authorized a job for work that's already done, they'll go through the overhead. You know we're not supposed to operate this way. Remember the last time the San Diego Shipyard complained to your boss?"

"Leo, I'm just trying to fix the ship. I'll take the heat. One of these days the Navy's going to wake up and see the bill of goods these shipyards have sold them. You know how they hire each other so they both can get an award fee. It costs much more to get work done with this new teaming arrangement."

"I hear you, but there are rules I have to follow. Listen, I'll do it this time, but send me an email in case somebody wants to know who authorized this."

"No problem. Somebody has to put the ship first and not the rules. With this davit we need all the help we can get. I'll explain it to the shore-side command after they chew my butt out."

"Okay, Jake, but I must have that email."

"Keep your shirt on. You'll get it," Jake said, then hung up and dialed the next number.

"Willie, we need to take the davit techs out to sea with us. I give you my word that the project manager will cover it."

"Jake, you know I can't do that. Your command has come down hard on us for working like this. We need a work statement sent to us by computer; then we have to estimate it, get approval for the work specification, a proposal, and then you fund it. I wish you'd asked me two weeks ago; we could easily have done it, but you know how much paperwork is involved."

"I'll give it to you when we get back. After twenty-one years on the waterfront, have I ever stiffed you or anybody else?"

"No, Jake. Your word is good, but we've got to abide by the new Shipview rules. I don't want to screw up the metrics."

"Don't tell me about some phony numbers that don't amount to a hill of beans. Look, Willie, our jobs haven't changed. We're here to fix ships, and they're going to change the rules from now until eternity, but my word never changes. Leo will process the paperwork while we're out at sea, and if anyone gives you any heat, just put the blame on me. It won't be the first time I got chewed out for breaking the rules so that the readiness of the ship improved."

Willie paused, and Jake held his breath until he finally heard the answer he wanted. "Well, okay, but this isn't like the old days. Navy management is watching us like a hawk, and we have to deal with metrics."

"Metrics don't fix ships; people do! Besides, what's more important, a bunch of numbers on a flow chart that make accountants happy or a ship getting underway and battle-ready? Is anybody listening?"

"I hear you, Jake. If it were anybody else, I wouldn't do it. If I get into trouble over this with my boss, I'm coming for you."

"Go right ahead. Everybody else uses the port engineer as the scapegoat. If your boss gives you a hard time, I'll go talk to him. You know Rizzo put thirty years in the Navy before retiring. He used to be my boss at San Diego Maintenance Center, so I won't have any problem getting my butt chewed by him."

"Okay. Have your project manager call me first thing in the morning, and we'll take care of the paperwork."

"Thanks, Willie. I owe you one."

"Don't sweat it. I want you to know I wouldn't do it for just any port engineer. I've been stiffed by a couple of your comrades."

"I know, and that's a crying shame. It won't happen this time, I promise. The ship leaves at 0700 tomorrow morning. I'll see you when I get back," Jake said, ending the conversation. Then he called his project manager, who squawked some more because Jake was again bending the rules for the good of the ship and the Navy. He was in direct violation of the new Shipview rules. Finally Jake called Captain Davey to tell him the techs would be aboard when the ship pulled out in the morning.

26

Marriot Hotel near the San Diego airport

Gently Jim slid Elena's feet onto the chair, as he got up and quietly checked his cell phone to see if the ship or Military Intelligence had tried to contact him. He knew the USS Sheboygan was getting underway tomorrow and staying out the night. He looked out the hotel window, as the gusting winds had quieted and shadows began to bathe the San Diego Harbor in the twilight. Multi-colored neon lights lit up the downtown buildings, casting full-toned dimensional images on the bay's quiet reflecting water. Returning sailboats and speedy military craft crisscrossed the water like gnats on an inland Minnesota lake. Jim wondered about his future in the Navy and Military Intelligence, especially if he and Elena got really serious.

Because of his dual tasking, he knew his free time would be quite limited. Late one night in his previous ship's wardroom, he had listened to a couple of officers tell horror stories about wives who couldn't wait the six-month deployment and found other love interests. He'd seen what it had done to his buddies and wasn't sure he wanted to chance going through that. Going to sea was always tough on the spouses and children, and Jim began to wonder if his love for the sea and adventure was slowly being replaced by something even greater. He hoped and prayed the good Lord would protect and guide him in all his future decisions.

⌒

"Qu 'est – ce – que tu pense, cheri?" Elena asked in a soft, sensuous tone, as she came up behind him and pressed her womanly body into his back, wrapping her arms around his waist and squeezing him tightly. She loved the feeling of strength that radiated from his body to hers.

"Say again?" he asked.

"I wondered what you were thinking."

Jim covered her hands with his. "I was thinking about you and how we met and how comfortable I feel around you."

"I feel the same way. You're a good man, a special man."

"I'm glad you feel that way," Jim said, as he turned around in her arms and pulled her close to his chest in a secure hug, all the time gazing down into her engaging eyes.

"I thought you came to help me with my studies, Jim," she teased, purposely rolling her J.

"I did too, but I think your books will have to wait," he said, leaning down to kiss her. Elena arched her back slightly and met his lips, as their bodies surged together. Their kiss spoke of gentleness, with quiet, unfulfilled desire. Elena had never been kissed like this before. Her whole body tingled, feeling good in a clean, natural way. The other men she had been with never touched her the way Jim did. There was something so different about him…so right.

She wondered if he felt the same warmth in his heart that she did in hers. Then she noticed a slight tear roll down his cheek. Her eyes widened with surprise. Never had she experienced such an innocent love from anyone, especially a man. The men she'd known took what they could get and left her to deal with her emotions.

Quickly she pulled away from him, taking a few steps and hoping he would pursue her.

"What's wrong, Elena? I know this is too fast. I'm sorry, but I never thought this would happen."

Oh, Jim, she thought, *if you only knew. What am I going to do?*

You must go!" she blurted out, instantly regretting her words.

"Yes, you're right," he said. "I can't do this."

Elena was still shocked and confused at her own reaction, as well as Jim's. "I don't want you to go, but you must," she insisted.

"I know. You're absolutely right. I have to go—now."

Quickly changing her mind, she no longer cared about what was right; she cared only that Jim not leave. "No, Jim," she begged, "please stay."

"Elena, I want to, but something might happen between us, and—I can't let it."

"What are talking about?" she asked, truly puzzled by his remarks. "Don't you think something already has happened?"

"Yes, I know. And that's what I'm afraid of."

"Jim, I don't understand you. What are you afraid of? Are you afraid of me?"

He turned his back on her and went to the window again, running his hands through his hair, his distress obvious. "Elena," he said, his back still to her, "my ship's leaving tomorrow morning. If I stay here, I know things are going to happen between us."

"Is that wrong, *cheri?*"

"Yes. I mean, no. Oh, I don't know." He turned and looked at her. "Elena, I have to be true to you and to God."

"What's God got to do with us?"

"Everything. Look, I'll be back in a couple of days. Do you still want to come to the barbeque on Saturday?"

"Of course. Your mother invited me."

"Are you sure?"

"It would be wrong for me not to go. I still don't know what's bothering you. Is it something I've said or done?"

"No."

"What is it?"

Jim sighed. "I'll call you Saturday morning, and we can discuss this further. You've got to study, and I've got to be on the ship at four in the morning. After the barbeque on Saturday I'll tell you everything. Now I must go," he said, walking slowly but determinedly toward the door.

Elena caught up with him and gently grabbed his hand. Slowly he turned to face her.

"Where do you think you're going, *mon cheri*?" she said, melting into his waiting arms.

They held each other for a long moment, and he kissed her again, as that same warm feeling of rightness flooded her body, welcoming his touch. Gently releasing her, he reached for the door, and walked out.

Almost without her realizing what she was doing, Elena followed him, stopping only when Jim pushed the button for the elevator. Their eyes met in the reflection of the shining brass elevator plate beside the door.

"Saturday?" he asked without turning around.

"*Oui*, Jim. Saturday." She waited until the elevator door closed behind him, and wondered why he had mentioned God in connection with their relationship.

27

Liz's apartment

"Great news, Abdullah. The Americans are going to let me ride the ship tomorrow," Liz said into her cell phone, as she drove to her apartment in La Mesa.

"That's good. Will you be able to take some of our men with you?"

"Of course. All I've got to do is put them on the contractor list that I hand the First Lieutenant when I go aboard tomorrow. I'll need to have them on the shipyard's list of people who work for San Diego."

"Why?"

"Some eager-beaver might check with their security, and the list must match the shipyard's rolls or we're in trouble."

"That's not necessary," Abdullah said gruffly.

Liz, sensing Abdullah's disdain for admitting his lack of knowledge and for forfeiting control of the mission to a woman, tried another tact. "Abdullah, if we have the names on the list this time, the next time the ship goes to sea, it will be so much easier. The Navy will recognize your men. If we wait, they might balk at a new list. If we establish precedence now, we'll have less trouble in the future."

Liz knew Abdullah was a control freak, but he wasn't a fool. She waited, giving him a moment to see the wisdom of her logic. "Perhaps you're right," he said finally, his resentment evident. "Tell Haviv to put their names on the San Diego shipyard's list of employees. You had a good idea, but you didn't know how to implement it."

"You're right, Abdullah. I'll call him immediately," Liz replied, forcing a tone of sincerity into her voice before she hung up the phone and laughed. She shook her head at how easily she played him, and then she called Haviv with her plan. Liz parked her car and went up to her apartment and put her purse on the counter.

The doorbell rang and Liz wondered who it could be.

"Elena!" Liz exclaimed as the two sisters embraced. "What are you doing here?"

"I have to tell you some wonderful news."

Liz looked at her dreamy-eyed sister and wondered what she was talking about. "Come into the bedroom and help me pack for a few days."

"Where are you going?"

"Shhh! Let me think," Liz said as she analyzed what she would need, going through a mental checklist.

"Please, stop thinking, Lizzy! That's all you ever do. I've got wonderful news."

Liz wasn't happy to be interrupted while she was mentally preparing for her trip, but she turned around with a sour look on her face. "Okay, out with it."

"I think I've fallen in love for the first time."

"What! Are you insane? Don't tell me you've fallen for Abdullah's son!"

"Yes, and it's so wonderful. He treats me like a princess. I've never had anyone hold me so tenderly, so caringly."

"Just a minute; I've got to vomit. Do you realize what will happen if Khalif suspects that you've become attached to Jim? Have you forgotten the sewers we lived in after we ran away from the orphanage? Don't you remember making fires to stay alive during the freezing winters? Remember the street boys we found dead in the sewers because they made a fire down there and it asphyxiated them? Have you forgotten the many days we went without food or how others sniffed the glue in a paper bag to get high and escape the hunger's constant pain? Elena, Khalif took us from that life. Our family abandoned us. Khalif saved us from a living hell, but if he finds out that you're in love with Jim, he'll probably kill us both."

"Lizzy, how could I forget? You're so smart and I always listen to you, but this is so different."

"You've got to control your emotions and do your job. That's why we're here. The Americans have killed our comrades and their families."

"Liz, we're Romanians, not Arabs. I can see that now; they're just using us."

"Look, you may be right, but you can't compromise the mission. You've got to do your part."

"I can still do my part. That hasn't changed."

"Elena, the next thing you'll tell me is that you're going to church and that you're becoming a Christian."

"I was coming to that," she answered softly.

"Are you totally out of your mind? Where are your loyalties? We're at war with the infidels! Who pulled us out of the sewers and gave us a future? Who gave us food and clothing?"

"Lizzy, we've been brainwashed."

"Elena! If you don't get control of yourself, I'll have to tell Khalif."

"No, I beg you! Please don't tell him. Please don't take Jim away from me."

"The mission comes first; I have no choice."

"Elizabeth, don't act so self-righteous with me. You know Abdullah is just waiting for the opportunity to slit your throat.

I see the way he looks at you when you come up with a better idea than him. He hates you. Can't you see that?"

"I can handle Abdullah."

"Don't be so sure, Lizzy. Abdullah longs for the day this mission is over so he can cut you up and throw you in a dumpster like he did his sister after she went out on a date with an infidel. I've seen the contempt he has for you. You're a threat to him, because you're smarter than him."

"Khalif will protect me."

"Don't be so sure, Lizzy. Khalif comes and goes like the wind. Do you really think anything will happen to Abdullah if he kills you? You're not much higher than a dog in his eyes."

"I've provided many good ideas. Khalif wants me to help him plan the next attack."

"If...you live through this one. Abdullah will slit your throat without thinking twice. In his moment of rage, Khalif won't matter. Lizzy, I love Jim. I thought you'd be happy for me, but all you talk about is this mission. You better wake up. There's more to life than killing people to take over the world. I think you're lying to yourself. I notice the way you talk about him."

"About who?" Liz asked softly at the discovery of a hidden secret sin deep within her heart.

"You don't even know." Elena laughed, shaking her head in obvious disbelief as her sister fidgeted and looked away

"What are you talking about?"

Liz smiled. "You and the bosun?"

28

Ensenada, Mexico

The S.S. Dauphine, an old freighter with running rust streaming down her sides, slowly pulled into the busy port of Ensenada, Mexico, after a long trek across the Pacific Ocean. Many other ships were in port, offloading their containers. The Liberian flag, flying from the Dauphine's main mast, gave its country of registry but not its Greek ownership. The Mexican customs and immigration officials, including Horate Ruiz, waited with the ship's agent on the wooden pier, as the gangway was lowered down with the vessel's crane. The SS Dauphine was in the older section of the port because they had only eleven containers to offload and a couple of tractors. The chief mate of the Dauphine waited at the quarterdeck until his men had finished rigging the gangway before he welcomed the officials aboard.

"Please, follow me," he beckoned, as they proceeded up the gangway to the quarterdeck. He led the officials, headed by Ruiz, up to the captain's office, where five bottles of Johnny Walker Black stood at attention guarding five cartons of American cigarettes on the table.

"*Senors*, I am Captain Andryuk; welcome to the Dauphene. This is the first time we've come into your country, and I was hoping you could join me in a drink," the Greek captain said, not waiting for a response and pouring them each three fingers of whiskey. He had hosted many of these meetings that always were accompanied by cumshaw for the officials that came aboard. "Ice?"

Ignoring the captain's question, Horate asked one of his own. "What will you be offloading?"

Handing out the drinks he looked at the official's nameplate. "Farm equipment, *Senor* Ruiz. We have three tractors, plows, a couple of seeders, and spare parts, all made in Japan."

"*Capitan* Andryuk, what was your last port of call?"

"As you can see from the ship's manifest, we were in Yokohama." The captain handed over the official documents.

"Where will the equipment be going?"

"I don't know, but here's a copy of the final delivery point," Andryruk said, handing Ruiz a large brown envelope with a clasp on it. He opened the clasp and peeked inside. He spotted a couple sheets of paperwork, with several one-hundred-dollar bills mixed in. Not bothering to count the bills, he quickly closed the envelope, determined that this unexpected bonus would remain in his possession.

"The containers have been sealed since we left Japan, but if you want, we could open them."

"I think we should—just to be on the safe side, of course," Ruiz insisted. "It's quite hot today. Perhaps we could look at the one closest to the gangway."

"Certainly." Andryuk smiled and then lifted his glass. "Please, let's enjoy our drink."

The agents joined the captain in downing their libations. "Will you be needing supplies while you're here?" the shipping agent asked.

"Yes. I've drawn up a list of things the cook needs, and here's the money. If it costs more than that, please let me know, but I'll need receipts for the company's books." He slid the list and another stack of hundred dollar bills into the agent's waiting hand, and it was obvious that it was much more than necessary.

"I will get you receipts, of course, but I think you probably have enough here." He glanced at the list and added, "It will only take a few hours to gather these supplies."

"Good; we're on a tight schedule."

With the financial transactions completed, Andryuk asked, "So how did you get that beached container ship off the sand?"

"*Aye, aye, aye*, it was very hard," Ruiz replied, knowing immediately that the captain was referring to the vessel that had gone aground a year earlier, making international news. "We pumped off the fuel and jettisoned the ballast, and threw off as much cargo and equipment as we could. Then we got four ocean-going tugboats and pulled her into deep water when the tides were the highest."

"That must have been dangerous."

"*Si*, we snapped two towing wires. Finally we got her out to blue water."

"I'm surprised it didn't rip her bottom."

"It did. But without cargo or bunkers it wasn't too bad. We made temporary underwater hull repairs so she could sail to a Taiwanese shipyard."

The captain drained what was left in his glass, as did the others. "So, are you ready to look at the cargo?" He turned to his Chief Mate. "Show the customs official the container, and have one of the sailors escort the shipping agent off the ship."

"It's too bad, *Capitan*, that you won't have time to enjoy our country and the senoritas," Ruiz said, smiling.

"*Amigo*, you're right about that. But we haven't got much to unload, and then we're headed back to sea. This ship doesn't make any money when it's in port."

The three men moved toward the door with their eyes lingering on the remaining unopened soldiers standing at attention on the captain's table.

"You might get thirsty a little later," the Greek skipper said. "Please, take a bottle with you."

As the men were leaving, with the whiskey tucked under their arms, the captain stopped Horate at the door. "Oh, I almost forgot. One of my sailors will be leaving the ship; I'll need to talk with you about that."

Ruiz stayed behind after the others were gone. Accepting the captain's invitation to sit down, he listened with guarded interest to what the commanding officer was about to propose.

"I have a little problem with one of my sailors. He wants to return home, but he seems to have lost his seaman's card. I can vouch for him that he's been on this ship for the last five months and has been an excellent worker. Getting him exit papers could be quite difficult."

"*Si, Capitan,*" Ruiz said, openly eyeing the remaining bottle of whiskey that sat on the desk between them. "It's most unfortunate that one of your sailors lost his shipping card. Does he at least have a passport?"

Andryuk, obviously following the Mexican's line of sight, quickly poured the official another three fingers of whiskey. "He had his passport and shipping card with him when we picked up the tractors in Japan. The night before we left, he went into the back alleys of Yokohama to the tempura bars, where Japanese businessmen take their mistresses. He didn't realize it, but the girl he was talking to was the concubine of the president of an electronics factory. You know how the Japanese can be when a Chinese tries to interfere with their women. Within minutes he was escorted out of the bar by three Yakuza and almost beaten to death. It's a wonder he survived. He didn't tell me he had lost all his papers until we were at sea."

Ruiz swirled the rich liquid in his mouth, then swallowed, enjoying its warmth all the way down. "Losing your shipping papers costs the shipping company twenty-five thousand dollars and it will delay the sailing of this vessel until we can straighten things out. You're better off going to the next port and wiring ahead to his embassy to get the proper paperwork."

"Normally I would," the captain agreed, still smiling, "but it's not that easy. He wants to be at home for the birth of his first son."

Horate Ruiz studied Andryuk, knowing his smile was forced. "I don't know how I can help you," he said, setting his empty glass on the desk.

The captain refilled the glass and pulled out five thousand dollars from the top drawer, then laid it down in front of Ruiz. "Perhaps there is a way he could get off the ship and fly back to Taiwan."

The Mexican official eyed the money. It was more than he would make in a year, and he quickly made a decision. "You're going to need the right man to get his papers so he can fly out of our country without problems."

"That's what I was thinking. I could never find that type of man in a short period of time. Perhaps you could help."

"Yes, of course. But there would be a small, additional fee."

The captain's smile widened. "I understand. What would such a fee be?"

"It will take a few days to make the necessary arrangements," Ruiz said, doing his best to keep his voice steady, "and I believe probably an additional ten thousand American dollars."

"I don't have that much money. How about two thousand?"

Horate knew he should just take it, but he couldn't help but think of all this once-in-a-lifetime opportunity could mean to him and his family. "That's a little low. Why should I risk my career for you and a sailor I don't know? If you want me to help get him out of the port area, it will take eight thousand dollars."

"Six thousand is the best I can do. Take it, or the man will have to miss his son's birth. I'm sure you can understand his feelings. You have children, don't you?"

Ruiz realized he wasn't going to get any more out of him. "*Si*. For the birth of a son, I agree."

"Done," the captain said quickly, adding another five thousand to the pile on the desk. "Here's the money."

The official snatched it and stuffed it into the envelope with the paperwork and uncounted hundred dollar bills, even as he quickly formulated a plan. "I was thinking. The undercover immigration official goes off the clock at four tonight. If your man could get in the container at six, it will be dark by then. It will take him out of the harbor area. Then he is out of your hair and mine. What do you think?"

"Sounds like a good plan. Thank you for your personal involvement. Please, take a bottle of my best." Andryuk went to his cabinet and pulled out a bottle of Crown Royal.

"*Gracias*, Capitan."

"Chan, can you come in here," the captain bellowed. Seconds later a Chinese man in blue coveralls entered the room. "Be ready to leave at six tonight."

"Yes, Sir."

Ruiz frowned. "It's unusual to have a Chinese sailor in your crew, isn't it, *Capitan*?"

"When we left Greece we were short one man, and the company hired him in Taiwan," the captain explained, smiling yet again. "Thank you for your understanding."

Horate nodded. "*Gracias, Capitan*."

Andryuk observed from his office porthole the Japanese tractors being offloaded from the bow of his ship. Using guide ropes and the ship's booms, the stevedores handled them easily. He watched as Ruiz opened the container and Chan slipped past him unnoticed. When the inspection was completed and the container closed and sealed, the offloading began. As the men began lifting the container, the crane's wire slipped, and the container crashed to the ship's deck, making a terrific noise. Work on the pier stopped, as the crew looked around to see if anyone was hurt and then checked out the ship's crane.

"Go get the chief engineer!" the angry mate yelled to one of the sailors. A few minutes later an older man with white coveralls, smudged with grease and loaded down with tools hanging out of the pockets, went inside the crane housing. Fifteen minutes later he re-emerged.

"What did you find?" the chief mate asked the ship's engineer.

"You overheated the motor and fried the windings. It'll take me about two hours to replace it and get the winch back online."

"What the devil's going on?" the captain hollered from the bridge wing, disgusted with the delay.

"The winch motor failed," the mate replied to the skipper.

"Why's that container door open?"

"It must have popped open when it hit the deck," the mate answered.

Andryuk rushed down the ladderway to the main deck and went through the sailors standing around the accident. "Get out of the way," he said pushing a seaman away and going into the container. Chan was lying on the floor with a box on his legs.

The captain picked up the box and checked the Chinese scientist out. He was unhurt and the captain walked out.

"Mate, close it up, and reseal it. Let me know when the crane is repaired."

By the end of the afternoon, the motor had been replaced and tested, and the captain was assured that all was in working order. With a signal to the waiting stevedores, the crane was fired up again, and the container was offloaded to the waiting truck. The captain watched as the driver reached for the paperwork from the ship's crew and then sped off the pier and out toward the yard gate. The stevedores unloaded the rest of the containers on ten other trucks, and the SS Dauphine got ready to leave.

The captain, his mission accomplished, signed a few documents, and the SS Dauphine steamed out of port.

29

Engine room, USS Sheboygan

Booker stayed late to finish changing the lube oil filters on the main engines before leaving the ship. With the Sheboygan sailing in the morning, he didn't dare leave anything undone.

Everything was finally completed and Booker drove to a local bar called the Tom Cat, anxious to taste the cool suds as they slipped over his tongue and slid down his throat. The chief had once again given Petty Officer James the afternoon off, and Booker was disgusted with the command structure on the Sheboygan. It wasn't fair. He had tried to go to medical again, but Doc was gone for the day. Booker put in another liberty chit, but it had been rejected because they had to finish their maintenance on the main engine cylinder heads. Booker had thought he would be able to take the previous day off, but instead James was allowed to take the day off, leaving him to do her work.

Booker knew his wife would be furious with him when he came home late. She never understood, and when he tried to get his Mexican mother-in-law to help, she claimed she didn't want to interfere. His home life was hell on earth, and he longed for a divorce, but they had three children. For the time being, at least, he was stuck.

⌐

Jamal had been patiently watching and waiting across the street from the Tom Cat. At last he saw Booker pull up in front, and he watched as the man went into the bar. Liz had hacked into USS Sheboygan's computer system and found out that Booker had a poor credit rating and was always behind in his bills—the perfect target.

Jamal entered the building a few minutes behind his mark and eased up to the beer-stained bar. Out of the corner of his eye, he observed what Booker was drinking and ordered a brew. When it came he pulled out a twenty and drank slowly. He noticed a pool table, walked over and picked up a stick, and then put in four quarters and racked the balls. When Jamal had finished his beer, he abandoned the game and went to the bar, this time right next to Booker, though he didn't try too hard to get the bartender's attention.

"Man, what's up with the bartender?" he asked, aiming his question in Booker's direction. "Doesn't he see me? Does he think I'm invisible?"

"I know what you mean," Booker said.

"A man could die of thirst around here. Hey, I've got the table set up. You want to play me in a friendly game of pool?"

"Me? I've got about ten dollars on me," Booker answered. "Just enough for another beer, and then I've got to go home. So if you're thinking of hustling me, it ain't going to happen."

"No way, man. Just a friendly game. No bets." He turned his attention back to the bartender and raised his voice. "Hey, bartender, can I get a couple of beers for my friend and me?"

The bartender, wearing a snide look on his face, reluctantly poured a couple of tap beers and then slammed them down in front of Jamal before snatching his twenty-dollar bill.

"Geez, what an attitude," Jamal said to Booker. "So, how about that game? Look, it's no fun to play alone, and there's nobody else in here, so have a beer and join me. What do you say?"

Booker shrugged. "I can't pass up a free beer and a game of pool."

"We'll flip for the break. Call it in the air."

Booker won the toss, aimed the cue ball, and broke the rack. He didn't get any in, and Jamal followed, narrowly missing the side pocket and leaving Booker with an easy shot, just the way he'd planned. Booker took a swig of beer and sunk the ball before missing. To keep it close Jamal sunk a shot, but then left himself nothing to shoot at on the table, so he tried a bank shot and scratched. Booker was obviously becoming more confident, and after another swallow of beer, ran the table and sank the eight ball to win the game.

"Nice run. What's your name?" Jamal asked.

"People call me Booker."

"Glad to meet you, Booker. My name's Jamal. What do you do for a living?"

"I'm in the Navy."

"Really?" Jamal smiled broadly. "You're in the military. Well, then, I'm going to buy you a drink. Bartender, bring us a couple of shooters. So how's life in the Navy?"

"It sucks, but thanks for the drinks," Booker said, apparently warming to the attention. "Let me tell you, it's changed a lot over the last five years."

"I hope for the better."

"No, not even maybe. We've got over fifty percent women on my ship, and let me tell you, that can be a pain."

"Fifty percent women! I'd think it would great to have a few girls around, especially with long trips to sea." Jamal smiled and took a seat at a table.

Booker joined him and began to spill his frustrations. When Jamal asked about his wife, Booker shrugged and said he'd called his wife from the ship and told her he'd be late. "Going to sea doesn't bother me, but sometimes those young women, especially if they're good looking, get a lot of breaks. I'm telling you, I work harder, do more, and yet I can't get a day off."

Jamal nodded and spoke in his most sympathetic tone. "I understand. You're too valuable, and somebody's got to do the work. It isn't right, but it happens. I work in a shop where the owner's son runs the jobs, and he always has his special workers who kiss up to him. I refuse to do it, and naturally I get stuck with the worst jobs."

"I know exactly what you mean," Booker said, nodding his agreement. "Life on the USS Sheboygan just isn't fair. Then I go home, and my wife complains that I don't spend enough time with her. I can't win."

Jamal laughed. "My old lady's the same way."

"How long you been married?"

"Too long. Her parents split up, and she's forever going over to her dad's house and buying and fixing him dinner with my money. She's over there right now; that's why I'm here."

"I hear you, man. My wife's mother is living with us, and it's like having two wives."

"Whoa, man, I don't know how you can handle that. Two hens in the same coop! I don't envy you, Booker. I don't know how you do it."

"Look, I've got ten bucks left," Booker offered. "Let me get the next round, and then I've got to run."

"Hey, thanks. You're okay."

Booker went up to the bar and flipped down his last bill. The bartender came back with two beers, and then Booker returned to the table, carrying a mug in each hand. His face looked longer than it had a moment earlier.

"What's the matter?" Jamal inquired.

"My wife's going to kill me."

"Why? What didn't you do now, partner?"

"I was supposed to bring milk home for the kids, and now I've spent my last ten on beer."

"Look, man, here's a twenty. You've got it a lot rougher than I do, and it's not going to hurt me."

Booker shook his head. "No way. I can't take your money. I never should have told you about the milk."

"Hey, man, don't sweat it. Next time you see me, if you have the money you can pay me back. If I have to wait for next payday, that's no big deal. I'll see you in here again. Twenty bucks isn't going to break me, so lighten up. Besides, you're defending our country, and from the sounds of it, you don't get many bonuses."

"You heard that right. Hey, thanks. You're a real friend."

"Don't mention it," Jamal said, draining his beer and getting up. "Well, I've got to get going. I'll see you around."

Booker nodded. "Thanks again, Jamal. I'll pay you the next time I see you."

"Whatever," he replied. Then he left the bar, got in his car, and drove away, knowing full well that the majority of that twenty would be spent on beer before Booker went to the store to buy milk for his kids.

30

USS Sheboygan, Pier 6, Naval Base

USS Sheboygan's engineers arrived at 0200 to light off the auxiliary boiler and get the engines warmed up. Liberty expired for them four hours before the rest of the crew so they could get equipment online. The ship's engineers were always the first to arrive for sea duty and the last to leave once they returned. The captain relied on his engineers to get him under away and to keep commitments. So far they hadn't missed any. They'd been late once, but his engineers were innovative enough to make voyage repairs to the malfunctioning equipment. In the last few years the Navy had been cutting back on repair dollars so they could build new ships. Captain Davey always made it a point to be onboard when the engineers lit off the plant. Oftentimes he would go below with the Chief Engineer, just so the engineers knew he cared about them and was aware of what they did for his ship. Captain Davey's wife, however, wasn't so happy when he rolled out of bed at 0100, but he did it anyway.

Once onboard the captain went to the wardroom and made himself a fresh pot of coffee. No one was around, and he knew the CHENG would be in to have a cup of joe, along with his Main Propulsion Assistant (MPA). Davey had served as an engineer and was glad he had survived that job. He'd seen many fine naval careers shipwrecked because a chief engineer didn't understand his power plant or didn't have a good MPA.

As he poured his coffee, the door to the wardroom opened, and Bosun Browder entered the mess.

"Good morning, Captain. You ready to take the old girl out?"

"You bet, Boats. What are you doing up so early—or should I ask if you're just rolling in from a night ashore?" Captain Davey asked, grinning at his bosun.

"Ooh, Captain, you know how to hurt a guy. But, no, I spent the night aboard. They were working the davit late, so I just turned in, but I couldn't sleep."

"Something bothering you?"

"I don't know. I got a feeling something ain't right, but I just can't put my finger on it."

"What do you mean?" the Captain asked with a grin. "You fall in love again?"

"Shoot, Captain," Boats said, laughing a little. "If that's all I had to worry about, I'd still be sleeping. No, that's not what I'm talking about."

"Is it your retirement?"

"Nah, nothing like that. I've just got something gnawing at my gut."

"You worried that lifeboat davit won't work again?"

"Maybe, but we did three tests with it last night, and it seems to be working fine."

"Did you eat onboard last night? Maybe something didn't agree with you."

"Nah, Captain, I've been eating Navy chow for twenty-eight years. No, it's something else. I was tossing and turning all night long. I got maybe an hour's worth of sleep."

Larry Swanson, the ship's CHENG, walked into the wardroom and pulled down his mug from the rack on the bulkhead. "Good morning, Captain, Boats. Is the coffee fresh?"

"You bet it is. Your engines going to be ready by 0700?" Davey asked.

"Yes, Sir. The MPA is testing that valve Jake found for the steam line, so we should be good to go, as long as it doesn't leak. I'm headed down to main control now."

"Great. I might come down a little later," the CO said, letting the CHENG know he'd be down in case there was any last-minute cleanup that needed to be done. Rarely did he walk in the CHENG's spaces unannounced.

"Boats, what are you doing up?" Larry asked.

Boats shrugged. "I don't know. Couldn't sleep."

"Must be that French tech rep for the boat davit," the CHENG teased. "She's a cutie. She turn you down for a date?"

"No, she didn't. Matter of fact, once we're finished with this underway, I might take her out. She works for the shipyard here in San Diego."

"Speaking of tech reps, Boats," Captain Davey interjected, "I received an email last night. There's a couple reps coming to launch the Sea Flyer again."

"I hope we don't have to go out and rescue that little un-manned reconnaissance boat again," Boats said, looking none too happy about the extra work his crew would have.

"The company did some upgrades and wants to put some techs aboard to monitor the signals and make sure it makes the right turns and speed changes," the captain explained.

"Well, I think we're a long way away from making that craft reliable. It's not like the UAV's we deployed with last year. I think when the little boat dips in the swells, it loses its signals and then gets off course, but I could be wrong."

"Boats, if it saves lives, I'm all for it. Have the crane detail ready to go once we clear the last sea buoy. I'll see you later. I'm going to my office."

"Roger that, Captain. The crane crew will be standing by to launch Sea Flyer once we hit open water."

The captain left the wardroom and returned to his office. He drained the last bit of his coffee and set his cup down, all the time wondering what was eating the bosun. Walking aft he opened the watertight hatch and went outside, then stood by the railing on the 05 level, looking over his ship. The house lights were on, but there was no one moving about. He looked at the retractable flight deck and wondered how it would work. This time at sea, as always, they had plenty of things to do. They'd have a full schedule, testing engines, the lifeboat davit, the new missile launchers, and now the Sea Flyer. The UMV was the least of his worries, but everything else had better work.

The captain looked across the bay at the still waters of San Diego Harbor. Now that he'd served twenty years he could retire, and San Diego was a great place to live, if you could afford it. The weather was fabulous, and he could sell his house in Eastlake, now that the kids were almost out of college. He and his wife could downsize and move into a condo. The payments would fit his retirement budget, and he wouldn't have to mow the lawn, but all of that was in the future. For now he descended the metal steps, going down five levels to the boat deck for another look around his ship before going below to main control.

31

Ensenada, Mexico

Khalif was waiting at the farm when the ten trucks arrived with tractors and farm equipment. The drivers pulled into the shed and immediately began to unload the containers with heavy forklifts. Launcher parts were carefully taken out and put in an area to begin assembly before installation in the plane. Most of the critical circuitry and mechanical parts were intact, so it would take only two weeks to be fully assembled and electronically tested. The Light of Allah had hired some retired Soviet army technicians to put the launcher together and to operate it. He made sure they were all single men, so that questions from their families wouldn't be raised when they didn't return home as expected. The Chinese scientist emerged from one of the containers and immediately walked over to Khalif.

"Dr. Chan, I see you made it. You have ten days to get everything ready. Will that be enough?"

"Yes, Khalif, as long as I don't get bounced around and have all that I need."

A puzzled look came across Khalif's face. "Hussan, make sure Doctor Chan has everything he needs to assemble the bomb. Everything must run according to the Light of Allah's timetable. It is key to our success."

"Don't worry, we shall be ready," Chan confirmed. "I'll begin at once."

"Allah will be pleased. I'll be back in ten days to inspect the work." Turning to Hussan he ordered, "Be sure to run the tractors and plant the fields. I don't want Satan's spy satellite taking pictures with all the equipment we've just brought here and not see the fields plowed. The infidels aren't stupid, so begin to work the ground and plant some crops."

"As you wish," Hussan said.

Khalif smiled to himself. It was no accident that Hussan had been assigned to this job. In the dry farming community in Yemen where Hussan had lived as a boy, everything was done with old, outdated equipment that barely ran or was pulled by a worn-out horse. Their family hardly had enough to eat, and they spent much of their time waiting on the rain that seldom came. When the opportunity came for him to better his life by following the militant Islamic movement, Hussan had jumped at the chance to attend one of the training camps in Pakistan near the Afghan border. Khalif knew that though Hussan had found great meaning for his life in being part of the movement that would bring an American city to its knees to worship Allah, he also knew that the former farm boy was anxious to drive the tractors and plow the fields.

"Do you see this long strip of land, Hussan?" Khalif asked.

"Of course, Khalif."

"Do you think you can make it level?"

"Sure, if I could find a road-grader or a bulldozer."

"See what's in the village. Maybe there's an old grader you could attach to a tractor."

"I will look, but why do you want a strip of graded land? I thought I was going to plow the ground and plant the seeds you've given me."

"You will, but we'll need to land a plane here."

"All will be ready for Allah," Hussan said.

Khalif continued instructing Hussan, all the time wondering if the farmer-turned-fighter was ready to die a martyr's death. "When you grade the strip, tell the others that you will need a staging area for harvesting the crops and shipment. We won't have enough room in the barns. Then when you get done grading it, spread some dirt on the strip so it won't be noticed from the skies. Don't tell anyone the real reason for the strip. Only you and I shall know. Is that understood?"

"Yes, of course, Khalif."

"Good. Make sure you keep it that way. The Light of Allah's plan cannot be compromised. Now that you are here, when you go to the village make sure you drink some liquor. No one must know that you are Muslim."

"Of course, Khalif. I will do as you say."

Khalif didn't like the idea of Hussan going into town, but the townspeople would get suspicious if he didn't. Hopefully he wouldn't drink too much and allow his words to slip.

Walking to the car, Khalif felt his excitement level rising. It had taken four years to plan this operation. If the other sects of the militant movement did their part, America would be caught unaware, devastated with little choice but to bow to Allah's orders or die!

32

USS Sheboygan, Pier 6

The crew of USS Sheboygan began filtering onto the ship before liberty expired at 0500. Chow was being served on the mess decks, and everyone changed into their working uniforms before getting something to eat.

"Navigation brief, wardroom," sounded over the loud speakers as the ship came alive. The captain, his officers, the chiefs, and the leading petty officers of the deck and navigation department went into the wardroom for a final brief on the navigation detail before transiting the ship out of the harbor. The captain sat in his chair and listened as Jim briefed him as to how the events would unfold.

Twenty minutes into the brief a chief petty officer came into the wardroom and quietly whispered to the CO, "Captain, the tugs are alongside, and the pilot is coming aboard."

"Very well," the commanding officer replied, and then announced to the rest, "Let's wrap this up and get going."

The first lieutenant quickly finished the Power Point presentation and looked to the captain for any final comments.

"Dismissed," the captain said, smiling. He loved going to sea with the ship under his command. There was no better experience in the Navy than commanding a naval warship at sea, and he dreaded the day he would turn command of his ship over to a perfect stranger. The last four months of his tour were going by faster than he had expected. Every time they left port, he knew he'd better make the most of it. Other than the lifeboat davit failing, he hadn't had any incidents that would cause him concern.

"First, I'll be on the bridge if you need me," Davey said, leaving the wardroom by the side door. No one else ever entered or departed the wardroom using that door; it was for the captain alone. Every once in awhile the port engineer would use the door, but he always made sure he took off his cap upon entering. It was a sign of respect, and he always honored it.

⟿

"Man sea and anchor detail," the announcement came over the loudspeaker. The crew on the mess decks took a last-minute forkful of food from their half-eaten breakfasts and then took their plates to the scullery before scurrying out to their sea detail stations so they wouldn't get chewed out.

The orange and green tractor tug blew its whistle, and a couple of heaving lines were thrown over the side and onto the deck of the powerful boat. Deckhands on the tug quickly grabbed the monkey fists and pulled on the taglines as the ship paid out their mooring lines.

"Not so fast, you apes," Boats cautioned. "Can't you see the line's going into the water? Johnson, you awake yet?"

"Yes sir, Bosun."

"Son, pay attention to what you're doing. I don't want my lines going into the water. You hear me?"

Johnson appeared a little hung-over, and the bosun didn't doubt that the sailor had a killer headache. He and some of the others had gone to a bar last night, knowing they wouldn't have anything to drink for the next few days, and they had stayed out a little too long.

"I said, 'Did you hear me?'" Browder growled, now inches from Johnson's face.

The young man kept his eyes on the lines, as he slowly paid out the line so the tugboat crew could make it up to their cleats.

"Yes, Sir, Bosun. I heard you. I'm watching it," he said, as Boats checked out the kid's bloodshot eyes.

"Well, you'd better be or you're going to be walking around with a size twelve shoe sticking out your butt!"

The other sailors looked over at Johnson and began to laugh a little but stopped the moment the bosun shot them a look. Everybody did what Boats wanted, when he wanted. He knew his old school verbal tirades were a welcomed diversion to their lives at sea.

"What you smiling at, Perkins?" Browder roared to a young woman paying out line behind Johnson.

"Nothing, Boats," she answered good-naturedly.

On the ship's bow the men and women worked alongside each other in the task of making up the tug to the ship.

"Tighten up that line," Browder hollered to a third-class seaman, who had the end of the line wrapped around a mooring cleat. "Take out the slack," he yelled again, watching everything like a hawk. Twenty years ago he'd seen a line part and a man cut in half because of sloppy line handling, so Browder was all business when his crew was working on his forecastle. As a result he'd never had a major injury on his watch.

⌣

The tugboat gave a couple of blasts with its whistle, and then the OOD announced over the 1MC, "Underway. Shift colors."

The American flag was hoisted up the mainmast as a couple of sailors lowered the ensign from the aft end of the flight deck, and the Sheboygan slowly drifted away from the pier.

"One-third ahead," the harbor pilot called from the bridge wing, as he leaned over the side and watched the ship's bow pull away from the big floating black fenders that protected the dock.

"One-third ahead," repeated the helmsman.

A heavy puff of black smoke came out of both Sheboygan's stacks, as the engines ramped up. The ship pulled farther away from the pier and was now into the harbor and heading between the bridge pilings. Everything was running like clockwork, as the ship headed beneath the tall bridge. From the flying bridge it looked as if the mast would hit the underside of the Coronado Bridge, but it cleared it easily, and the ship soon passed two national assets, the nuclear carriers John Stennis and Ronald Regean, docked at North Island Naval Air Station. The Sheboygan slowed a little as they let the pilot climb down the Jacob's ladder and onto the deck of the tugboat. The ship was now under Captain Davey's command, as a heavily armed patrol boat, equipped with two fifty-caliber machine guns, shot by doing fifteen knots.

Heading toward Point Loma they passed a red buoy where seals were basking in the early morning sun, taking a break from their fishing. They barked their greetings at the big ship, as if passing their own salute to a ship of the line. If seals were this far into the harbor, the water was clean and fish were near. Of course, it helped that a bait barge was throwing day-old anchovies over the side and providing the barking sea dogs a scrumptious breakfast. They quieted down as the ship passed the Point Loma sub-base.

"Ahead two-thirds," Davey ordered, as the Sheboygan cleared the final channel buoy. The ship kept the same course and speed for the next hour until it was fifteen miles off shore.

⌒

After lunch the captain slowed the ship down, and Bosun Browder got his "deck apes" together to lower the RHIB boat from the lifeboat davit. Liz Ferrari and a male colleague were standing by as they went through the computer checks to lower the boat.

"Bosun, how much time do we have before we lower the boat?" Liz asked.

"As much as you want. We're going to slow down and use the crane to lower the Sea Flyer into the water and test its guidance systems. When that's finished, we'll lower the lifeboat."

"Great, Bosun," Liz said, throwing a quick wink at Browder. "We found a malfunction with the programming, and we're correcting it now. We should be ready in an hour."

The bosun walked to the starboard side of the boat deck and got his crew together to hook up the slings for the Sea Flyer. Technicians from the parent company were also aboard to work the guidance system on the remote operating vehicle.

"Careful," the bosun hollered, as the ship took a heavy roll in one of the swells. A new seaman recruit lost his balance and quickly grabbed the shoulder of the sailor next to him, preventing him from falling overboard. He hadn't gotten his sea legs and wasn't expecting the first heavy roll of the trip.

"Put the shackle through the eye of the sling, and slip the pin in. Then jump off," one of the chiefs ordered, overseeing the sailors who were standing on the deck of the Sea Flyer. The chief rotated his index finger, pointing upward, signaling the crane operator to raise the small boat. It left the deck of the ship and swung over the side. The captain slowed Sheboygan to five knots and turned broadside to the wind to make the launching a little smoother. The technicians remotely started the Sea Flyer's engines as it was lowered into the water. Automatically the special hooks from the wire rope slings detached. The little recon boat began to leave the side of the ship.

"All right!" one of the tech reps exclaimed, as he played with the joystick. The boat responded beautifully, and the bosun just shook his head. Why couldn't the davit operate like that, he wondered?

The technicians turned the Sea Flyer in all different directions and then turned the camera on so they could see the video feed. The image blurred every time a wave washed the lens, but an automatic flushing device instantly cleared it.

Curious about the image the Sea Flyer was broadcasting, Bosun Browder poked his head into the converted container every now and then and looked at the monitor. The little unmanned boat was scanning the horizon and picking up a fully loaded Japanese car carrier steaming toward San Diego Harbor.

"That works pretty good," Boats said. "Does it ever fail?"

"We still have a bit of a problem if it gets out of range," the techie explained. "Then the ship can alter course and track it down, and we can reestablish contact and control."

"How about your controls? They look like something you'd buy at a toy store."

The techie laughed. "I've heard that before. We keep them simple and they work like a champ. To be honest, we didn't try and reinvent the wheel, just upgraded one of the remote airplane controls. Of course, we had to add controls for the camera, but we haven't had much problem with either of them."

"I wish I could say the same for the boat davit. I think the Frenchies over-designed it so they could make tons of money fixing it. What a rip-off. That davit hasn't worked right since we did the op test in the shipyard. Let me know if you need anything from us."

Boats walked out of the container and over to the boat davit. "Liz, are you and the crew ready?"

"Sure are."

"Good. I've done this before. Once the boat is over the side, that's when the real fun begins. I'm not manning it, so we'll just lower the boat to the water line."

"That'd be great," Liz replied cheerfully.

The bosun lowered the eleven-meter RHIB boat over the side, and everything went smoothly until it hit the water line. Suddenly the forward winch started to jerk the bow up every time it touched the water, hammering the lifting stanchion and hooks.

"Have you seen enough?" Boats yelled. "Because you've got about ten seconds, and then I've got to take control before that winch rips that boat to pieces."

"We've seen enough. Bring it back on board, and we'll look at the programming again," Liz said. "We'll be ready later."

"Anything you say," Boats said, more than just a little tired of the whole davit but certainly not of Liz. Once he secured the davit, he went over to the helicopter flight deck and got ready to retract the deck once more to test the launch sequences for the tomahawks. He was watching as one of the chiefs worked the controls as the steel deck retracted. The hefty panels were moving smoothly, powered by heavy-duty hydraulic pumps.

"Bosun, Bosun!" the techie from the unmanned surveillance boat shouted, running out of his container. "We've just lost Sea Flyer."

"Just hold your horses," Boats said. "I'll go up on the bridge and talk to the old man. I'm sure we can pick it up on radar and change course."

The bosun left the boat deck and climbed the five ladders to the bridge, where he found the captain sitting in his chair on the bridge wing, enjoying the clean, fresh sea air. He raised his eyebrows as the bosun approached.

"Boats, I know you didn't make this trip all the way up here to get some sun."

"No, Sir, Captain. They've lost control of the Sea Flyer, and the techs want us to change course to find and retrieve it."

The captain laughed for a moment and then got out of his chair and went inside the bridge. He went over to the surface-to-surface radar and pointed to the little craft.

"Change course to two-nine-zero. Speed one-third."

"Change course to two-nine-zero, speed one-third," the OOD repeated

The captain picked up his binoculars and scanned the horizon. "Boats, are you done with your tests? The engineers want to do full-power on the main engines."

"Soon as we bring that little UMV back, we're all done."

"How'd the davit do?"

"It didn't, but they're working on it."

"Let me know when you've got the Sea Flyer onboard, and then I'll turn the engines over to the engineers."

The bosun and his crew retrieved the Sea Flyer and stowed it in its skid, and the Sheboygan ran a straight course, slowly increasing speed to twenty-two knots. For the next eight hours the engineers below took readings and made adjustments to the main engines.

Early the next morning they did a successful launching of the lifeboats from the davit, but again didn't put anyone in them. The Captain wanted to do a couple of fire drills, so the crew responded to the numerous bells and whistles throughout the day and night.

The following morning the exhausted crew of the USS Sheboygan pulled back to San Diego Harbor with most of the equipment tested and a weekend of liberty awaiting them.

33

White House, Oval Office

At eight A.M. the highly classified Threat Matrix aired by secure video to the President's office as he and Director Stevens watched.

"In eight days we will celebrate freedom for all Muslims," the Light of Allah announced on the Al Jazeera television station, which was broadcasting live throughout the Arab world. "The hope of a new world rests in our hands."

"What do you make of this, William?" President Ryland asked, his eyes focused on the screen as it went to blue. He reached over and shut the monitor off.

"We didn't respond to his first threat, so we have eight days to find out if this next threat is real," Director Stevens replied.

"What have you found out about him?"

"He calls himself 'The Light of Allah.' He seems to think either the end of the world is coming, or the militant Islamic movement is going to take over the world with him as the head."

The President was frustrated. They needed more information than that to know how to deal with this self-proclaimed Light of Allah. "That's all? He sounds like most of the other radical leaders of the Islamic movement. Surely you know something else."

"Getting Intel out of the Arab community is very tough, but we've monitored the jail cells in Guantanamo Bay and heard two inmates talking about this Light of Allah. It seems—and I don't know if this is totally true—that he fought alongside

Osama bin Laden during the war against the Russians in Afghanistan. We don't have much more except that he followed bin Laden to the Sudan when he set up his network there. We had a hunter looking for Carlos the Jackal in the Sudan, and he gave a report on bin Laden. It seems when bin Laden left in 1996, The Light of Allah took over and began his own movement."

"Have you been able to establish his true identity?"

"That's a strange one. From his face we haven't been able to discern if he's had plastic surgery."

"We'd better keep an eye on him. How's he received in the Arab world?"

"From our contacts, very well. As you can see, he's an attractive man who's very charismatic. He doesn't seem to have any enemies within the Arab world, which we find very unique. Usually the Arabs fight among themselves, but he's been able to bring them together."

"That's not good. If he brings the Arabs together, we could have a real problem on our hands." He turned his attention completely to his colleague. "What's he really after?"

"Like the rest of the militant Islamic terrorists, to bring down the financial empire of the United States and wipe the Jews off the face of the earth. As you well know, the militant Islamic movement is a social, educational, economic, and religious network that's attempting to take over the world. They want to impose the *shari'ah* or Islamic law on all the countries of the world. This would make the earth one big *ummah*, or Muslim community, living under the rule of Allah. I know you refuse to negotiate with terrorists, Mr. President, so we've kept threat con Bravo for our borders and military bases. We're checking ID's even closer now. Your immigration policy has taken a lot of heat, but our borders are starting to tighten up. For years I believe we've let all kinds of people into our country that have done us great harm and potentially more."

"I wish the press would print that," the President said. "It seems every time I make a move to increase the security of our citizens, the left comes out against me."

"You're tough, Sir; you can handle them."

The President nodded. "As long as you give me the right Intel, I can deal with the pressure. Keep digging on this Light of Allah. We may have a problem on our hands in eight days."

Rising from his desk, the President went to the window and looked out at the rose garden. "The average citizen has no idea how intense the militant Islamic movement is. Any time suicide bombers are sent out with the promise of paradise, wine, and seventy-two virgins for blowing themselves up, that's difficult to stop. It can be a huge incentive to someone who's had nothing in this life. Many believe we can negotiate with these terrorists, but what they don't understand is that they are at war with the world, and they are slowly growing within many countries. We have to decrease the risk to our people by decreasing our vulnerability."

"Mr. President, I appreciate the position you've taken. Many men wouldn't have the courage to stand up to them."

"Somebody has to. Keep digging, William. I've got faith in you. What about the nukes?"

"We haven't located them, but we overlooked one of the relatives of the man we found at the morgue."

"Really, who?"

"It turns out that one of the ships that loaded up at Seal Beach has a bosun who was married to the man's niece who is at the morgue."

"Have you talked to the bosun?"

"No, because he's been at sea, but we pulled his record."

"What did you find?"

"He lost his wife eight years ago, went on a drinking spree and got into some trouble. The niece's uncle put up the money to bail him out and pay his legal bills. We didn't pick it up at first because he was married into the man's family."

"What's his name?"

"Browder."

"I want him thoroughly but quietly investigated. Don't take him off the ship," the President said picking up his hat and coat.

"Sir, if I can have another moment of your time, I have a delicate issue to talk to you about."

The President, already late for his next appointment, turned back to face Stevens. "Go ahead."

"From what my analysts have put together, we believe this Light of Allah may be operating out of the northern part of Sudan."

"Really? Where?"

"In the eastern tip of the Sahara Desert."

"Can we send someone in there to investigate?"

"It's not that easy. It would be like finding a needle in the haystack. There might be a way to get some help."

"And what would that be?"

"Black Ice Corporation. They could be contracted to gather Intel. For the past twenty years there's been a civil war in Uganda. The Lord's Resistance Army has been fighting the Ugandan government troops because of the atrocities of the present regime. This small but well organized army has one-tenth the manpower as the government troops, yet they've forced them to negotiate peace."

"What's your point?"

"Peace talks are now being held in Sudan between the LRA and the Uganda government. As part of the peace talks the LRA has been told to leave Northern Uganda. They're in Southern Sudan, and I believe we could quietly approach them to ask their help in traveling to the Sahara. I'm sure we could hire a squad of them to take our special forces to Northern Sudan to see if we can find the Light of Allah's base camp."

"Aren't the leaders of the LRA indicted by the International Court of Criminals?"

"Yes, but those indictments were brought by the government of Uganda, who themselves have committed many atrocities to their own people."

"Why do they call themselves the Lord's Resistance Army?"

"Their leader considers himself a prophet of God."

"We don't recognize this army. We only recognize the government of Uganda."

"Correct. So our mission would have to be very secretive. The rebels are living in a foreign country, and I know they could use the money. Until the negotiations are complete they can't return to their homeland, and crossing the country of Sudan could be quite dangerous for us."

"Do they speak English?"

"Uganda was colonized by the Brits and Catholic priests, so many speak English quite well. I believe we could approach the LRA leaders at the peace conference and ask to hire some of their soldiers as guides. We'll purchase a couple of old but well-built trucks and drive up to the northern part of the Sahara Desert. We'll keep in contact with satellite uplinks."

"I don't like the idea, but if we use this Black Ice Corporation maybe we can keep it quiet. I need intelligence about this Light of Allah. If you believe hiring a couple of men to guide you through Northern Sudan will work, then do it, but do it quietly. I don't want to start a controversy with the government of Uganda, especially if they're in peace talks. I don't want this thing blown out of proportion. Do you understand?"

"Yes, Sir, Mr. President. We'll proceed accordingly."

34

Islamic Headquarters, National City

"Haviv, may Allah be praised! Khalif told me we go operational in eight days."

"I know, Abdullah. I've discovered a way to get our men on the ship without anyone knowing."

Abdullah's euphoria at the victory that was right around the corner began to fade. "What do you mean? My plan is already set!" he exploded.

"Yes, but Liz has told me about a special unmanned reconnaissance vessel that's being tested. We don't need to use their lifeboat, and this boat is covered."

Abdullah's rage and resentment grew at the mention of Liz's involvement in this new part of the plan. "She's only a dog! What could she know?"

"She was on the Sheboygan for two days and watched how they operated their gear. They have a container stowed on deck that operates an unmanned craft. Liz also thought of a very easy way to get the men onboard the ship without anyone being aware."

"What would she know about strategy?" Abdullah challenged, glaring at Haviv. "Have you talked to Khalif about it?"

"Yes."

Abdullah scowled. Haviv was smart and that Khalif probably liked the new plan better. He didn't like it when others were acknowledged ahead of him.

"Listen, Abdullah, the plan combines the best of both of our plans, just like old times. Let me tell you—"

"You mean before you went soft," Abdullah interrupted, determined to regain the upper hand, even though he didn't know the details of Haviv's new plan. "No, this new plan will never work."

"The Light of Allah has already approved it."

"What!" Abdullah thundered. "You dare to go over my head? Why, I ought to cut your heart out right now and throw you in a dumpster, just like I did to my sister who was seen coming out of a nightclub with a Westerner."

"I had nothing to do with this plan," Haviv assured him. "Liz was talking to Khalif, and he liked her ideas."

The only thing worse than Haviv taking credit for this new plan was passing the credit to a woman. "Living in America has made everyone soft. Since when does a woman have any ideas worth anything?"

"Abdullah, Allah has used her to discover a weakness in their training operation that will help us."

"Maybe. But let's see what she can do under pressure. Can she fight like a man?"

"The Light of Allah has also moved up the timetable for the attack. The next time the ship gets underway, we strike."

"I can't believe all this has happened without anyone consulting me," Abdullah fumed. "A woman comes along, offers what she thinks is a better plan, and the Light of Allah accepts it and changes everything."

"Perhaps it is Allah's plan. Maybe he is using a woman to transmit his ideas."

"Don't be ridiculous! I suppose the next thing you'll tell me is that Elena is a virgin, and she's going to run the mission."

"Of course not, Abdullah. You are our leader."

Abdullah clenched his jaw before answering. "And don't forget it, Haviv!"

35

USS Sheboygan, Pier 6

Jim waited until the ship was docked and the sailors had finished stowing the gear. As much as he wanted to run down
the gangway and call Elena, he walked aft on the flight deck and
checked the stern lines. Curiously, he checked to see if the rat
guards were in place now that he'd learned so much more about
them from bosun.

"How much longer before we lower the gangway?" Jim asked,
as Boats walked toward him across the flight deck.

"About fifteen minutes. I want to make sure the lines are good
and tight before we let the shore crane lower the accom ladder.
If you want, Lieutenant, you can leave as soon as we lower it to
the pier."

"I appreciate that, but I'll wait until everything is finished."

The bosun didn't say anything, but the look of respect on
his face told Jim he'd impressed him by staying to see the job
done. Jim had heard stories of first lieutenants who were less
conscientious about their duties, and he was sure Browder had
run across several of them during his military career. As far as
Jim was concerned, good leadership dictated that leaders serve
their department and their people, and he wasn't about to initiate
morale problems by leaving early.

"Lieutenant, the gangway is secure," the bosun said a few minutes later. Jim immediately went up to the captain and reported
the condition of the deck department.

"If you've nothing else for me, Captain," Jim said, "I'd like to shove off."

"You go ahead, Jim. I know you just got back in town and have a lot to do. Be sure to be here tomorrow morning. We have a department head meeting."

"Yes, Sir, Captain," Jim said, as he raced down the stairway to heaven to the boat deck, and then down the ladder to main deck and to the ship's quarterdeck. In five minutes he was in his car and quickly pulled out his cell phone in hopes of catching Elena. He called the hotel, and they put him through to her room, but there was no answer. He figured she was probably still in school, so Jim left a message and headed home. He drove his car off base and got on the I-5 freeway, quickly shifting into fourth gear and flooring his old Porsche Carrerra. Like a well-trained racehorse, the car jumped at the opportunity to gallop down the freeway. Just as he took the Carlsbad exit, his cell phone rang. Excitedly, he grabbed it, fully expecting to hear Elena's voice.

"Hello, Jim, this is Captain Fullerton."

Jim felt as if he'd been doused by a bucket of cold ice water. "Yes, Sir," he responded.

"I need to see you in my office immediately. Urgent Intel from Washington arrived an hour ago."

"I'll be there in twenty minutes," Jim said, clenching his cell phone tightly, the air in his love-inflated heart escaping. Then he wondered what was so important and how much time it would take. Suddenly his mind was alive with all kinds of thoughts. Maybe there was a special op that they needed him on now that the Sheboygan was pier-side. His phone rang again, but gone was the growing excitement and tender fragrance of young love.

"Welcome back, Jim," Elena said, rolling her "J" and making Jim's heart do summersaults. "I'd love to see you. I missed you."

"And I'd love to see you too, but I've just been recalled."

"Oh, Jim," she said, the disappointment evident in her voice.

Jim's heart skipped a beat, recognizing her sincerity and wishing he hadn't volunteered for double-duty. He'd once looked at his secret double-life as quite exciting, but now the additional duty of military intelligence was keeping him away from the woman his heart pursued. With all his being he wanted to be with Elena, but duty came first. He hoped she would understand.

"When will you be off?" she asked sadly.

Bummed by the unexpected turn of events he replied, "I don't know. Something's come up."

"That's okay, *cheri*," she said in sad, melodic notes. "Call me when you're free."

"Trust me, Elena, I will," Jim said fervently.

"Of course I trust you, *cheri*."

"Did you think about me?"

"Of course, *cheri*. I thought of you every day while you were at sea and wished I could be with you. I even dreamed about you."

"Really? What was the dream about?"

"Oh, I can't tell you over the phone, but later when we're together I'll tell you. *Au revoir*," she said, her voice soft and seductive, leaving Jim wanting her even more as she clicked off the line.

With all his heart he wanted to pass the Coast Guard Station and Homeland Security and drive straight to Elena's hotel, but he followed the call of duty and pulled up to the gate. After showing his CAC card he parked his car and quickly went to the CO's outer office.

"He's expecting you," the secretary said.

Jim knocked on the door and looked in. When the Captain in Military Intelligence looked up Jim said, "Sir, I got here as quickly as I could."

"Come in, Jim. While you were out at sea the border patrol captured six men crossing the border on dirt bikes."

"Why's that so unusual?" Jim asked, wondering why the capture of a few men coming across the border merited his returning to base and to Captain Fuller's office.

"They were all Muslim. As you know, we've limited the number of citizens from certain Arab countries to enter the United States because of the terrorist activities that have happened over the years."

"Where are they now?" Jim asked, still wondering why this pertained to him.

"We've shipped them off to Gitmo."

"Well, I guess the intelligence community will be interrogating them."

"I'm sure they will, but what concerns me is that they had fake CAC cards. I can only imagine that they were headed to one of our bases as suicide bombers," Fullerton explained.

"Why would you think they'd be blowing themselves up?"

"Because they had small Russian detonators on them. I don't know if we caught all of them. There could have been some that came over before we captured this bunch."

"Sir, what would you like me to do?"

"I need you to take a look at something in Mexico."

"Yes, Sir."

"I want you to go to Ensenada. We have a report of three Arabs meeting with a Mexican customs official in Rosarita Beach, but this man works in Ensenada. Now he may have been in Rosarita Beach for pleasure, but I'm not so sure. These two events might be tied together, and if they are, then maybe this is just the tip of the iceberg. I can't spare another agent to send with you, and I know you just arrived here, but if you've got a girlfriend, maybe you could take her with you as a cover."

"Sir?"

"Intel has confirmed that foreign interests bought a farm down there and built a large barn on it. One of our analysts was curious about it, so he used a satellite and zoomed in on the image of the barn. It didn't look quite right to him, so he kept monitoring the place. In addition to building the barn, they brought in some farm machinery and plowed the fields."

"Sounds about right to me."

"Except it was late July. The analyst happened to be from Iowa and noticed that they planted their corn in the hottest part of the year and watered it."

"Did the corn come up?"

"It did, but this guy's from corn country, and he never saw them cultivate between the rows and didn't hire any laborers to do it either. Some of the photos show armed guards patrolling the perimeter."

"Maybe they're afraid of the drug cartels or bandits. You know how Mexico is."

"Maybe. But we need more Intel on the matter. I need you to talk to your commanding officer and get permission to go down there for a few days. If you have any trouble getting the time off, let me know."

"Yes, Sir."

"Check with the yeoman for travel money. I would prefer you pay everything in cash. Just act like a tourist. Any questions?"

"No, Sir," Jim said, already imagining himself on the beach with Elena.

"Fine. Report back to me in four days. What do you know about Bosun Browder?"

"He seems squared away."

"Okay, but keep an eye on him."

"Yes, Sir," Jim said and wondered what the bosun had done to attract the attention of military intelligence. He quickly went back to the ship and told the CO that he needed a few days off to pursue an intelligence matter, but didn't mention Browder to him. Captain Davey gave his permission for leave, and Jim hurried to his car, hoping Elena could take a few days off from her diamond school.

He dialed her number, and she answered right away. "Elena, you'll never guess what just happened."

"*Oui*, I have no idea, Jim."

"I've been given four days off, and I want to know if you can come to Mexico with me for a little vacation."

"Mexico! I'd love to go with you, but I've just started this school."

"I was thinking of leaving Friday and being back in town on Tuesday, so you'd only miss two days of class."

"Oh, Jim, I don't know. I'll have to check with my teachers."

"See if they'll give you the assignments ahead of time, and you can take them with you. Remember the last time we studied together?"

"I do," she said warmly.

Jim envisioned the smile he heard in her voice. "We could do some sightseeing and then I could leave you alone to study."

"And what would you do?"

"I could work out and go for a run. Ask your teachers, and when we meet tonight we can talk."

"Oh, I don't know if we can meet tonight."

Jim's heart sank. "Really? Why not?"

"The school is having a dinner and fashion show tonight in Los Angeles. One of the cutters is in from India with a new collection."

"Can you bring a date?"

"I'm sorry, Jim, but the diamonds are very valuable and are normally not open for public viewing, so only the students from the school are allowed to attend. You can imagine how security is around them."

"I suppose," Jim said, crestfallen as he realized how very much he wanted to be with her—this moment, and many moments to come.

36

University District

The Light of Allah's messenger returned to San Diego, where Abdullah and Haviv met him at a coffee shop.

"I'm afraid we have some bad news, Khalif," Abdullah said, uneasy at being the one to deliver this bad news.

"What is it?" Khalif asked, his eyes displaying his displeasure.

"The team you sent here was captured by the border patrol and has been put in jail." Abdullah waited, watching Khalif's face closely. There was only a flicker of anger before he answered.

"When will they get out?"

"I don't know," Abdullah admitted, "but I think they had their detonators with them. Haviv thought we shouldn't go and inquire of their situation, as it might draw attention to us. I don't know…"

Khalif cut him off. "That was good thinking. We need to get more men into this country, and I don't think it will be easy. They'll be watching their borders much more closely now."

"Which brings me to another plan," Abdullah said. It was, of course, Haviv's plan, but Abdullah needed the credit in Khalif's eyes. "The woman we sent on the ship said they are testing a new boat called the Sea Flyer. It's an unmanned, remote-controlled vessel that is launched over the side of the ship and used to gain intelligence without putting the Americans in harm's way. Instead of bringing our men across the border, why not bring them up by fishing boat. They could be in place off the coast and then we could use the Americans boat against themselves."

Khalif rewarded him with a smile. "Brilliant plan, Abdullah. Allah has truly inspired you."

"Thank you, Khalif. If you can get more trained men, then we'll be ready."

"The Light of Allah wants the attack to commence in eight days."

"Yes, I know!" Abdullah exclaimed, shaking his head. "We've just begun our work."

"Do you question Allah?" Khalif demanded.

"No, of course not," Abdullah answered, lowering his head. Then he looked to Haviv, not knowing what else to say.

"We shall be ready," Haviv quickly interjected, though Abdullah detected the hesitation in his voice, and he was sure that Khalif did as well.

37

Carlsbad

Jim immediately went home and began packing for his trip to Mexico. Though he was disappointed at first that he wouldn't get to see Elena tonight, he now saw it as an opportunity to go to church, which he hadn't been able to do since he arrived on the West Coast. His life had been a whirlwind, and he hoped God would understand. He put on a clean shirt, went downstairs, and headed for the front door. Before he could make his escape, Abdullah came out of the kitchen, intercepting him. "Where are you going, Jim? Do you have a date?"

"No, I'm just meeting some friends tonight," Jim answered, anxious to stop the conversation before it got started.

"What happened to that pretty girl you met at the airport?"

"She's busy tonight. Besides, I need a little time by myself."

"Is everything okay between the two of you?"

Jim was mystified. He wondered what had happened in the four years since he'd been on the East Coast. He was hesitant to believe it, but it appeared that his father was actually starting to act human.

"Everything's great between Elena and me. She had to go to LA on a business trip. It's all part of her schooling."

"Really? Well, have a good time tonight, and don't get into trouble."

"Um, sure, Dad," Jim said, and then hurried out the door before this very strange conversation could go any further. He headed to a

Christian bookstore in his area, "Loaves and Fishes," and wondered if he could find a church nearby with a relatively young congregation that was on fire for the Lord. If his dad ever found out about his new religious persuasion, he'd go through the roof.

Jim quickly dismissed the envisioned confrontation from his mind, as he knew it would be ugly and probably violent. His dad didn't know a lot about him or his secret military work. Jim knew how Abdullah would respond, so he decided it was better left unsaid.

Once in Vista he spotted the bookstore, pulled up and parked, and then walked in the front door. After browsing for a while, he was approached by a young man, obviously an employee.

"Is there anything I can help you with?"

"I'm looking for an action-packed adventure novel," Jim said.

"That's easy." The tall, slender man smiled. "I'd recommend *Spirit Warrior*. It's outsold all of our books in this store, and I know the author personally. He's a great guy, pretty tough. You'd enjoy it."

"What's it about?"

"It's a science fiction novel set in the Blue Ring Galaxy, with a lot of high-tech, action-packed scenes. It's a fast read, and nearly everyone that buys it loves it. I've been trying to get the author to write a sequel."

"Sounds good. I'll take a copy. Say, you wouldn't know of a good church that has a service tonight, would you? I'm new in the area, and I'd like to check one out."

"I sure do. There's a church called the Builder's Stone, pastored by a former Olympic wrestler, a really cool guy, and he attracts a lot of young people of all races."

"Great. Do you have directions?"

"Sure, no problem. It's here in *The Good Newspaper*. It's even got a map." The clerk reached under the counter and pulled up the monthly paper.

"Hey, that's great! You've been very helpful." Jim smiled and offered his hand. "I'm Jim. What's your name?"

"Dave. Good to meet you, Jim. And if you don't like this church, come back. I know of a few others that are quite good."

Jim paid for his copy of *Spirit Warrior* and left the bookstore with his newspaper. He opened it and found the ad for the church, along with the directions. He had a couple of hours to kill before the service started, so he went to a coffee shop and began reading the book he had just bought. It was every bit as good as the salesperson said, and soon he became engrossed in this fast-paced book filled with action, plot twists, new worlds, and the classic battle between good and evil.

Suddenly his cell phone rang. When he saw the incoming number on the caller ID, he smiled, anticipating Elena's lovely voice. He wasn't disappointed.

"Hello, Jim," she said, her voice warm and as sweet as honey.

"Elena, how's the diamond show going?"

"It's not. I made a mistake and thought it was tonight, but it's really next week. What are you doing?"

"I was going to a special place tonight."

"By yourself? Could you use some company?"

Jim hesitated. He'd never mentioned to Elena his relationship with God, and he wasn't sure how she would respond.

"Jim, are you there?"

He cleared his throat. "Yeah, sure. I'm here."

"Would you like me to go with you? I wouldn't be a bore."

"Sure, of course, Elena."

The tone in her voice changed. "You don't sound too excited. Maybe we should make it another night."

"No, no, I'd love your company," he assured her. "It's just that…well, there's a part of my life I've never told you about."

There was a pause, and when Elena spoke, Jim knew she was wondering what his deep, dark secret might be. "Whatever it is, don't worry, *mon cheri*. I would be happy to go with you—if you want me."

Jim quickly made his decision. If this relationship was going anywhere, he had to tell her about his Christian walk.

"Okay. Do you agree to go any place with me tonight?" he asked, hoping in one sense that she would turn him down, afraid of the consequence, yet hoping even more that she'd accept.

"Of course," she answered without hesitation, "but after that you've got to go anyplace that I choose. *Oui?*"

Relieved, Jim wondered what this compromise would entail. Taking a deep breath, he answered, "Okay, I'll pick you up in thirty minutes."

"That's not much time for a woman to get ready. What should I wear?"

"Something casual."

"Okay. I'll see you in thirty minutes."

⌒

It was the first time in Elena's life that she wasn't in control of a relationship, and she wasn't sure she liked it. She knew she was beautiful and charming, and most of the time she could turn the heart of any man, unless he was mentally unbalanced—and obviously that wasn't the case with Jim.

She shook her head. This relationship was too good to be true. No man had ever treated her with so much love and respect.

Usually the men she was assigned to believed they were God's gift to women and that she should fall at their feet, when in fact they were lower than the vultures that fed off the dead carcasses in the sand. Caring about her assignment was a new experience for Elena, and she couldn't help but wonder how it would ultimately play out for her.

⌒

Jim returned to his car and drove to the hotel to pick up Elena. Usually he raced down the I-5 freeway, but this time he traveled in the slow lane, deep in thought. This was the first time he wasn't excited about being with her, and he wondered if it would be the last time they went out together.

He parked the car, went up to her room, and knocked. When she opened the door, Jim walked in, scarcely noticing how absolutely beautiful she looked. All he could think of was how she might react when he took her to church.

⌒

The last time Elena had put on a tight red sweater with a plunging neckline the man she was with couldn't pull his eyes from her shapely figure.

"What's the matter?" she asked, reaching out to lay a hand on his arm. "Is everything alright? Should I change?"

"No, no. You look great," he answered, standing at the window and gazing out at the San Diego harbor. "Everything's fine. We've got to get going, or we'll be late."

"Oh, Jim," she said, inserting a playful tone into her voice, "why do we have to rush? You Americans are always moving too fast. You have to learn to slow down and enjoy life."

"If I slow down tonight, we both could be in trouble."

Elena laughed. "Oh, don't worry, I won't bite you." She removed her hand from his arm and stood behind him, then reached out and wrapped her arms around his chest.

"We'd better go now," he said, his voice husky as he turned around in her arms. "I really want to take you to this place."

Sensing his frustration, Elena's temper ignited and she snatched her purse and flounced out the door, leaving Jim standing in the room. She went to the elevator and pushed the button. When the door opened, she got in before Jim could reach her, but as the doors began to close, he stuck his hand inside and they opened again.

"What's wrong, Elena?"

"You! That's what's wrong!"

"What do you mean?" The look of concern on his face was genuine, but she was still annoyed that he had resisted her advances.

"I called you up because I wanted to be with you," she said, pouting as the elevator descended, "and you treat me as if I have some strange disease! You didn't kiss me, hug me, or even look at me."

His face softened. "Look, Elena, I'm sorry. I've had a hard day, and there's a lot on my mind."

"You don't have to take it out on me! What happened to the Jim I met, the one who is warm and kind and considerate?"

A war of emotions wrestled on his face, and then he said, "I'm not who you think I am."

"Really? And just who are you?" she demanded.

"This place I'm taking you tonight must remain a secret between you and me. My father must never know."

She felt her annoyance dissipating, replaced by genuine curiosity. "This means a lot to you?"

"More than you know. I don't want to tell you about it just yet. I want you to experience it first, and then we'll talk about it."

Now she was intrigued. "Sounds mysterious," she said, allowing the first hint of a smile to return to her face. "I can't wait."

The closer they got to the church, the more nervous Jim became. He was worried the service would be unusual and Elena might not like it. Maybe this wasn't such a good idea. He'd never been here before and didn't know what to expect. He followed the directions from the newspaper until they pulled up in front of a warehouse.

"What is this place?" she asked, looking at the building and then back to him.

"You'll find out soon enough," he assured her.

They got out of their car and walked inside, where they were warmly greeted at the door by an older couple and then took their seats. A few minutes later a couple of young people with guitars and a drummer took the stage and began playing some music. The beat was up-tempo and lively.

"Is this some sort of a dance party?"

"Not really," Jim said, "but the music is pretty good."

The other people in the room began singing, lifting their arms and worshipping God. Soon a short, powerfully built man with mangled ears walked to the podium. The music ended, and the man began to preach about a Kingdom that wasn't under the law. He spoke of a Kingdom that operated on grace and mercy, not rules. The sermon lasted about thirty minutes, and after a few more songs, they were dismissed.

Elena was silent until they got into the car. "Where is this kingdom that is above the law?"

"It's in my heart," Jim answered, praying silently that she would understand.

"Really. What are you talking about, Jim? Does this mean you're a Christian?"

"Yes, but don't tell anyone, especially my dad."

"Why? Why keep this a secret?"

"Because I was once a Muslim, but I've changed."

Elena raised her eyebrows. "Why did you become a Christian?"

"It's a better way," Jim answered. "The right way." He paused and then asked, "Are you religious?"

Elena shrugged. "I don't know. Until I came to America, I thought I was Muslim."

Now it was Jim's turn to raise his eyebrows in surprise.

"Recently I heard a black man speak on the *telly* about this Christian way of love…and now tonight. That's all I know about it."

"You said you thought you were a Muslim. Elena, are you or aren't you?"

She waited a moment before answering. "Truthfully, I've been one for many years, but since coming to San Diego, I've been questioning why some of our people are trying to destroy this country."

"You mean the militant terrorists?" Jim asked, suddenly quite interested in what she had to say about the matter.

"Yes."

"No country is perfect. America has its challenges, but at least throughout the world we try to help other nations."

"Some people might not agree with you."

"What about you? Do you think you would ever consider being a Christian?" he asked, hoping she would respond favorably.

"I don't know. It's something I must think about before I can answer that."

"That's fair enough. So, now that you've gone to church with me, where do you want me to take you?"

"To my room," Elena said, her eyes shining. "We can have dinner, and you can spend the night with me."

Jim was stunned, not having expected to deal with two major life issues on the same night. He wondered how to answer without offending her.

"What's the matter, Jim?" she asked, the joy fading from her eyes.

"I just can't do that," he said.

"What?" Anger flooded her features and she blew up. "You promised me that if I went with you, then you would go wherever I wanted! I remember the holy man saying, 'A man is only as good as his word.'"

Jim was caught. "He's right," he admitted, "and so are you, but..." He paused, and then answered with a sigh. "Okay, I'll spend the night with you, but we aren't going to have sex."

Elena's brows drew together in a frown. "What's wrong with you, Jim? Don't you want me?"

"Of course I want you. But... I can't have sex with you."

"You can't... or you won't?"

He waited a moment before answering. "Both."

"You don't find me attractive enough?"

"Elena, you know that's not it. You're a knockout, and every part of me wants to be with you in a very intimate way, but... I'm saving myself."

"Don't tell me you're a virgin!"

"Not hardly. I've had sex before."

"With whom? Another man? Is that it?"

"No, of course not. Elena, I—"

"Jim, I know I'm an attractive woman, but you've been refusing my advances. Tell me why."

"Because the next time I have sex, it's going to be on my wedding night."

Elena's eyes opened wide, as Jim waited. Would this be the end of their relationship? If so, he knew he'd done the right thing, as hard as it was.

"All right," she said at last. "I still want you to have dinner with me and stay with me tonight. I just want you to hold me."

Jim hesitated. He knew it wouldn't be easy, but he saw no other way to keep his word to Elena—and his allegiance to God. "I'll hold you in my arms. I'll even sleep with you, but on the opposite side of the bed."

She smiled sweetly, and Jim wondered if she had accepted his terms or was planning to try to sabotage them. It looked like he was going to have to be strong tonight.

El Cajon coffee shop, El Cajon, CA

Khalif pulled up in his car and went into the coffee shop. Immediately Abdullah arose as Khalif approached.

"*Salaam alaikum.*"

"*Alaikum salaam,*" Khalif replied, as they took their seats. "Abdullah, may Allah be highly praised! Our moment has arrived. The Light of Allah has ordered the attack when the moon is full."

"Will the bomb be ready?"

"You let me worry about that," Khalif cautioned. "Just have your men in position. Will your son be ready?"

"Elena is working on that right now. He'll be ready. The others have arrived. Will the fishing boat be ready?"

"Yes," Khalif assured him, pleased that things were nearly in place. "All will be ready. The Great Satan will finally be brought to his knees, and Israel will be defenseless."

"It will be a good day for *jihad*," Abdullah agreed.

"Indeed. Now it's time for you to act. This will be our last meeting, but I wanted you to know that the Light of Allah is counting on you. When you succeed he told me to tell you that he wants you by his side. He wants your fire and he wants to give you the name *Avenger.*"

"He won't be disappointed."

"I know," Khalif said sincerely.

Oval Office

The President met in the Oval Office with his Director of National Intelligence before the specially convened Congressional meeting in the West Wing of the White House. He knew the strain of the past weeks showed on his face, but he was determined to stand strong.

"William, I don't have much time. Have we found out any more about the Light of Allah?"

"Not yet, Sir. But one team in Northern Sudan is watching a suspicious oasis, and the other team is searching the desert. There's a lot of ground to cover. The eight days will expire next week, and we haven't heard anything."

"Perhaps it was a hoax," the President suggested, though he doubted that was the case.

"I don't think so. There have been terrorist attacks in England and Spain this week. I'm sure you've seen the al-Qaeda world map and how they've carved up countries. Their empire stretches from Spain to Iran."

"It'll never happen. They won't be able to conquer all those countries."

"I don't know," Stevens said.

"If the Bible is right, this could be how the one-world empire comes into existence before the second coming of Christ. This Militant Islamic religion could be the devil's tool for world domination."

William looked surprised. "Do you really believe that, Mr. President?"

"One country has never been able to dominate the world. It makes sense that only a religion could spread to all countries and unite them."

"Maybe," Stevens said, his skepticism obvious.

"Continue your investigation on the Light of Allah," the President instructed, knowing their time was growing short. "I want to find out all you can about him. I only hope those nuclear missiles aren't in his hands!"

40

Tom Cat Bar in El Cajon, California

"Hey, Booker, how's the Navy been treating you?" Jamal asked from across the room, as he watched the weary sailor walk through the front door of the Tom Cat and make his way across the bar.

"We've been working fourteen-hour days, and my wife is mad as can be. That's why I don't want to go home. All she does is complain. I get yelled at on the job, and when I go home it's the same. I have no place for myself. I can't win," Booker answered and then reached for his wallet. "Here's the twenty dollars I owe you."

"Thanks. Hey, have a beer. This one's on me. Let's play a game of pool."

"Sure," Booker agreed. "That'd be great."

Jamal kept buying the beer, and around midnight he slipped something into Booker's glass. A few minutes later Booker passed out on the barstool, and Jamal helped him out of the bar, where two men grabbed the passed-out sailor and carried him to Jamal's car. They searched and found Booker's keys and ID in his pocket.

"Have you got the CAC card?" Jamal asked.

"We have it. What's next?"

"Put him in the trunk of my car, and let's get going."

〜

One of the men was dressed in a naval uniform, complete with Booker's nameplate. He bore a similar resemblance to Booker and, with makeup, could easily pass for him, so long as he didn't run into anyone Booker knew, which was his main concern. The look-alike jumped into the front seat and started Booker's car, and then drove to the naval base. The tired gate guard waved him through, showing no signs of suspicion. The man drove to the pier where the USS Sheboygan was berthed, did a quick once-over of the area, and then let the others out of the trunk, glad that he'd had the good fortune to look most like their victim so he could drive instead of being crammed into the trunk with the others.

The three men changed into contractor's coveralls and went through the automatic security gate at the pier, each swiping Booker's CAC card and then handing it back through the fence so the next man could swipe it. Using false credentials and carrying large toolboxes, they boarded the ship, went down to the missile launch room in the welldeck, and chained their locked toolboxes to the bulkhead. The heavy metal boxes had the words "San Diego Shipyard" stenciled on them. Then the men left the ship and drove off base. They pulled the sleeping Booker out of Jamal's trunk and put him in the front seat of Jamal's car, then gave him a sniff of ammonia and disappeared.

〜

"Hey, Booker, wake up," Jamal said, shaking him from his heavy sleep. "You okay, man?"

Booker groaned, "What happened? How did I get here?"

"We were going to go to another bar, but you passed out. Are you okay?"

"Yeah, sure, other than a killer headache. What time is it?"

"Two A.M."

Booker groaned again. "My wife's going to kill me. What happened?"

"One minute I was talking to you, and the next minute you fell asleep."

"Man, I don't remember a thing," Booker said, reaching for the door handle.

"Don't sweat it. We had a few drinks and talked to some women, and then I helped you out here to get some fresh air. Nothing to worry about, my friend."

Booker got out of Jamal's car. "Really? I can't remember anything."

"Like I said, it's cool. Hey, I have to go now, but I'll see you next week."

⌣

Groggily Booker stumbled over to his own car, started it, and drove home. His wife had already gone to bed, but when he quietly slipped into the house and slid between the sheets, she awakened.

"You were drinking again!" she shouted. "I'm home all day, cleaning and taking care of the babies, and you go out drinking! I need a break too, you know. I don't think you even love me anymore. If it wasn't for my mother, I couldn't make it."

Booker knew better than to say anything. His head hurt even more now that his wife was yelling at him. Then the babies started crying, and his mother-in-law came into the bedroom and began berating him in Spanish. All Booker could do was take a blanket and head for the car. His wife's angry words chased after him.

"Why don't you just go back to the ship? You're not even man enough to take care of your wife!"

Booker felt his temper rising as he climbed into the backseat of his car and stretched out. Within minutes he was fast asleep, as the car across the street slowly drove away with its lights off.

41

Mexican coastline, past Rosarita Beach

The winding road and sheer drop of the rock cliffs, combined with the natural beauty of the ocean pummeling the shore below, was breathtaking, as Jim and Elena headed toward Rosarito Beach.

"Oh, Jim, this reminds me of the drive along the beaches in Southern France. It feels so good to be away from the city," Elena said, smiling brightly. She had chosen a powder blue, loose-fitting gym outfit, which accented her blonde hair and blue eyes.

"We have a reservation for Rosarita Beach Resort Hotel and Spa, but the weather is so nice I think we should go further down the coast. I'm sure they'll have some good rooms in Ensenada."

Elena's antenna went up. She remembered hearing Khalif talking about an operation area based in Ensenada, but she couldn't remember what it involved. Then again, Abdullah would know about her being on this trip, so she decided not to worry. Besides, how could Jim possibly know about their Ensenada operation?

Two hours later they pulled into Puerto Nuevo where a sign advertised lobster dinners.

"Are you hungry, Elena? I think we still have about a hundred kilometers to go before we reach Ensenada."

"*Oui*, Jim, I'm getting very hungry."

He pulled the old Porsche over, steering clear of the potholes, and then drove up to a small beach hotel at the edge of town.

Captivated by the quaintness and closeness to the water, Elena suggested, "We could stay here."

"We could eat here, but this isn't the place I had in mind for you. I want only the best for you. We've got a couple of days, and I really want to relax."

"*Oui, monsieur*, only the best," Elena repeated, smiling at his consideration.

They walked into the restaurant and were greeted by an exquisite culinary aroma that enticed their senses. Jim grabbed a menu and quickly read the twenty-five ways lobsters could be served.

"This is going to be good," he said.

"A table for two, Senor?" the waiter asked.

"Absolutely," Jim replied with hearty approval.

"Would you care for a Margarita?"

Jim hadn't had a chance to unwind, and they were close to the hotel he had already picked out, so he nodded his assent.

Elena was thirsty and quickly drank her Margarita. "Wow! They make their drinks a little strong down here," she commented, and then smiled coyly. "Are you trying to get me a little tipsy to take advantage of me?"

"The thought never crossed my mind," Jim said with a smile.

The broiled lobsters arrived, and they enjoyed the fine Mexican cuisine, complete with beans, tortillas, and rice. After a cup of strong Mexican coffee they headed back down the highway and finally arrived at Ensenada. Jim picked out a beautiful beachfront hotel and immediately booked a room. He carried their two small bags inside and opened the curtain. The hotel was built on some pilings, and the rolling of the waves washed their room with peace and tranquility.

"This is so relaxing," Elena said, stretching provocatively on the bed and watching Jim's reaction out of the corner of her eye.

"I could fall asleep. Can you rub my feet again?" she purred invitingly, rubbing her foot against his thigh.

"Sure, Elena, but then I want to get a workout. I checked and there's a gym in town."

"What? You're going to leave me? I thought we came on this trip to get closer!"

"We did, but I've got to stay in shape for the Navy," Jim reminded her, "and you've got to study."

"The Navy! What about me?"

"Just relax," he said, sitting on the edge of the bed and lifting her feet for a massage.

Elena closed her eyes and pretended to drift off to sleep, but when he gently placed her feet on the bed and quietly slipped out of the room, she opened her eyes and glared at the closed door, wondering where he was going.

↪

Jim went to his car and unlocked the glove compartment, and then he looked at the map and began to drive inland. He drove off the blacktop and immediately regretted not renting a jeep; the terrain was tough on his old sports car. With a film of dust blanketing his ride, he finally arrived near the site's location. He parked behind some shade trees, pulled out the satellite pictures and some binoculars, and began to check the place out. Even with the binoculars he couldn't see anything unusual, so he slowly made his way along the dirt road toward the farm. Carefully he scanned the area and noticed a chain-link fence around the property. Keeping out of sight, he explored a little more until he spotted a lone guard, lazily sitting near a tractor with his automatic weapon resting against the big rear tire. Jim thought he looked too relaxed and wondered if this was the right place. A young crop was growing in rows, as if this were a regular farm.

He crept closer and found another shade tree. Watching and waiting in the shadows, he drew a quick sketch of the area surrounding the farm. After an hour he walked back to his car and drove to the hotel.

"How was your workout?" Elena asked, a smug look on her face. "It seems you've been gone for hours."

"Oh, it was great," he said, regretting the subterfuge. "They had all the right equipment. I must have lost track of time. Would you like to go for a walk on the beach before dinner?"

"Sounds wonderful." She glanced down at Jim's shoes and frowned. "Where was this gym? Out in some field?"

"Oh, that," he said, forcing a smile. "The parking lot was pretty dusty." He hoped she believed him, but it was hard to tell from her expression. "Come on," he said, trying to lighten the tone, "let's go for that walk before it gets any later."

A couple of tourists rode horses on the beach as the sun was making its daily descent to the ocean's surface. Jim and Elena walked hand-in-hand, keeping conversation to a minimum until they got back to the hotel in time for dinner. While they ate, a band began playing in another part of the hotel, and the music sounded modern and upbeat.

"Jim, we never danced the other night. How about tonight?"

"Do you like to dance?"

"*Oui*, of course, Jim. Do you?" she questioned with one eyebrow raised.

"Sure, but I'm not that good."

"*Bon*, I'll teach you—after dinner," she said, grinning, her eyes sparkling with confidence and expectation.

The meal was excellent, but neither ate much. They spent most of their time gazing at each other from across the table.

"Anything else?" the waiter asked.

"Just the check," Jim replied, and the man hurried off. When he returned, Jim signed the bill, adding his room number.

"Come on, Jim," Elena said, anxious to get him out on the dance floor. "Let's see what you've got."

Though Jim danced, he devoted most of his energy to watching Elena, as she closed her eyes and moved freely to the flowing rhythm of the lively music. Jim was proud to be her man. Her picturesque beauty ignited the growing feelings he had. When the music slowed, he quickly drew her into his arms. She eagerly embraced him, laying her head against his shoulder, as he enveloped her. With bodies pressed tightly together, the combustion of love started slowly, but blazed when Jim reached down and kissed her on the neck. Elena opened her eyes and smiled, and then passionately pulled his head to her and kissed him on the lips. He pulled her tighter to him, but not so hard that he would hurt her. The music sped up, but they had no more desire to dance and instead walked back to their room. Elena held Jim's arm closely to her body, and once they got into the room they kissed again, this time with abandon. Jim could feel his body temperature rising and quickly pulled away, but just as suddenly he pulled her back again. Then he gazed down at her with tender love in his eyes.

"I know you don't understand me, but I just can't do this," he said, wishing with all his heart that he didn't have to say it. "I've only known you for two weeks, but I think of you all the time. A few years ago I got sexual with a girl back at the academy, and it wrecked our relationship. Let's just sleep as friends—you on your side and me on the other."

Elena's lower lip came out in a pout. "Then why didn't we get separate rooms?"

"Because I want to be with you, but not in a sexual way. Okay?"

"*Oui*, but you are a crazy American."

Jim put on his pajamas while Elena was changing in the bathroom, and then slipped into the bed. A couple of minutes later she came, dressed in a revealing red teddy.

"You are very beautiful, but I'm still going to keep my vow. I hope you understand."

"I don't understand, and this has never happened to me before. But if nothing else, hold me, Jim, while I sleep."

Jim knew he couldn't stay with her in Mexico for two days and nights without something happening, so he decided to return to San Diego the next day. The secret farm had been observed, but nothing seemed to be happening. There was no valid excuse for staying any longer.

42

San Diego Naval Base, Pier 6

A week later Jim was aboard the USS Sheboygan, as it made preps to get underway to test the new Tomahawk launch system, retest the lifeboat davit, and deploy Sea Flyer. The crew had returned to the base early that morning, as liberty expired for all hands at 0600. Contractors got on the ship before 0700, and the brow was lifted thirty minutes later, as the 'Sea and Anchor' detail was set. With a blast from their whistles, harbor tugs pulled up, and the crew used lines to tie them to their ship.

The pilot arrived a little later, and the ship pulled away from the pier. Once in the harbor the tug let the ship's lines go, and the crew pulled them back aboard. Under her own power, the USS Sheboygan approached the Coronado Bridge. Slowing down, one of the tugs pulled up mid-ships, and the pilot climbed down the Jacob's ladder until he reached a raised platform on the bow of the orange and green tractor tug. Two deckhands then helped the pilot onto the boat.

Captain Davey oversaw all this from the far edge of the bridge-wing, fifty feet above the waterline. He leaned over as the tugboat pulled away from the warship and called "All ahead one-third" to the OOD, who repeated the command to the helmsman.

Doing five knots as it crossed under the Coronado Bridge, the Sheboygan passed as two F-18 Super Hornets rumbled down the tarmac at North Island Naval Air Station and quickly shot up into the early morning sunrise.

Jim looked toward Elena's hotel near San Diego airport, wishing he didn't have to get underway. He was in the Navy, and ships and their crews were meant to be at sea. As the ship continued to move ahead, Jim fondly remembered the time he and Elena spent together in Mexico—the food, walking on the beach, late-night dancing, and, most importantly, holding each other.

"Jim, go and check on Sea Flyer," the captain ordered, jarring him back to reality. "We're going to launch her first, and I want to make sure all is ready."

"Yes, Sir," Jim replied, quickly leaving his spot on the bridge to follow the CO's command. He found the bosun on the forecastle, getting all the lines stowed, so Jim went to see if the techs in the connex box were ready to launch the Navy's newest science project.

"The captain wants to deploy this once we clear the sea buoys. Will you be ready?"

"Sure, Lieutenant," the lead techie responded. "We'll probably have to make a few changes to the software in our receiver. It's been acting up a little."

"Hurry up then, because we've got a full day with a bunch of other systems to test. He wants you to use the sixty-ton crane to put Sea Flyer into the water. Then you can have the whole day to play with it."

"We'll be ready in about thirty minutes."

Jim nodded. "That'll work. It'll take us about that long to get clear of the shipping lanes. The old man is pretty punctual, though, so you'd better be ready."

"Will do, Lieutenant. Thanks." The lead technician turned back to his radio receiver and computer keyboard and began punching in frequencies, which were changed every day for security purposes.

Jim went to check out the lifeboat davit. Both RHIB boats were nestled in the davit. The upper RHIB was seven meters in length and looked fast. The eleven-meter RHIB had a house on it, and it was bigger and looked slower.

The port engineer was looking at the controls with Liz. "The last time they tested this at sea, the automatic features malfunctioned."

"I realize that," Liz said, "but we've reprogrammed the computer, and we should be in good shape."

Jim smiled, wondering how this little *tête-à-tête* would play out.

"I'm not doubting you," Jake insisted, "but I think we should be handling this in manual mode."

"Trust me," Liz countered. "I know what I'm doing. The new software will take care of all the variables."

Jake looked unconvinced. "I don't know. Let's launch it in manual and see if everything works, and then we can try automatic." Jake looked at Jim in an obvious bid for support. "Don't you agree?"

"If the port engineer says we ought to try it in manual, then we probably should. He ought to know," Jim said, and then turned and walked to the ladders leading to the bridge, not wanting to get dragged any further into their conversation. As he walked away he overheard a final statement from each of them.

"The captain isn't too fond of this new davit," Jake said. "If you can at least prove it in manual, he'll feel a lot better. This is the ready lifeboat, Liz."

"That's fine," she conceded. "If you want to try it in manual first, I have no problem with that."

Jim smiled and kept walking. There were too many other matters to consider that took precedence over a minor power play between Jake and Liz.

As the ship moved closer to Point Loma Submarine Base, they passed the Navy's mammal program. Caged in ocean pens the dolphins came to the surface to be fed. Some of them had put in a night of swimming with their handlers, patrolling the harbor underwater. They quickly swallowed their fish in large gulps, smiling at the humans and thanking them with squeals of delight. The dolphins, along with hidden cameras and high-speed Navy patrol craft, kept the San Diego Harbor secure from seafaring intruders. San Diego Naval Base and the Coronado Bridge had been prime targets during the attack on the World Trade Center buildings, but grounding of the commercial jets throughout the United States had successfully stopped any further terrorist actions on September 11.

⌇

With the sea air blowing in his face, Davey was in his element. His entire military career he had wanted to captain a ship. He remembered looking around the room the day he was commissioned, at the hundred or so faces in the room, all no doubt wondering who would screen for command. To date he had heard of only one other classmate who had been given command at sea. It was the best job in the Navy, and he knew it. It was an awesome responsibility and very demanding, but it filled a man's heart like nothing else.

As Davey stood there, considering his good fortune in having received his command, he heard someone approaching. Turning, he came face to face with his First Lieutenant.

"There's nothing quite like the open ocean, is there?" he asked. When Jim nodded his agreement, the captain got down to business.

"Once we get twenty miles out, I want to launch Sea Flyer," he said. "Let them play with it while we do the missile shoot."

"What about retesting the lifeboat davit?"

"Don't remind me. That's my biggest headache. I've never seen anything with so many problems." After the missile shoot, we'll deploy a RHIB."

"Yes, Sir," Jim responded before leaving the bridge.

"Ahead two-thirds," the captain called out to the lee helmsman, steering clear of the kelp beds. A company located on the waterfront next to the San Diego Shipyard harvested the leafy seaweed and made sweetener from it.

With a puff of smoke the engines responded, and the Sheboygan surged into open water.

"Captain, permission to launch the Sea Flyer?" Bosun asked over his side phone.

"Permission granted. Let the techs know we won't be picking their boat up any time soon."

"Aye, aye, Captain."

⤶

Jim walked down to the tech's connex box, which was chained to the boat deck, and opened the door. The box had electrical power and was kept very cool because of the computer. They had a brand new air conditioner installed in it to keep the heat from building up in the small steel enclosed space.

"The captain says you can launch your boat," he announced, "but we won't be able to recover it till later in the day."

"We heard," the lead tech said. "We'll be operating the boat all day. We've got plenty of tests to do. When do you think your crane will be ready to launch?"

"We're running the operating chits right now, and as soon as the bosun is done up forward he'll come back and take care of you. What speed do you need for launching?"

"About five knots."

"Roger that. I'll tell the Captain. I'll be back in about ten minutes."

"Thanks, Lieutenant."

Jim spoke to the CO over his side phone and then walked over to the lifeboat davit and examined it. Liz was looking at the display console and checking its programming with her laptop. "You ready to try this out, Liz?"

"Just making some last-minute adjustments. When do you think we can try a launch?"

"In about an hour."

"Great. We'll be ready. Are you going to take the boat out for a run?"

"Not till we see the davit operate flawlessly. You know what happened the last time."

"Trust me, Jim. We know what the problem was, and we've corrected it. We downloaded a whole new program with software changes from the factory, and we'll try it in manual before we operate in automatic."

"Good," Jim answered. "The captain's going to want to see it run a few times before he puts anybody in it."

Leaving Liz to complete her task, Jim walked away, as the Sheboygan steamed further out to sea. A hazy mist rolled in, obstructing their view of the shoreline. The ship began a gentle rolling, as they entered a fogbank, limiting visibility to 500 yards. At the edge of the fogbank, Jim saw a spout of water from a migrating whale. He looked for others but couldn't see any more water sprays.

"Lieutenant, we're finished stowing lines," Bosun Browder announced, walking up to him. "Is A-gang ready to run the crane?"

Before Jim answered he wondered why he had to keep an eye on the bosun. He noticed that Boats was friendly with the davit tech rep and wondered if there was a connection between them that wasn't professional. Finally he said, "I'll call the CHENG. Do you have some people standing by?"

"Yes, Sir. We're ready to launch Sea Flyer. This model looks bigger than the last one we carried."

"I think they modified it so they could carry more cameras. Here comes the senior chief from A-gang. Senior, are you ready to run the crane?"

"Yes, Sir. We've got the operator coming up now."

The first class from A-gang climbed up the steel ladder on the side of the crane and went into the cab. A loud whine could be heard, as he turned on the electric hoist motors. The bosun got his people on station, tending the lines so the unmanned boat could be kept away from the side of the ship as it launched.

"Lieutenant, are the techs ready?" Boats asked.

"I don't know. Let's check."

The two of them walked to the connex box and opened the door. The techs had their systems up and running.

"We're ready to raise the boat and put it in the water," the bosun announced.

"Wait one, Bosun," the lead techie responded. "We're not getting a backup signal from the vessel. We need to make an adjustment."

"How long will that take?"

"We need about five minutes, and we should have it."

"Roger that," the bosun said, as they left the connex box. "It never fails, Lieutenant. Every time we get ready to test some of this new equipment, something happens. I just hope the missile shoot is okay. We've got a lot of steel to move on the flight deck to send one of those birds to San Clemente Island. With a little bit of rocking and rolling, it might bind up."

"That's why the port engineer is onboard," Jim said. "He can analyze the problem and have somebody standing by to fix it when we get to port."

Sam, the tech from Dynamic Systems Incorporated, came up to them. "We're ready to put Sea Flyer in the water," he said.

"Great," Jim replied, as they walked over to the crane. "Let's do it."

A first class boatswain mate gave the crane operator signals, as two sailors tended the guide ropes. The Sea Flyer went up into the air and was slowly rotated until it was hanging over the side of the ship. Then the tech remotely started the engine. The first class, with his right thumb pointing down, signaled the crane operator to pay out the hoist and lower the boat into the water. Slightly banging the side of the ship, the Sea Flyer was lowered into the water. With no one onboard, the techs automatically released the lifting hooks. Giving the boat a hard right rudder, it quickly moved away from the ship.

"Lieutenant, do you see how easy it is to launch this boat? I don't know why we've got that multi-million dollar davit on the port side of the ship just to launch a ready lifeboat," the bosun said in disgust.

"I hear you, Boats; sometimes money, politics, and technology get mixed up in some of these decisions, but we at the deck plates have to make their decisions look good no matter what it takes. At least we have the techs onboard. Last time I heard, the French company who built the davit refused to go to sea unless we paid them another two hundred thousand dollars to buy spare parts."

"That's true. I wish we had the simple old-fashioned davit. It always worked. I don't know why the Navy went to such a sophisticated piece of junk. It's going to be a nightmare to maintain."

"Just talk to the port engineer about repairs. He'll take care of it."

"Jake will do the best he can, but sometimes even he can't get any support. Well, there goes the Sea Flyer. I hope they can keep track of it this time."

The unmanned reconnaissance boat headed away from Sheboygan on a course that would take it beyond the horizon. With the camera up and running, Sea Flyer could view 360 degrees, with the capability of zooming in on anything their special Ziess lenses picked up. The feed to the ship was instantaneous. Sea Flyer disappeared into the fogbank, and the video from the boat showed two shades of gray, one for the water and the other for the fog.

"Let's start testing the lifeboat davit. Stow those lines and go to the port side of the ship," the bosun barked to his sailors.

The port engineer was talking to Liz, while viewing the open controller. They were looking at the automatic sequencing of the davit, as Jim walked up to them.

"Are you ready, ma'am?" Jim asked.

"As soon as you are. We can start the op test to the waterline," she answered.

"Let me tell the captain. He might want to come down and witness this himself," Jim replied, as he got on his side phone and called Captain Davey. "Hold fast," he said, after completing his call. "The captain will be right down. He wants to personally see this operation."

About fifteen deck sailors gathered around the davit. None of them wanted to ride the boat down to the waterline, and no one could blame them, especially after the first test.

Captain Davey joined them, and they saluted. "Jake, are we ready to run this?"

"Yes, Sir. Let's give it a try."

"Good. Jim, Boats, get your people ready, but I want to see this put to the waterline and brought back up before we man it."

"Yes, Sir," Jim said.

"All right then," the captain ordered, "lower the boat and let's see what happens."

The eleven-meter RHIB boat was lowered over the side. Everyone watched and waited to see if the winch would suddenly let loose, but nothing happened. It barely touched the splashing waves, with the ship making five knots. Liz operated the controls and brought the boat back up without any repeat of the problems on the first sea trial.

"That went pretty good," Boats said. "Try it again."

Before noon they had lowered the boat four more times, and the davit worked flawlessly each time.

"Lunch for the crew," the OOD said over the 1 MC.

"Liz, shut it down for a while," Jake said. "Our time for the missile shoot is at 1300, so we'll have to wait till 1600 before we launch the boat with people in it."

"That's fine. I'll check out the software one more time to see that we're ready."

The sailors headed up to the mess decks to enjoy the fine Navy chow. After the mess line was secured, they all reported back on station and watched as Jim opened the flight deck panels, exposing the Tomahawk missile launcher. This was a first for the amphib Navy. No amphibious ship had ever been equipped with Tomahawks, but as the number of naval ships continued to decrease, missile capabilities were increasing on these platforms. The destroyers and cruisers could only fire missiles, but a ship that was able to deliver ordnance on target and launch an amphibious attack force would prove to be even more effective in theater.

~

Captain Davey made his way down the ramp into the well deck, as the missile control system was powered up. He walked into the newly installed launch booth and noticed some of the shipyard toolboxes locked to one of the I-beams.

"I see the yardbirds left some of their tools behind," the captain said to Jim. "I hope they won't need them. What's our range?"

Jim pointed to the grid on the radar screen. "We're about forty miles off. That's where our missile is supposed to hit."

"How are we going to know if we hit the target?"

"Techs are on shore and will evaluate, but there's also telemetry gear on the missile and the target."

The Tactical Action Officer inserted his key into the launch enable panel. "Missile ready, Captain."

"Fire when ready."

"Range fouled," the voice from range control interjected.

The TAO repeated, "Captain, range fouled."

"What's the problem?" the captain asked.

"Some buffalo have moved onto the missile range," TAO explained. "They're herding them off in ATV's."

"What? I thought they built a fence around the range so they wouldn't wander in."

"They did," TAO answered. "But the buffalo knocked it down."

"Call the range and see how much time they need to clear the buffalo."

TAO keyed the mic. "Range control, this is Sheboygan. Are the buffalo still roaming?"

"We've almost got them off; it won't be but a few minutes now. They're in the upper quadrant, so they shouldn't be a problem, but just in case we're clearing them. Stand by, Sheboygan."

"Standing by," TAO replied.

"They've really put a lot of new technology on this ship," the bosun said, pride evident in his voice. "Once we're up and running, we're going to be a tough ship."

"We still have to op-test everything to see if it all works," Captain Davey added.

"Sheboygan, this is the range," came the announcement. "We're all clear over here. Commence testing."

TAO repeated, "Commence testing."

The captain pushed the launch button sequence, and within thirty seconds a fiery dart shot out from the Tomahawk tube. The crew kept quiet and watched the ship's black and white monitor. It was fuzzy and hard to see and every few seconds it went blank momentarily, as the satellite feed was disturbed. Finally the missile exploded on target, and a cheer broke out from the crew.

"Well done, Sheboygan. Good shot," the range master said over the radio. "You were off by about two hundred yards to the north. Recommend making an adjustment to your navigation circuit by one quarter turn clockwise, and test fire again," range control relayed from the shore techs.

"Roger that, range," replied TAO.

The fire control man made the corrections and then CIC locked in the new coordinates. "Ready, Sir," TAO said.

"Range, this is Sheboygan. We're ready for the next firing. Are the buffalo off the range?"

"All clear, Sheboygan. Fire when ready."

"Go ahead, Jim. Push the button," Captain Davey ordered.

With a smile on his face, Jim pushed the sequencing button, and thirty seconds later another fiery missile headed skyward, while the crew watched the monitor and saw the missile land on target.

"Great shot, Sheboygan," the range master said over the radio. "Test completed."

"Roger that, range," TAO said.

"What about the other missiles, Captain?" Jim asked.

"We'll probably drop them back off at Seal Beach. They were placed aboard in case we had problems with one of the launchers. Boats, let's lower the lifeboat."

"Roger that, Captain," Boats said, as he headed up to the boat deck.

43

Boat deck, USS Sheboygan

"Liz, we're ready to try a manned launch of the lifeboat," the bosun announced. "Instead of sending the normal boat team, the gunnery sergeant and I will take the boat out." Then he turned to his senior chief. "Wait till we get in before you lower it."

Looking puzzled, Liz said, "I thought the captain wanted to see the boat launch."

"No, he's on the bridge," Boats explained.

Boats and Deek got into the boat, and under Liz's guidance and Jim's watchful eye, the ship's crew used the manual control to lower the RHIB to the waterline. Once it crested the waves the bosun released the hooks while Deek started the engine. Boats immediately took the helm and pushed the engine throttle forward, steering the boat away from the ship. The RHIB quickly headed to the horizon

Suddenly a cheer went up from the other side of the boat deck from the techies looking for their unmanned boat. Sea Flyer appeared near the ship, as the techs finally got control of their unmanned boat and steered it back to the ship.

"Lieutenant, boy, are we lucky," the lead tech rep said. "We lost control of the Sea Flyer but somehow got it back. I don't know what happened out there, but we'd better bring it aboard."

"Sure thing," Jim replied. "As soon as it comes alongside, we'll pick it up with the crane."

The Sea Flyer made some turns and headed back. It was quickly alongside the Sheboygan, and one of the sailors used a Jacob's ladder to climb over the side and drop into the boat, where he hooked up the lifting pad-eyes to the crane's hook. Once that was accomplished the boat was lifted out of the water, and the sailors guided it into its boat skid.

"Thanks, Lieutenant. We'll take it from here," the technician said.

With that the Sheboygan's crew shifted back to the port side of the boat deck and watched, as the bosun and gunny sergeant rode the waves in the RHIB and Jim headed to the bridge to report to the captain.

As the crew was absorbed in watching the bosun riding the waves in the RHIB, Sea Flyer's false bulkhead was quietly dismantled, and the terrorists grabbed their loaded weapons. Abdullah was the first to slip out of the boat and move to the outboard side of the craft, as his men, one by one, stealthily disembarked. With weapons drawn they boldly walked across the boat deck.

"Nobody move!" Abdullah shouted.

Stunned, the crew spun around. Directly in front of them stood ten armed terrorists. Dressed in black tactical assault gear, they pointed their guns at them. Abdullah, Liz, and four others quickly climbed the outside ladders to the bridge deck. Four shipyard workers took off their coveralls and slipped into black gear and headed to missile control to open their tool boxes and retrieve their weapons. Then they headed up the ladder to the bridge.

Moving slowly a chief reached down and picked up a pipe wrench holding it behind his back.

"I wouldn't do that if I were you," one of the terrorists warned a sailor. "Drop it!"

The chief dropped the wrench, but a couple of senior sailors tried to make a break for the truck tunnel in the house. Bullets ricochet off the steel deck, stopping them in their tracks.

Captain Davey jerked around at the sound of the gunshots. "Go to security alert!"

"That won't be necessary," Abdullah cautioned, making his presence known on the bridge. "If you want to try, go ahead. So far none of your crew has been killed, but we will start if you don't do what we say."

"Dad!" Jim blurted, "what in the world is going on?"

Abdullah turned to his son, his dark eyes cold and determined. "Son, it's time to take your rightful place beside me. You will help me in this."

"You're insane. I can't do that. I won't!"

Abdullah smiled. "Of course you will. You have no choice."

Jim's mind flashed back to the summers when his father had insisted he attend the secret terrorist camps in Oregon, but never would he have believed his father would lead an armed attack on the United States of America. Then he remembered how fervent and violent his dad's temper could be, and he knew Abdullah was serious.

"You won't get away with this!" Captain Davey said.

"We already have," Abdullah countered. "And this is just the beginning. Order that boat to return to the ship, or we'll blow it out of the water."

Captain Davey picked up a mic and keyed it. "Boats, bring the RHIB alongside of the ship. Now!"

"No, Sir. I won't do that," the bosun replied. Jim tensed for the response he knew would come.

Crack snapped the machine pistol, and the helmsman dropped to the deck, blood splattered on the bulkhead where he had been standing.

"Tell your bosun that if he doesn't comply with my orders," Abdullah told the captain, "I will continue killing your sailors one at a time until he returns."

"Boats," Davey said over the mic, "they've just killed Mendez. Return to the ship at once, or they'll keep killing more of our men."

"Understood, Captain."

"Tell your bosun to watch the side of the ship," Abdullah ordered. Then, turning to his men, he said, "Throw the body off over the side, just in case the bosun has any second thoughts about disobeying my commands."

Two of the terrorists lifted the lifeless body of the helmsman, carried him to the port bridge wing, and threw him overboard. Enraged, Jim watched as the body tumbled down to the waterline, making a big splash.

"Train the machine gun on the bosun and the boat," Abdullah said, "just in case he has any thoughts of bravery." Then he watched, as the speedy RHIB came dashing across the waves toward the Sheboygan.

"Open fire," Abdullah commanded, as the RHIB pulled to within fifty yards of the ship.

Captain Davey lowered his head and Jim glared at his father, as the fifty-cal spit out bullets and shredded the eleven-meter RHIB.

⟿

"Mother of God, they're shooting at us!" Boats exclaimed, an instant before he and Deek jumped into the water. They both dove deep, as the heavy bullets whizzed by them. Moments later they came up for air, hiding behind one of the pontoons that had somehow remained intact.

"We need to contact someone shore-side," Deek said between gulps of air and water.

"Not likely!" Boats yelled as a wave crashed over him.

The fifty-cal again opened fire, and they dove back into the depths of the ocean. Slowly they resurfaced again behind the shredded pontoon, but the ship had drifted on.

"We need to return to port and get help," Deek shouted.

"I hear you, Gunny, but by the time we get help, many more of the crew might die. We can't allow that. We've got to get back aboard and find a way to retake the ship."

"Man, you heard the automatic weapons. Nobody on Sheboygan is armed, and we're floatin' out here like ducks on a pond."

"Work with me on this, Gunny. We've got to return to Sheboygan," Boats said.

Without hesitation, Gunny nodded his angry agreement, and they began swimming toward the ship, ready to dive under water if they were shot at again.

44

Washington D.C.

"The President of the United States has one day left before we take out an American city," the Light of Allah announced on the Al Jazeera network. "It is divinely appointed for all Muslims to rise up and seize control of the empire that Allah has promised us."

The Director of National Intelligence immediately headed for the White House with a DVD of the speech. Already there had been an outbreak of suicide bombings in Spain, England, France, New York, and Indonesia. Using his cell phone Stevens called the President's secretary to let her know he was coming. When he entered the White House he immediately headed for the Oval Office.

"He's expecting you," the secretary said, holding the door open.

"Thanks," the director said, entering the room. "Mr. President," he began immediately, "I believe an al-Qaeda attack has struck the Western World. I don't think we've seen the worst of it. We must release the prisoners in Guantanamo Bay!"

The President looked at Stevens with firm resolve and fire in his eyes. "I'm not negotiating with terrorists! Call a meeting of the joint chiefs and the intelligence community in the Situation Room. We've got to use every means possible to pursue these people on our home front."

Stevens had expected this response but hoped to change it. "We can't shift our total focus within our borders."

"I agree. We've been fighting most of our battles on other people's soil, but I think we need to defend our own as well."

"Mr. President, there's something else you should see." Stevens inserted a compact disc in the player. When the Light of Allah's message was complete, he said, "I don't think the suicide bomber in New York is the attack he's talking about, Mr. President. I've ordered all military bases to Threat Con Charlie, but we still don't have much to go on. One of the areas that might be a target is the West Coast. A couple of weeks ago we caught five Islamic men sneaking across the border. They could have been heading to San Diego, Los Angeles, or San Francisco."

The President frowned. "Increase security at the borders, airports, and seaports. Order the Coast Guard to get all their cutters out on patrol. Make sure the checkpoints for INS are fully manned and they conduct thorough searches. We can't let them fan out if they get through our patrols."

"What if they're already here, Mr. President?"

"We're going to have to deal with that, but for now, let's do all we can. Any word from Sudan?"

"We've found a massive grave in the desert near an oasis. We believe a huge complex was built under the desert floor, and it could be where this so-called Light of Allah is operating."

"Find him, William. Send more men in if you have to. I need the coordinates of that bunker."

"Yes, Sir. We've already sent another team."

45

USS Sheboygan

Abdullah checked his watch and turned to the captain. "Stop the ship. In an hour San Diego should be in flames. We can't allow the satellites to think we have power. Keep two people on the bridge to maintain course. Order your crew to report to the mess decks with their cell phones." Abdullah handed the captain the mic.

"This is the captain speaking. All personnel on watch and off watch are to report to the mess decks immediately. Failure to do so could result in the loss of life."

Davey handed the mic back to Abdullah, as the crew of the USS Sheboygan headed to the mess decks under the careful scrutiny of Abdullah's armed men. Using heavy-duty plastic tie wraps the terrorists secured the sailors back to back and made them sit on the mess deck. One of the sleeper cell agents, educated in the United States and now working for a controls company in San Diego, headed to the engine room. He knew the diesel ship's operating procedures because civilian contractors were accomplishing more and more repairs and calibrations. He had been to sea several times with different ships and knew how to run the diesels controls and understood what the engine operating alarms meant when they sounded. As long as the main engines and generators stayed on line, they'd be able to maneuver.

Back on the helm a young woman sailor pleaded with a terrorist who stood nearby, "Sir, I really need to use the bathroom."

"That's not my problem. You're going to stay here till we're done with you."

"Please," she pleaded.

While Abdullah and the captain watched, the terrorist back-handed the woman across the face, and she fell to the deck. Blood ran from her nose, as she tried to right herself. With one hand Abdullah reached down and lifted her up so she could stand, though not for her sake, but rather so the others could see what would happen to anyone who stepped out of line.

"Abdullah, it would be my pleasure to send this one to Hades," the terrorist offered, as he jammed a gun to the woman's head.

"Her life is of no consequence to me," Abdullah said, squeezing the sailor's neck until her face turned red.

"Let go of her!" the captain shouted. "If you want me to cooperate, don't harm my crew."

Abdullah lessened his grip around her neck. "Very well, Captain. Make your next announcement. Tell your crew what has happened to your ship."

Abdullah watched carefully, as Captain Davey picked up the black mic and squeezed the trigger on the side. "This is the captain. Our ship has been taken over by terrorists, and they have already killed Seaman Mendez and thrown his body over the side. Do as they say, and don't try anything. I repeat, don't try anything."

Abdullah retrieved the mic and then said, "Captain, you won't be going anywhere. Take a seat." Abdullah pointed to the only chair on the bridge and issued an order to his men. "Secure his arms."

Two of the terrorists quickly moved forward. Clothed in black but with their bearded faces exposed, they tightly cinched the captain's arms to the chair, drawing a little blood in the process.

"Abdullah, do you want lookouts posted?" one of the terrorists asked.

"Yes. Immediately. Have someone monitor the radars. Go around to all outside decks, and make sure there are no lights on. Liz, turn off the running lights. It must appear that we've lost all power."

"Will do," she replied.

"You touch any more of my crewmembers," the captain growled, "and you'll have to answer to me. I don't care if I have to chase you to hell and back."

"Really, Captain," Abdullah smirked. "You're in no position to give me orders, nor will you be allowed in Allah's paradise, where I will be. I control you and your ship."

"As God is my witness, if you touch my crew, I will hunt you down like the dog you are and crush the life out of you."

"Who is in charge here, your God or Allah? Look who's tied up. You fail to realize the chances of either one of us surviving are quite remote."

An hour later, Liz came back on the bridge with her laptop open. She plugged it in and struck the keys, setting up a satellite feed.

"Son," Abdullah said, speaking again to Jim for the first time since he had declared his refusal to help him, "I'm going to need you to pilot the ship into San Diego. Do you think you can do that?"

Jim looked horrified. "Why would you even ask? You might as well shoot me. I'm a citizen of the United States, not the Nation of Islam. I will never help you!"

Abdullah's face reddened and he spoke in a loud whisper. "You listen and you listen good, Son. There's a whole lot more at stake than this ship. There is a *jihad*, and we're again attacking the great Satan's homeland." He pulled away and redirected his attention to Liz. "Show him what's happening!"

She clicked a few keys, and a live television broadcast came up on her screen.

"We go now live to the White House, where the President will address the nation," one of the talking heads announced.

"Like Pearl Harbor and 9/11, the United States has been attacked," the President announced. "At two-thirty-three Pacific Standard Time, an electromagnetic pulse bomb detonated over San Diego. The estimated death toll is in the thousands, and the bomb destroyed all electrical circuits. Power lines carrying electricity to the city are damaged beyond repair. All electrical devices, unless shielded, are out of commission. The Marines, Army, and National Guard will be moving toward the city and taking people to the outlying areas, where there is power and shelter. This is a national emergency. We are in a state of war against those who have attacked America. Our intelligence reports indicate that this is the work of a new al-Qaeda terrorist, the Light of Allah. Thirty days ago he demanded that all Islamic prisoners held in Guantanamo Bay be released and returned to their countries. As you know, I do not negotiate with terrorists. In the meantime, I'm asking the American people not to go to San Diego. Survivors are being evacuated in an orderly fashion. The military and Highway Patrol will be sealing off the highways. All lanes will be used for the mass exodus from San Diego. I will address the nation again tonight at eight P.M. Thank you for your cooperation . . . and pray for America. I pray that God will bless and protect this nation in its hour of need. Good night."

The talking heads began their rebuttal of the President's speech, and Liz disconnected the satellite link-up.

"You see," Abdullah said, his thin smile nearly as cold as his eyes, "this ship is but a small player in all this."

46

White House

The Situation room in the West Wing of the White House was jammed. The Vice-President, members of the Cabinet, senior members of the Senate and House, all sixteen directors of the intelligence agencies, and high-ranking military officers silenced their cell phones. Everyone turned their full attention to the Commander-in-Chief.

The President steeled himself for what lay ahead. "I will not negotiate with these terrorists. Israel has been under constant attack, whether they have peace accords or not. We must fight back! Where is the Light of Allah based? What planes can we get into the sky to put the pressure on him? William, what are your thoughts?"

"We still don't know his location, Mr. President. Al Jazeera has been broadcasting his messages, but they're delivered to the station by courier and then put on the air," Director Stevens reported.

"Have we had analysts look at the background to see where the tapes are being made?"

"Yes, Mr. President, and they're all coming from the same room, but we have no idea where that room is. At least with bin Laden we could check the landscape, but these broadcasts could be from anywhere."

"Mr. President," the Democratic leader of the Senate interjected, "I think it's time we released the prisoners in Guantanamo Bay, or we'll be attacked again."

"Howard, before we start talking that way," the President responded, redirecting his attention to Director Stevens, "where did the bomb come from?"

"Satellite pictures taken moments before the bomb detonated showed that a plane violated international airspace and flew close to the border without filing a flight plan with Mexican authorities. It fired a missile while in the air that detonated over the city. The plane was knocked out of the sky when the bomb went off."

"Do we have people on the ground looking for the wreckage?" the President asked.

"Yes, Sir, but it's not that easy. The fuselage is scattered throughout the Mexican border, and we're having a hard time finding it."

"Find it. I want answers, and I want them now!" He turned to the Commandant of the Marine Corps. "How many vehicles do you have heading toward San Diego?"

The short, no-nonsense general paused briefly before responding. "Every bus and truck that has an engine has either left Camp Pendleton or is leaving as we speak, Sir. Twenty-Nine Palms and the other bases in California and Arizona are responding with helicopters, buses, and trucks. We'll have the first five thousand people picked up within the hour."

Turning to the blue suitor the President asked, "Admiral, what about the Navy?"

"Our bases are responding, but we've got to get our own people re-supplied with generators. I don't like the idea of not being able to patrol the harbor, so I'm sending the two Sea Fighters in from San Francisco. They aren't equipped with much fire power, but they can patrol, and they can launch a couple of swift boats."

"What about the National Guard?"

"Sir, most of our people are in Iraq. We just deployed our California Division," the General of the Guard said.

"Is Miramar Marine Corps Air Station back up and running?"

"It will be, Sir," answered the Marine Corps General. "We're flying in generators and are hooking up temporary wiring."

"Declare San Diego a no-fly zone. I don't want anything in the air that isn't military. All military air patrols have orders to shoot down any unauthorized or suspicious aircraft. We're not taking any chances."

"Mr. President, I have family members in San Diego," a liberal female Senator said. "Isn't there something we can do? Maybe we could release at least some prisoners. After all, we don't know where this Light of Allah will strike next."

"I understand and sympathize with you," the President responded softly. "I must look at the nation as a whole. I don't know where they will strike again, but we have our military in the air. If any unidentifiable bird comes into our airspace, we'll knock it down. But that's not what I'm worried about. If I put myself in this Light of Allah's shoes, I'd already have another attack planned and ready for execution. We've got to find out what it is."

"Mr. President," a cabinet member said, "you saw what a disaster New Orleans was. This is much worse. There was no warning in San Diego, but at least the backcountry didn't burn again. Some of the survivors are leaving their homes and trying to walk out."

The President suppressed a sigh and turned the question over to Director Stevens. "William, what's your assessment?"

"All of our weapons systems are down in that area, but we'll have ships on station in the next twenty-four hours. The Air Force is flying B-52's throughout our country with AWAC's up. From our satellite pictures, the only thing moving are the trucks and humvbees we're sending and a couple of remote vehicles that were on the edge of the blast zone. I'm sending every available chopper to San Diego, loaded with water and supplies."

"Why didn't our missile-tracking system pick up this plane?"

"Sir, that's the odd part of the attack. We had a satellite picture, but the computer system went down before we ever saw the plane. I believe someone cracked our cyber codes and erased any signal that had the plane on radar. I don't know how that's possible, but if it's true, we're in big trouble."

"Could they have hacked into our system, dummied up the signals, and then destroyed it without our knowing?"

"Mr. President, because all the computers were fried, we may never know. I hate to say this, but San Diego might be a diversion," Stevens warned.

The President's heart constricted at the Director's words. "What are you saying, William?"

"Sir, the war with the terrorists could be a full-scale cyber attack, or they could have other attacks lined up and have already compromised our defense systems. Last month a computer complex was raided, two dogs and a security guard were shot and killed, and the only thing taken was a CAC card."

"We've got to get our anti-cyber hackers hot on their trail," the President insisted. "I thought it was only the Chinese we had to worry about."

"Yes, Sir, I thought that too. Maybe the Chinese are sharing information with them."

"Admiral, what about our ships off San Diego?"

"Mr. President, we have two ready-strike groups within three hundred miles of San Diego. I've ordered all salvage tugs from Pearl Harbor and San Francisco to make flank-speed toward San Diego because we have two carriers down. We'll tow them to Bremerton to be rewired."

"How long will that take?"

"At best, six months," the Admiral replied. "We've deployed four F-18 squadrons to the area, but we have to refuel them with our airborne tankers. They need to land at Miramar Marine Corps Air Station, and hopefully within the hour we'll have the fuel farm up and running with emergency generators. We're using March Air Reserve Base in Riverside as a staging area."

The President clenched his jaws. "Does anyone here not think the enemy knows that San Diego is a wide-open target?"

"I don't know, Mr. President, but I agree with Stevens," the Homeland Security Chief replied. "It could be a diversion."

"That's one heck of a diversion. I want our recovery timeline decreased and the rest of our defenses up and ready for the next attack. William, I want more information about this Light of Allah. I don't care what you have to do to get it. I want results! We're involved in a war of spiritual dimensions, and it isn't going to get any better any time soon."

"Yes, Sir, Mr. President."

"General, get down to Gitmo and start interrogating those prisoners again. I'm sure one of them will know who this Light of Allah is and where his base camp is. Do what you need to do. We've been at war since 9/11, and our country is vulnerable. Share what you find with the CIA and the FBI. Some of the terrorists are living here in the United States, and I want them found."

"Mr. President, if you just release the prisoners, this whole thing will blow over," the female senator said, repeating her plea for negotiations.

"It won't, Senator, but don't ever stop telling me that. People's lives have been lost by my decisions, and I always need to hear the other side. If there's a better way to keep our people out of harm's way, I'm all for it. Let me tell you, when I was a second lieutenant in Vietnam, there was a captain that took just the course you're advocating. He was in command of a firebase and convinced the colonel to stop sending out nightly patrols because he was taking heavy casualties. Permission was given to stop the patrols, and three days later his entire camp was wiped out. Every living thing was killed. That's the mentality we're up against, ladies and gentlemen. The militant Muslims want to take over the world in the name of Allah, and I refuse to negotiate. We'll meet again at eleven tonight. Dismissed."

The politicians and military men and women got up from their seats and filed out. In their wake cell phones began chirping and vibrating. Kate, the President's secretary, rushed into the room and whispered something in the Chief Executive's ear and then turned on the television set.

The President got up from his chair and called out, "Will everyone please quiet down. General, go out and call everybody back into the room. Threat Matrix has picked up a video feed from Al Jazeera television."

The men and women quickly returned, and Kate increased the volume of the television until it drowned out the voices of those still drifting in. The handsome Arabic man on the screen, known as the Light of Allah, was dressed in white, with a red inner garment and a black cloak.

"To the President of the United States. My informants have told me that nothing is being done to release my brethren from Guantanamo Bay, so you force me to do something that I did not want to do," he said, his mood somber. "It was never my plan to destroy ten cities in the United States, but you leave me no options."

"Oh, baloney," someone said, loud enough for everyone to hear.

"It will be unfortunate for the people of the United States that you have disregarded my humble requests," the Light of Allah continued. "Already too many of your people have died on your soil, and yet you will not negotiate with me. I could have used a bigger, more destructive bomb, but I wanted to limit your loss of life. You see, I am a man of peace. Again, I offer you a peaceful settlement. Release one planeload of my brethren as a token of good negotiations, and I will delay my next attack. The cities of America are defenseless against me. You have one hour. At eleven o'clock I will initiate the next strike, but far more deadly than the first. I hope, for the sake of innocent American lives, that you listen and agree to my generous peace offering."

The Light of Allah's sad expression faded from the screen, as the television switched to Al Jazeera studios, and one of the Arabic newscasters reported, "The Light of Allah is doing what he said he would. The eighth largest city in America has been crippled. He is humbling the Great Satan to release Islamic prisoners held against their will. Muslims everywhere should be very grateful to him," he decreed, as the President's secretary turned the television off.

"Thank you, Kate," the President said, as she exited the room.

"William, have someone contact Al Jazeera and see if they can arrange a meeting with this Light of Allah."

"I'll try, Sir, but this guy is pretty slick. He delivers tapes to the station, but we can't seem to crack into their computer system to access the pathway they're using."

"I don't care what it takes," the President repeated. "We must find him!"

47

The bridge of the USS Sheboygan

"Jim, I need you to pilot this ship into San Diego Harbor," Abdullah said. "It's time you returned to your roots. Remember the camps?"

Jim bristled. "I hated those camps. I told you before, Dad, I'm not doing it!"

"We'll see about that. Bring the whore in here," he ordered one of the terrorists. Jim flinched as he heard the sound of flesh being struck, but then his heart froze, as a woman stumbled into the room, dragged by her hair to stand before Abdullah. The woman's mouth was secured with duct tape, and her hands were tie-wrapped behind her body. Her head was down but the familiarity didn't escape him. He didn't want to believe his gut feeling, but deep down he knew, even before Abdullah yanked her head up.

"No!" Jim groaned, as he saw Elena's reddened, swollen face. "You grotesque pig of a man! May the God of the Jews strike you dead, you horror of a human being!" Then he launched himself at his father with every intent to kill him or die trying, but Abdullah sidestepped him and slapped him viciously across the face. Then he grabbed his son and threw him up against the bulkhead, pinning him.

"Elena's life hangs by your decision. It's up to you. We can steer the ship into port, but it would be better if you did it. It would be safer for all the lives onboard. Think about that!"

"You can't do this," Jim shouted, looking past his father to Elena, suddenly understanding why his dad had been so interested and helpful in his relationship.

Without warning Abdullah pulled a pistol out from his waistband and fired. Captain Davey winced as the bullet grazed his thigh.

"I can, and I will. It's up to you, my son. Have you forgotten what happened to your mother when she didn't obey?"

Anger flushed Jim's face, as he remembered how brutal his father could be. "All right, all right. I'll pilot the ship."

"And handle the comms."

"What comms? You wiped them out when you blew up San Diego."

"I will need you to handle comms with other ships or planes coming to San Diego. I'm sure the Great Satan has already sent reinforcements to help out his crippled city. For now we don't want to go back to port until we get the word, so I've stopped the ship."

⤿

The terrorists separated the chief petty officers from the sailors. Then they looked at the nametags and checked everyone's name off a list that Liz had printed out from the XO's update, just before they got underway. When the list was complete, one of the terrorists hurried to the bridge and gave it to Abdullah.

"Very good, Mosel. Only two missing, but we know where they are," Abdullah said, smiling as he considered the fate of the men aboard the RHIB. "Go back down and remind the others what happens to those who don't cooperate." Mosel hurried off the bridge to obey.

Suddenly the bridge lights dimmed, then went off.

"What's that? Liz, take a couple of our technicians and find out what's causing the lights to flicker," Abdullah ordered. "I need power restored immediately!"

"Yes, Abdullah. I'll check one space and our engine techs can check the other," Liz said, as she ran from the bridge to find out what had happened.

The port engineer had been on the wing wall when he heard the gunfire. He watched the fifty-cal spit out bullets and shred the RHIB. Because he wasn't an official member of the ship's crew, his name wasn't on the ship's manifest, and he wondered if the terrorists would realize that he was unaccounted for. Carefully he made his way down to the number-two auxiliary engine space. All the engineers had left the space and reported to the mess decks. If the terrorists had sent anyone to the engine room, it would be the forward space, main control.

Jake took a moment and said a quick prayer to the Lord. He looked around and spotted a bent piece of scrap metal. He pop-riveted a heavy electrical wire onto the back of it, then tripped another lighting breaker and wired it to the dead side of the buss and placed it over the breaker handle and painted it black. After that he opened a sample cock and let seawater puddle on the steel deck plates. Quickly grabbing an eighteen-inch steel pipe wrench, he slid into a corner behind the switchboard and then watched, as two black-clad terrorists rushed down the ladder into the auxiliary machinery space and checked out the machinery. He could easily have taken one of them out, but he didn't want to give away his position or the fact that he was onboard. The terrorists had automatic weapons, but Jake knew that if he kept his wits and trusted in the Lord, God would show him how to defeat them.

"Here it is," one of the terrorists announced. "One of the lighting circuits tripped. I'll just close it and we'll get back to the mess decks." He stepped into the puddle of water and reached out his hand to close it.

The other man screamed something in Arabic and immediately jumped back. "You idiot! Do you want to get yourself killed? You've got water all over your boots. Get back, and I'll close the breaker," he said, as he reached out and closed the generator circuit breaker. Instantly 440 volts and 2000 amps shot across the wire and plate and arced into his body. He jumped like a lightning bolt had hit him and flopped around, trying to pull his hand away from the energized breaker, but he couldn't pull free. Sparks flew everywhere, and then the breaker exploded and a piece of burning metal caught him in the throat. The other terrorist watched in horror and then grabbed a fire extinguisher to put out the smoldering breaker.

Jake rushed out of his hiding place and swung the pipe wrench with all his might, hitting the man in the head. The terrorist reeled but didn't go down, so Jake hit him again. This time he fell to the deck plates. Jake bent over and checked for a pulse, but there was none. Black burn marks covered the other man where electricity had leapt out of his body. Jake checked their pockets to see if they had any identification, but instead found a cell phone. Then he heard footsteps up above, rushing down the ladder to the engine room, and he quickly looked for a place to hide. There wasn't any nearby, so he took a chance and ran across the space and into the escape trunk, hoping they wouldn't see him. The door closed behind him, as he quickly climbed the rungs up to the next deck and lifted his head out of the escape hatch to see if anyone was in the passageway. Every part of his body tingled as he climbed out. He ran aft and rushed up another set of steel stairs, opened a hatch, and climbed out onto the starboard wing wall.

The sun was setting, and it was getting dark at sea. Jake noticed the ship wasn't making any headway. He tried using the cell phone, but there was no service, and he wondered how far offshore they were. Then he ducked, as he heard two men talking on the flight deck, one deck above him.

Jake sat quietly, shaking. He'd never killed a man before. Pushing his thoughts and emotions from his mind, he was trying to figure out what to do next when he noticed something bobbing in the water.

48

Starboard wing-wall, USS Sheboygan

Jake looked again at the darkened sea. The ship had stopped moving, and he thought his eyes were playing tricks on him. Then he saw it again! Something was moving in the water. Maybe it was just a piece of pontoon from the lifeboat, floating near the stern. He wondered if he should climb down the side of the stern gate and swim out to the pontoon. Was God giving him a way to make it to shore and get help? He looked all around but couldn't see land. Peering into the growing darkness he tried to see if there were any gulls or birds of any kind, but it was too dark. Trying to swim to shore would take too long. He had to think of more ways to take out terrorists without being caught.

Again he closed his eyes, prayed, and asked the Lord for help. He sat there for a while and began contemplating his next move. Maybe he could break into the armory and get guns and ammunition. He thought about rigging up a cutting torch so he could cut through the heavy steel hatch. He got up to go, but then glanced again at the floating pontoon. It seemed to be drifting toward him. Maybe God was giving him an escape off the ship, but Jake couldn't go. He knew that was the easy way out. He'd worked on this ship for eighteen years and wasn't about to abandon it now. Somehow he had to stay onboard and fight the terrorists—even if it cost him his life.

He began to consider ways to disable the main engines. Just before leaving to go back down into the engine room, he once again glanced toward the water. He couldn't believe what he saw! A hand was waving to him and getting closer. Someone was swimming in the water, pushing the pontoon toward the ship. Then another!

Jake dashed forward and got a line. He tied it to a cleat and threw the line over the stern of the ship, trying to be as quiet as possible. When he looked over the side, he saw Boats and Deek in the water, grinning up at him. Overjoyed but cautious, he quickly glanced at the port wing-wall, where one of the lookouts had just walked down the ladder-way and was now looking around. Jake hoped he wouldn't look down into the water. Finally the man returned to the flight deck.

Jake motioned to Boats to wait and then ran to the engine room. He opened the boiler water test cabinet and grabbed a bottle of phenalthaleen from the test kit, then hurried back toward the stern of the ship on the port wing-wall. Either terrorist could turn around at any moment and shoot him, but Jake quietly climbed up the ladder near them. The two had a pot of coffee they were sharing, sitting behind them near the ladder. When they turned their backs, Jake quickly grabbed the pot off the flight deck, opened the lid, and poured the chemical in it. Quietly replacing the pot, he climbed back down the ladder and moved forward and then across to the starboard wing-wall. Going aft he hid behind the Nixie winch and motioned for Boats and Deek to continue waiting.

It didn't take long. Sixty seconds after the two lookouts refilled their cups and drank the coffee, they looked at each other in panic. One man reached behind himself and grasped his buttocks, as he ran off the flight deck toward the house. The other guard didn't have time to run to the head. He dropped his gun, pulled his pants down, and hung his buttocks over the side, as his intestines exploded, releasing all that he had eaten in the last twenty-four hours. The phenathaleen was colorless and tasteless, but Jake knew it could empty a man in less than a minute.

Jake ran on deck. The terrorist scrambled for his gun but was too late. With arms extended, he rushed Jake. The old wrestling coach used an over/under lateral drop and threw him off the aft end of the ship, but he landed in the safety nets surrounding the flight deck. Jake jumped into the net with him and crashed his head into the man's sternum, knocking him over the side. When the terrorist hit the water, Deek grabbed him. He held his head under until he stopped moving. Meanwhile, Jake scrambled back to the flight deck and picked up the gun. Then he headed back to the starboard wing-wall before the other lookout came back. Finally he helped Boats and Gunny climb up the stern and onto the ship.

"How in the world did you guys survive the shooting and swim over here?" Jake whispered loudly, still not believing his eyes, as his two friends stood dripping wet in front of him.

"You think some sand-sucker is going to take us out with our own weapons? Gunny and I dove deep and held our breath for as long as we could, and then came back up on the other side of that pontoon, took another breath of air, and headed back down again." Boats paused, looked around, and whispered, "What's going on here?"

"Terrorists have taken over the ship. All the crew is on the mess-decks. I guess they don't know I'm aboard, and they sure don't think you two are alive."

"It's going to take a little more than a couple of ragheads to take us out, Jake. Let me have that gun. I'm an excellent shot. I could start taking them out, one by one."

"I'm sure you could, Gunny," Jake said. "There are a whole lot of them. I don't mind giving you the gun, but we have to be smart or they'll kill more sailors."

49

Office of the Director
of National Intelligence

Director Stevens sat at his desk opposite the bleary-eyed Marine general in charge of Gitmo. They were getting ready to report to the President, and the flight-weary general tried to rub sleep from his eyes. Still no information about the Light of Allah had come forth from the team in Sudan. They hadn't found any evidence of the hidden base or camp, and Stevens didn't have anything to report. So far the only thing they could track was that the DVD recordings had been sent over the Internet from Singapore. They could have been downloaded anywhere and re-sent. It was impossible to trace them. They left the office, and their driver headed to the White House, as Stevens envisioned the President's reaction to his empty report.

"General, how many Islamic terrorists do we have in Gitmo?"

"Sir, we have one hundred and thirty-seven. We've captured them from all over the globe."

"What do you think their Intel value is?"

"We've interrogated all of them. I believe we've extracted all we can from them."

Stevens sighed. This was not what he wanted to hear . . . and far less than what the President wanted to hear. "I'm inclined to advise the President to turn over the prisoners to the Light of Allah. Public outcry is at an all-time high. Even some members of the President's cabinet say we should release them."

"Good luck. You know what he's going to say."

They pulled up to the White House, and a Marine guard asked for their CAC cards while another used a mirror on a pole to check under the car. After they showed their ID's, they got out of the car and went to the Oval office.

"You look tired, General," the President said. "What have we got, Stevens?"

"Very little. We didn't get much information on the Light of Allah and don't know his location. I'm concerned that world opinion is suddenly swaying in his favor, and we've seen on CNN protests from around the globe that we should let the prisoners go."

"Stop right there," the President snapped. "I don't want to hear it. If we give in to their demands, we're bowing to their authority. Some people think I'm the great Satan, but I'll tell you right now, these militant Islamic fanatics are the ones following Satan. They've murdered a lot of innocent women and children in their holy *jihad*, and I'm not about to bow to their demands."

"Sir, can't you at least consider negotiating with them? Maybe we could release half of the prisoners," Stevens offered.

"No way! I'm not negotiating with the enemy. If I give a little here, they'll want more. It's my job to protect American lives, and that's exactly what I'm going to do. With God's help we'll find a way. God is going to protect His people who call on His name."

Stevens knew the Commander-in-Chief wasn't about to budge, so he tried another tack. "We do have one lead that we just rediscovered. About three weeks ago there was a lot of movement through Sudan by Islamic extremists. We had a report about a Chinese physicist spotted by a couple of operatives in Khartoum. We didn't think much of the report, but just the other day we decoded a message being sent to Mexico. We saw the same message on an obscure website being sent to other parts of the world."

"What did it say?"

"Not much. It just gave a time and a date."

"What was it?"

"Tomorrow at six P.M. there's supposed to be another attack on ten US cities. With that attack other terrorists are supposed to strike worldwide. I still think we ought to show some indication for negotiation, at least to buy more time."

"Stevens, when I was a second lieutenant in Vietnam the Viet Cong were only interested in negotiating when we were promising to leave. I think we can learn a lesson from that war. This war is on our soil, and I'm not negotiating with terrorists because it's not about their prisoners. It's about their trying to justify their attack to the world. Now let's have a word of prayer."

Without waiting for a response the President bowed his head and prayed, "Father, give me wisdom in this time of need. Help us defend our country and find this Light of Allah and bring him to justice. We pray in Jesus' name. Amen."

Stevens and the general followed the President as they exited the room.

50

Starboard wing-wall, USS Sheboygan

Bosun, Gunny, and Jake slowly moved forward in the shadows one deck below the flight deck.

"Quiet! I think I hear somebody coming our way," Jake whispered.

The three men ducked behind the tween deck near the inner catwalk, as the footsteps on the metal grating became louder and louder.

With his finger to his lips Deek whispered, "We need Intel. Let's drop this guy and get some."

The three men watched as the terrorist came closer. Just as he was upon them he turned and climbed back up the ladder to the flight deck.

"That's the other lookout," Gunny said. "We're going to have to take him out before he radios that his partner isn't on location."

Jake couldn't believe what he was hearing. "The flight deck's wide open. How are we going to cross to the other side of the ship? Somebody up in the pilot house will spot us."

"Maybe," Boats said, "but Gunny's right. We can't just stand around here. We've got to take a chance."

"Exactly. One of us might get killed, but if we don't try, a whole lot of people will die!" Deek declared fervently.

"Gunny," Jake argued, "if you want to run across the flight deck and try and take him out, I won't stop you, but if you miss we've lost our element of surprise."

"Then you pray, church boy! Cuz, I'm gonna take him out." Gunny popped his head over the steel hatch coaming and took a quick look. Then he pulled back down and handed the bosun his weapon. "Boats, cover me."

Boats raised the rifle while Jake kept watch. Deek climbed the tween deck ladder and popped his head slightly over the flight deck edge. Because of the darkened ship he was hard to spot in the shadows. Just as the lookout turned his back, Gunny exploded from his position. He got halfway across the flight deck before the man turned around. Recovering quickly, the terrorist jerked up his AK-47, ready to fire.

Deek launched a powerful crescent kick with his leg, striking the weapon, and followed with a solid body punch to the kidney. The gun fell to the steel deck with an unmistakable clang. Instinctively the terrorist pulled his arms up, expecting another punch, but Deek followed with a low round kick to the left knee. The knee buckled and the terrorist crashed to the deck in pain, but then rolled to his right and staggered to his feet. His training in martial arts was obvious, as the two men circled each other.

Boats watched with the gun ready but knew he couldn't fire or it would bring more terrorists. Jake split his attention between Deek's progress and the bridge, hoping no one wandered outside the deckhouse.

The two combatants continued to circle each other. Deek wasted no time and attacked again with a couple of jabs and then a sidekick to the ribs. The terrorist countered, deflecting the blows by lowering his arms. Without waiting, Gunny struck with a knee to the man's stomach, followed by an elbow strike to the temple. It was a perfect hit, and the man dropped to the deck like a sack of potatoes.

"You can stop right there or I'll cut you in half," Liz said, as she and two others stepped out of the shadows, her pistol pointed at Deek's chest. "I wondered about these so-called 'accidents' we've been having. Take him to the wardroom with the other officers. I'll make my report to Abdullah."

"That's messed up. I defended you against that man at the gym, and now you're turnin' on me. What kind of person are you?"

"Sometimes things aren't what they seem," Liz answered. "Put the ties on and take him to the bridge instead. I'm sure Abdullah will be happy to see him again. I've got to go down below." She waited till Deek's arms were secured behind his back and then walked away.

"We've got to do something, Bosun," Jake whispered in the shadows.

"I could take him out with the rifle after the woman leaves."

"Are you a good shot?"

"Not really, but we've got to stop him from taking Gunny to the bridge."

"God will have to show us what to do, and in a hurry," the port engineer said. Then he thought of something. "Wait a minute, Boats. Can we drop the crane's speed ball without turning it on?"

"You betcha!"

"Praise the Lord! Do you think you can hit the terrorist as he walks under it?"

"I'm already on it," the bosun said, as he ran through the shadows and climbed the outside handrails of the ship to the boat deck above. Then he scurried up the metal rungs on the crane and quietly entered the cab. He sat motionless in the operator's seat and positioned himself to use the foot pedals to drop the speedball on top of the terrorist who was now pushing Deek along the boat deck. He took in a deep breath and gauged how they were walking, but they were too far inboard. The crane was located near the life rails.

From the shadows Jake pointed his hand for Deek to move a couple of feet toward the crane. Just as they approached the crane, Deek tripped and fell to the deck.

"Get up," the guard ordered, as he poked the muzzle of his rifle into Deek's back.

Jake knew the terrorist still wasn't in position, but he had come closer. Deek slowly got to his feet and looked around. Jake knew Boats would have to power up the electrical system in order to move the boom, and the high whining sound of the hydraulic motors on startup would alert the terrorist, but they had no choice. Just then the ship took a huge roll to the port side, and the speedball slowly drifted in the terrorist's direction.

That was all Boats needed! Jake read Boats' movements from where he stood. Boats slammed down on the brake and clutch pedals and released the speedball, dropping it instantly and striking the terrorist on the shoulder, knocking him to the deck. Jake ran out of the shadows and grabbed the man in a rear naked chokehold before he could cry out for help. Boats quickly slid down the crane handrails and shoved a rag in his mouth, tying it off behind his head. Then he cut the plastic ties on Gunny's wrists.

Deek rubbed them and said, "Let's take him below and find out what he knows. We need to find out how many people are onboard and what they intend."

Just then the engines increased speed, and the ship leaned to starboard as they altered course.

"What are they doing?" Jake wondered aloud.

"I'd guess we're headed back to San Diego," Deek said, as he grabbed the terrorist and pushed him forward.

"Come on, let's take him to the deck storage locker two levels below," Boats said. "We'd better hurry up and see if we can get any information out of him."

Deek looked at him sternly. "I don't need your help on this. Why don't you two scout around and see if you can pick off another one?"

"Deek's right, Boats," Jake agreed. "Besides, I've got an idea. Remember when we repaired the ventilation last year?"

"I think so," Boats answered. "What's your point?"

"I think we can get up to the bridge deck by going through one of the fan rooms."

"Let's go."

As the bosun and Jake made their way to the main deck and crept along the outboard side of Sea Flyer's container, Liz and four terrorists came down the ladder-way from the bridge. They were very determined in their walk as they headed to the well deck.

"Wait one," Boats whispered.

Suddenly high-pitched hydraulic motors screamed out in the night. Then the big steel flight deck began folding back like a giant accordion. Even in the night the white missile box gleamed brightly.

"I don't like the looks of this," Boats whispered.

"You don't suppose they're going to fire missiles at San Diego?"

"I don't know."

"What did you load up in Seal Beach?"

"There was some confusion. Our message said we were to load two dummy rounds, but the Seal Beach paperwork had us loading twelve dummy rounds for a test firing. So we did."

"Think for a minute," Jake said, the hair on the back of his neck rising at the implications of his words. "Aren't they closing Seal Beach Naval Weapons Facility?"

"Yeah. So what?"

"Is there any way possible you could have loaded nuclear weapons?"

"No way," Boats said. "I was on a cruiser when we went to Seal Beach for nukes, and they had armed Marine guards checking everything out. The security was extremely tight."

Just then a couple of terrorists climbed up the side of the launcher and used their tools to remove a plastic cover over the nose cone of the missile. Red lettering appeared on the cone.

"Are those radioactive markings on the warhead?" Jake asked, pointing to the red markings on the side of the missile's fuselage.

Boats eyes opened wide. "Mother of God!"

51

Situation Room—West wing of the White House

The Director of National Intelligence turned on the monitor for a special Threat Matrix report. The President, along with the Vice-President, Cabinet members, Speaker of the House, the Joint Chiefs, and the Directors of the Intelligence community waited until the face of the Light of Allah appeared on the screen.

"Tonight ten American cities will be destroyed, and this time by nuclear weapons. The President of the United States has repeatedly refused my generous peace offers for the release of the prisoners that he has illegally captured and murdered at Guantanamo Bay. After the missile strike many Americans will be on their knees begging Allah for mercy."

The screen went blank, as murmuring filled the office.

"Ladies and gentlemen," the President said, wanting to regain control before fear took over, "before you speak, we have some Intel from Sudan. Director Stevens, what have you found?"

"We've discovered that somewhere in the Northern Sahara Desert the Light of Allah has made his base camp. We've captured a courier. He's Gurka, and no matter what method we use, he isn't revealing the location of the base camp."

"How was the last DVD delivered?" the President asked.

"During our stake-out of the Al Jazeera television station we noticed a new face in the crowd. When he went to the men's room, one of our men noticed a CD in the man's hand, and he followed him inside. When our man got close enough to him, he glanced down to try to read the CD's title, but the man quickly slid the disk into his jacket. Normally news people don't care if you read their release titles, but in that brief instant, our man was able to see the words 'Light' and 'Allah,' so he waited until the man came back out of the head, and then he and three others apprehended him."

"So did he confess that it was from the Light of Allah?" the President asked.

"No," Stevens answered. "He hasn't said a word, but we did a spectral analysis of the sand in his shoes, and it matches the sand in Sudan."

"Really?" The President felt a glimmer of hope. "How can that be? I thought all sand was the same."

"It's not. We had a hunch it was Sudan, so we analyzed the mineral content and granule size, and it was a match."

"Do you know where in the desert the camp is located?"

"No, Sir, we don't. We've been using satellites to monitor all the movement in the desert and still haven't spotted anything. I'm sending three more teams from Black Ice Corporation, and we've offered the locals a reward for the capture of the Light of Allah."

The President frowned, unsure of these particular tactics. "Will that work? They rarely go against their religion."

"It might. There are two groups of people over there. One of them is African and the other Arab. The *Janweed* are all Muslim. The African people of Sudan are very poor and have been persecuted by the *Janweed*, so we might get lucky."

"You mean God just may point us in the right direction," the President said.

"You could say that, Mr. President."

"I just did." The President suppressed a sigh, praying silently for God's intervention. "Keep me posted on the Sudan situation.

In the meantime, General," he said, turning to the Secretary of the Air Force, "are our internal defenses up?"

"Yes, Sir, they are. We've repositioned satellites over the US, and we're scanning any unusual activity. We have our B-52's equipped with AWACS up, and they're searching the skies for any launch. We scrambled squadrons from both coasts to knock out anything in the air, and we've secured all airports. Nothing should be up but our planes. All of our satellites and interceptor missiles are on full alert and are being monitored twenty-four-seven. All military installations have upgraded to Threat Con Delta."

The President nodded. He knew that everything that could be done at this point was being done. "Good. I want to shoot down any threat against the people of the United States. We will defend ourselves against *any* and *all* dangers!"

"I hope you're right, Mr. President," one of the women senators in attendance interjected. "I truly hope you're right."

52

USS Sheboygan

Boats and Jake opened a hatch to a fan room on the second deck and closed it behind them.

"I don't think this is such a good idea," Boats said. "If what you said is right about the other missiles, then we should be down there trying to stop them."

Jake looked down through a vent screen to the well deck. "Maybe you're right, but I know where the breakers are that supply power to the launcher. I've got to get to them and shut them down. It's our only real chance."

Boats shrugged. "Then go for it. I'm sure you know where they installed the circuit boxes."

"I should. I had them moved off the bulkhead in the well deck."

"Do you think anyone is around there?"

"I don't know," Jake answered, wishing that he did, "but even if they are, they wouldn't know where to look."

Boats nodded. "Okay then, but be careful."

"Don't worry. I know my way around this ship like the back of my hand."

"I'm sure you do, but we can't get overconfident," Boats cautioned. "I'll go get Gunny, and we'll head up to the bridge."

Jake nodded and exited the fan room, on a mission to shut down the launch breakers. He followed the shadows around the deck gear on the tween decks. Though the light was limited, he managed to find the control panel and pull the lever down, shutting off the circuit. He jumped when he realized he wasn't alone.

"I thought you might show up here," Liz said, slipping out from behind a metal stanchion and pointing her automatic pistol at the port engineer's head. "Actually, it was rewired in the shipyard so that it's live all the time, just in case. It's time the great Satan went to his knees. Now put your hands behind your back. Slowly. I don't want to have to put a bullet in your back, but then I wouldn't have to walk you up to the wardroom. Abdullah wouldn't care."

Just then two more terrorists arrived, escorting Deek.

"Here's one more for you," one of the terrorists said to Liz.

"Take the black one to the bridge," she ordered.

⌇

From the shadows the bosun couldn't believe it when he saw Liz leading Deek and Jake along, their hands behind their back. At his vantage point he could see three other terrorists starting up the missile system. He loved his country and was ready to die for it, but would his death be meaningful if he charged out, hoping he could dodge their bullets and disable the three terrorists? He knew better. The odds were greatly against him. Then he remembered something Jake had told him years ago, something about seeking the Lord with all your heart and not leaning on your own understanding. He wasn't sure he understood how to do that, but he knew he had to do something, and right now Jake's advice was all he had.

The bosun looked up to heaven and whispered, "Lord, you know I haven't served you. I've used your name in vain most of my life. I've chased women, drunk too much, and lived my life for myself. I know Jake says you help fools and drunks. Well, I'm both. If there's a way you can use me to stop this missile strike, I'm willing to make big changes in my life. I'm afraid a lot of innocent people are going to die if one of those birds takes off. Please, show me what to do."

Boats stood there and looked toward the missile. The panel was being energized, and the indicator lights on the control circuit brightened up. The three terrorists didn't have a problem with the ignition sequence. They inserted keys into the control circuits, and more lights on the panel went from red to green. Then he watched, as Liz climbed the stairway to heaven to the bridge. An idea popped into Boat's mind.

53

The bridge of the USS Sheboygan

Proudly Liz led her latest conquests, the captured port engineer and the gunnery sergeant, up to the bridge of the ship, expecting to be praised. "Abdullah, I've captured the rats that have been causing all our problems."

"Why didn't you just shoot them and throw their bodies overboard?" Abdullah asked. Then he turned around and looked at Deek and laughed. "You see how Allah delivers my enemies. So what do you think now? Are you man enough to fight me?" he asked as he punched the defenseless Marine in the stomach. Then he chopped him hard on the neck, and Deek's knees buckled and he fell to the deck.

"That's right. Bow to Allah. I can't wait till we're finished with the launch because I'm going to enjoy shooting you."

"We might need him later in case the ship has a problem when we begin to go into the harbor," Liz said.

Abdullah frowned. "Always thinking. Do you think Abdullah can't think for himself? Do you think you are the only one with a brain? I can't wait for this to be over, so I don't have to listen to your arrogant voice telling me some new idea. You may have fooled Khalif, but you haven't fooled me."

Liz swallowed the retort that yearned to be released, as wisdom and control prevailed. "Abdullah, you're the leader. I just thought you would be happy to know that we're ready for the attack."

"Of course we're ready for the attack! We're close enough to San Diego to fire the missiles. Is the system ready to go?"

"Yes. The others are powering it up."

"Dad, you're a fool. Everything you've taught me is wrong. The militant Muslim faith teaches violence. It's false. There isn't any love in it. It's all about rules and laws."

Liz cringed. Jim's tirade was certainly not going to help his father's already bad mood, and she didn't want to be the brunt of Abdullah's anger.

"What are you talking about?" Abdullah exploded, turning on his son. "It's our divine right to take over the world and subject all peoples to Islam, or they will die!"

"There's a better way."

"A better way? Hah! All my life I've been following the way of Mohammad, and now you tell me there's a better way. The great Satan has corrupted you. You're no longer my son, and that woman you love is nothing but a cheap French prostitute."

Elizabeth turned her head and glared at Abdullah.

"You say that about every woman," Jim countered, his reddening face revealing his feelings.

"If your mother knew you were in love with a whore, she would disown you," Abdullah spat.

"Mom would never disown me, and she told me she thinks Elena is very special."

"She's a dog. All women are nothing more than dogs!" Abdullah growled, "They are to be used for man's pleasure."

Liz's eyes locked onto Abdullah, but he didn't seem to notice her.

"So that's what you think of Mom?"

Enraged, Abdullah reached out and struck Jim, knocking him to the floor. His eyes widened as he looked at him. "Don't you ever talk like that about her! She's your mother."

"You're nothing but a degenerate fool. That woman over there," he said, nodding in acknowledgment of Elena, who sat crouched on the floor in the corner, "is ten times smarter than you. That's why they sent her out here—to keep an eye on you and make sure you don't screw up!"

Abdullah's face contorted in rage, and he lifted his hand to strike his son again, but stopped. His voice was cold and low, but it rose in volume as he spoke. "This is the nation that has helped the Jews survive in our land. America is filled with corruption, greed, drunkenness, drugs, and pornography. It's ripe for harvest, and Allah will have his way. It all begins today!"

"You've been brainwashed, Dad," Jim insisted, looking up at the man who had sired him. "There's another side to America, a very great side, one that isn't taught in the camps. America has extended its hands to the poor around the world. When have the Muslim countries ever done that?"

"America is an imperialistic country that helps others so they can get a foothold and then expose them to their capitalistic way of life. That life leads to enslavement. Look how they allow their women to run free, unchained. Women have little purpose except to breed and take care of the litters."

Liz's eyes opened wide, as Abdullah's words, though familiar, now hit home for the first time.

Jim got to his knees and began to get up when Abdullah slammed his knee under Jim's chin. He fell back down, groaning, then tried again to struggle to his feet, as Elena fought against her captors, finally breaking free and rushing to Jim's side.

"Have you told your son how you forced yourself upon me when I was sixteen?" Elena spat out.

"Silence, whore!" Abdullah roared. "You provoked me by your unholy dress. In my country you would have been killed. You and your sister need to be punished!"

"What difference does it make?" Elena asked. "We're all dead on this ship anyway. After you fire the missiles, America will retaliate."

"Enough! It's time your mouth is shut," Abdullah shouted, as he lifted his gun, smiled, and fired straight at her. Jim obviously saw it coming and jumped in front of the gun just as it fired. The bullet found its mark, and he crumpled to the deck.

Liz was too shocked to speak, as she watched Abdullah's reaction. With only the slightest acknowledgement of regret, he ordered one of the terrorists, "Shoot them all after we fire the missile."

With tears streaming down her face, she cradled Jim's head in her arms and cried, "Jim! Jim, can you hear me?" To her relief, his eyes fluttered.

"Why did you do it?" Elena sobbed.

"Because I love you," he whispered as his eyes blinked shut.

"Oh, Jim," she wailed, clutching his head to her chest. "Please, please don't die!"

54

04 Level, USS Sheboygan

Boats heard the gunshot and knew another of the crew had been shot. He had to get to the Combat Information Center. It was his only chance to stop the missile launch. He went into the deckhouse and ducked behind the blackout curtains to see if someone was coming.

Peering through a narrow slit in the black-out curtains, he saw Abdullah with Liz, walking down the passageway toward him. His blood boiled at the opportunity to face Abdullah again, but he knew facing him now wouldn't stop the missile launch, as they had already started the launch sequence. Checking his emotions, he quickly and noiselessly ducked back outside. He had no place to hide.

"Oh, Lord, if you're there, please help me save this ship," Boats prayed again. He looked all around but couldn't find a place to escape, other than jumping over the side. If he didn't take that chance, he was either going to be captured or shot when they saw him, and he couldn't allow that. He heard the footsteps coming down the passageway, and he knew he had to do something before the hatch opened, so he jumped over the life rail.

Grabbing the lowest round steel life rail before the deck coaming, he gritted his teeth and held on, as the watertight hatch opened.

"Are we ready to bring destruction to America?" he heard Abdullah ask.

"Yes," Liz replied. "We're just waiting for you to push the launch button."

Boats hung onto the lower life rail, as his body dangled over the side of the ship. His arms and shoulders slowly became inflamed with an unquenchable, internal fire.

"It will give me great pleasure to send these Americans to their graves," Abdullah gloated. "I just wish I could see the destruction when the warheads hit. Allah will be victorious!"

"The destruction will be great. Many will be killed, especially within a one-mile radius."

"It will be as Allah wills," Abdullah said solemnly.

Boats fumed at the verbal exchange, as he continued to hang on. But slowly he was losing his grip. The burning pain in his joints became more intense. He didn't know how much longer he could take it, but he couldn't give up. His training at the Lion's Lair had taught him to deal with pain, but that discipline might not be enough. Silently he again prayed to God for help.

"The Light of Allah will be most pleased with our victory."

"Yes, Abdullah. It will be another great victory, like the World Trade Center. The world will see they have no choice but to bow down to Allah or be killed. It is their choice to make."

Boats couldn't believe they were having a philosophical discussion about the fate of America while he hung from the railing. At least he hadn't been spotted. Finally they headed toward the ladder leading to the landing below, but then stopped.

Oh my God, thought Boats, I can't hold on much longer. If they don't move soon I'm going to lose my grip and drop to the ocean.

The pain intensified, but with a new burst of determination, he continued to hold on. Their backs faced him, so Boats decided to take a chance. He lifted one leg up and grabbed the edge of the deck coaming with his boot, bringing instant relief to his arms and shoulders. If they turned around, he'd be history.

At that very moment Liz turned and stared directly at him, her pistol at her side. They locked eyes, and he knew he was finished. He waited for the thunderclap of an exploding cartridge.

But she didn't fire. Astounded, Boats froze in place, feeling her gaze on him. Then, ever so slightly, she smiled.

Boats wondered if Liz was enjoying this, waiting for Abdullah to notice him and put a bullet in his defenseless body. Then she turned around and blocked any chance of Abdullah seeing the bosun. "Are you ready?"

"Yes. It's time," he replied, and they headed down the next three flights of steps to the boat deck.

Boats pulled the rest of his body over the coaming and lay there, breathing deeply and regaining his strength. He couldn't believe that Liz had spared him! Wasn't she one of them? Hadn't she captured Jake and Deek? Circulation gradually returned to his shoulders, arms, and fingers. He got up and bolted through the watertight door to CIC. If he could activate the remote-operated twenty-five millimeter deck gun and override the stops, he might have a chance to back the terrorists away from the missile controls. It wasn't much of a chance, but it was the only one he had.

Boats turned the knob to CIC, but it was locked. He looked at the screen above the door, spotted a fire extinguisher, and then grabbed it off the bulkhead and threw it with all his might at the metal vent. It bounced back, echoing down the passageway, but the metal didn't bend. Again he threw the steel bottle at the screen, but with little effect. He knew he had to hurry because someone would be coming from the bridge to investigate the banging noise. Valuable seconds were slipping away. The countdown to the destruction of American cities had begun. He had to get to the controls of the gun.

"Lord, help me," he prayed again, and then saw a slight crack in the door jam. Light spilled into the passageway. He looked around at the bulkheads and remembered a strip of metal exposed from the unfinished head renovation on that level. He ran to it, reached up, and ripped the metal off the overhead.

The bosun then rushed back to CIC and jammed the flat bar between the lock and the door jam. Then, with all his might, he threw the extinguisher at the door lock, and the door popped open. He hurried inside, looked around, and spotted the controls to the gun. He'd operated the old gun from the deck station, but this weapon was remote-operated and computer-controlled. He'd never fired it, but he remembered that the weapons officer had tested the gun. Since there was more testing to be done, the weapon was already loaded.

He hit the power button on the keyboard, bringing up a menu that required a password. Boats had no idea what the password could be, so he typed *Sheboygan* into the space, but it was rejected. Then he typed the captain's name, but that didn't work either. He knew he had just one more chance before he locked up the computer, so he sat for a moment. Twenty years ago he had taken a course in Fortran, but he couldn't remember a single thing from it.

A yellow sticky tacked on the side of the keyboard caught his eyes. "As Jake would say, praise the Lord!" He grabbed the yellow sticky and looked at the word *jackhammer.* Quickly he typed it in, and the screen came to life, but then went blank.

"What now?" he exclaimed, looking at the black screen and punching buttons on the keyboard, but nothing happened.

Then he saw faint movement on the screen. He looked again, and something splashed in the screen. He pushed the directional arrows keys on the keypad and the screen became lighter and lighter. The gun bore and camera were moving, and he pushed the directional arrow again. Finally he could see the boat deck and inside the well deck. Abdullah and Liz were in the control booth. He looked again at the screen and saw them pushing buttons. A command came up on Boats' screen: "Target Lock. Fire when ready."

Great, he thought. How do I make that happen?

Another command came on the screen: "Select firing mode." A box dropped down, offering the choice of rapid fire or single shot. Boats pushed rapid fire, and another box dropped down and said, "Ready to fire."

"Take your hands off the controls!" a voice commanded him from behind.

Boats couldn't believe they'd come so soon.

"Turn around very slowly and don't try anything," the tech rep from the unmanned boat said.

Boats wished he had a gun but spotted the steel flat bar on the desk.

"I didn't think you were in on this too."

"Shut your mouth and get over here."

Boats lunged for the flat bar and threw it as the gun went off. The bullet hit the steel as he lunged for the terrorist, grabbing the weapon and pointing it at his enemy. A shot fired and the man slumped to the deck with his eyes open, unblinking. Blood dripped from under his chin. Boats grabbed the weapon and ran back to the computer.

He refocused on his screen when he heard the unmistakable roar of rocket engines firing up. He'd run out of time! The missile was lifting off, but he didn't know how to fire the gun. Then, out of the corner of his eye, he saw a button to his right that said "manual fire control override." He pushed the button, and the twenty-five millimeter spat out a burst of thirty rounds.

In the screen he watched as Abdullah, Liz, and the rest of the terrorists ducked down in the control room. He hadn't hit anyone because the gun was pointed to the deck just above. Boats watched in horror, as flames started spewing out from the underside of the rocket. He adjusted the gun one more time and pushed the manual firing button.

Swoosh! The first missile departed the pad, with bullets flying in the air, heading for an American city.

55

Oval Office, the White House

The President's line buzzed and he punched the button. "Yes, Kate?"

"Sir, the director of National Intelligence, the CNO, and the Commandant of the Marines need to see you immediately."

"Send them in," the President said, anxious to hear what they had to say. The door opened and the two men walked in, stopping in front of his desk.

He nodded in greeting and then asked, "What brings you two here?"

"Some very strange news," Stevens replied.

"Really? What is it?"

"It seems a ship off the coast of California has just fired a Tomahawk at the United States. We thought the ship was drifting around, their electronics knocked out by the EMP bomb."

The Commander-in-Chief eyed the admiral. "Do you have radio contact with them?"

"No, Sir, but we sent out a signal identifier, much like airplanes, but it responded with an international maritime organizational number.

"Get to the point, Admiral."

"The ship is transmitting a signal that would identify it as a Chinese Naval Warship, but that doesn't make any sense. We'd have seen a Chinese warship coming to our coast from a long way out."

"So what do you suppose it is?"

"We think it may be the USS Sheboygan and now we know where our ten missing nuclear Tomahawks are…or were. The Sheboygan was out at sea when the EMP bomb hit San Diego. It was test-firing the first missile installation on an amphibious ship earlier this week, as planned and with great accuracy, using dummy cruise missiles," the CNO explained.

"We picked up a satellite image of another launch about fifteen minutes ago," Stevens added.

The President's heart felt as if it had stopped. "So you're telling me that nuclear warheads are heading for the American coast?"

"No, Sir. For some reason the Tomahawk crash-landed in the ocean without detonating. This could be the threat the Light of Allah has been using against us if we didn't free the prisoners at Guantanamo Bay."

"Why do you suspect more missiles on the Sheboygan?"

"Because they were officially fitted out with two dummy missiles from Seal Beach Weapons Station. A third firing wasn't planned because the records show they only took two missiles, but our satellite imagery tells us differently. Fortunately the missile never made it to the stratosphere but landed in the ocean intact."

"Last I checked, Admiral," the President said, "the Sheboygan's our ship."

"Yes, Sir. But maybe the ship has been taken over by terrorists."

"A U.S. Navy ship pirated off the coast of California! That's impossible."

"A member of the crew was married to the niece of the man in the morgue."

"And your point, Admiral?"

"One hundred thousand dollars was transferred to his account two weeks ago."

"Who was this man?"

"He's the ship's bosun and would have been in charge of the loading of the missiles at Seal Beach Naval Weapons Station."

"This isn't looking good. Have you tried to contact the ship?"

"Yes, Sir, but no one is responding."

"We have to take the ship out," Director Stevens said.

The CNO glared at Stevens. "And what about our sailors?"

"Sir, we can't take a chance. Do you know how many people will die if they successfully launch the next missile?" Stevens countered looking intently at the President.

"I need more information before I order an air strike on a Naval asset. I remember when that happened to me in Vietnam."

"Mr. President, we took these photographs of the ship and had them enlarged," Stevens added, pulling out a set of photographs from his briefcase and laying them out on the desk. "As you can see, no one is topside except these men. They're armed with AK-47's and don't look anything like our sailors."

"So where's the crew?"

"We don't know, but if they launched one missile, they'll try again with the others."

The President paused, a feeling of dread gripping his stomach. "Can't we track the missile and knock it out of the sky?"

"We can try, Mr. President, but the terrorists have been one step ahead of us every time."

There was no more time to waste. The President knew he had to act immediately. "Gentlemen, scramble our fighters and take the Sheboygan out."

"You can't do that, Mr. President," the admiral pleaded. "There's over three hundred sailors on that ship."

"And one Marine," the General stated.

"You're wrong. I *can* do that, and I don't see that I have any other choice. What do you want me to do? Jeopardize the lives of over fifty million people?"

"Mr. President, at least let us do a flyover before we sink her."

The President took a deep breath and nodded. "All right. You'd better make it quick, Admiral. I can't afford to have any cities destroyed. They've already fired one missile."

56
CIC, USS Sheboygan

The bosun saw movement in the screen and knew the terrorists would be coming to take him out, so he aimed the gun to starboard and fired again. Hot lead skipped across the steel deck and scattered them. They wouldn't be coming up that side of the ship with a gun boring down on them. The heavy slugs tore up the steel on the portside of the deckhouse.

Boats held his breath and waited. It seemed like an eternity, but soon he spotted four men climbing the ladder on the port side of the ship. He waited another long moment before training the gun and firing. Twenty-five millimeter slugs tore up the ladder, as the terrorists and lead went flying.

The bosun continued firing until there was no more movement. Then he moved the gun and scanned the area, looking for anyone else. They had gone inside the skin of the ship. He knew he had to be mobile, so he headed to Deek's room to get another weapon. The gunny always kept his side arm nearby. The door was unlocked, so Boats rushed in and looked around. He was a terrible shot with a pistol, but he had no choice. He opened the fold-down desktop, and a set of keys fell to the deck. Boats snatched them up and opened the small safe inside the desk. Then he grabbed the forty-four with five magazines and ran out of the room. He looked into the night before going out on deck, seeing no one, he ran up the ladder to the bridge.

Boats spotted two men with automatic weapons, standing on the aft edge of the bridge deck near the ladders. He picked up a shackle and threw it two decks below on the other side of the vessel. The terrorists opened fire. He made good use of the diversion to cut the distance between them and then emptied the clip, dropping them both before picking up their AK-47's.

Suddenly he heard Abdullah's voice over the loudspeaker, warning whoever was trying to retake the ship that the crew members would be shot, one by one, until the culprit surrendered.

"I don't think so," Boats said, firing the heavy pistol through the open bridge hatch where he knew one of Abdullah's men would be standing, then rushing through to check out the damage.

One terrorist lay motionless on the deck, a red swell of blood pooling around him. Laughter pierced the night.

"I thought I killed you in the boat," Abdullah said, grabbing Liz's gun and raising it to Captain Davey's head, "but you've come back to life. Now drop your gun, or I kill your captain!"

"Shoot him, Boats," Davey shouted. "That's an order!"

Boats looked at his CO, paused a moment, and then dropped his weapon.

Abdullah laughed again. "It's time for you to die! I should have killed you in the parking lot when we first met, but this is so much better. I will enjoy watching you squirm in pain as you die. I will shoot you in one arm to start, then a leg, and while you're suffering, you can watch me shoot your Captain. Oh, you're going to die, but real, real slow. Praise be to Allah! He has favored me this night to see my enemies die before my eyes. You two go get the African and bring the camera."

The two remaining terrorists exited the bridge, leaving Liz and Abdullah.

Abdullah slowly turned the pistol to the bosun. He took careful aim at his leg, and eased the hammer back, enjoying the moment to the fullest.

Boats' eyes darted about, seeking a way of escape. He wasn't close enough to get to Abdullah, and he couldn't protect his captain, but then he noticed Liz. Already her hand was coming down, and it slammed into Abdullah's fist. Her blow wasn't hard enough, as the gun went off, tearing up the stratica synthetic bridge deck covering. Amused, Abdullah turned and looked at her.

"I've been waiting to kill you for a long time," he said, raising the gun and pointing it at her. Before he could fire, Boats rushed forward and front-kicked Abdullah's chest.

He was late! The slug tore into flesh, and Liz fell to the deck. Boats crashed into Abdullah. The force of his attack knocked the gun to the floor, and they immediately began punching each other. Then they locked their hands around each other's neck, but Abdullah was stronger, and he began to squeeze the life out of Boats. The beginning of a starburst filled the bosun's brain, and he frantically hooked a leg around Abdullah and rolled him over, bouncing the other man's head off the deck. Abdullah's grip loosened.

With all his might Boats punched Abdullah in the nose, and blood splattered everywhere. The big man winced but punched back, and both men jumped to their feet. Each looked at the pistol that lay between them. Liz groaned in the corner, and that was all Boats needed to spike his adrenalin. He threw a powerful uppercut at the big man's chin, and Abdullah's head snapped back and he dropped his arms, as Boats hammered three quick blows to his kidneys. Then he head-butted Abdullah, and the big man fell to the deck right next to the gun.

Relaxing for just a moment, Boats quickly realized his mistake, as Abdullah grabbed the gun and laughed. "Now do you see Allah's will? You have been a worthy opponent, and I will give you the opportunity to accept Allah as your god."

Liz groaned again.

"Finally," Abdullah said. "The other whore is dying. Now make your decision! Did you really think you had the strength and power to beat me?"

Boats stood still, defiant—unafraid of death.

"Oh, you Americans are such pompous fools," Abdullah laughed, pulling back the hammer of the pistol. "Allah will reign supreme over this whole earth, and you and all the Jews will worship him or die!"

"Not on my ship!" the captain roared as he rose up and tore the mounting bracket of the chair from the deck. Still bound to it, he charged Abdullah like a wild bull, body-slamming him into the knife-edge of the metal hatch coaming, before he could fire the gun.

Amazed at the captain's strength, Bosun quickly grabbed the gun, as Abdullah slumped to the deck, his head bowed.

"I think he's dead, Captain."

"Don't be too sure. Check him out."

Boats slowly walked over to him, the gun ready to fire, but Abdullah hadn't moved. The ship took a roll and Abdullah's head lolled to one side before he fell to the deck on his face, his back covered in blood.

"I've got to get Doc. Maybe we can save Liz."

"Don't move, Boats. I hear others approaching with Deek," the captain ordered as he put his chair back in its position with him still bound to it. "Get down, Bosun!"

57

Oval Office, the White House

"Mr. President, Black Ice Ops has a location in the Sudan," Stevens announced, as he entered the Oval Office.

The President smiled. At last, some good news. "Great work, William. Give the coordinates to the Joint Chiefs, and execute an air strike immediately. What about your men in Sudan?"

"They'll move out quickly once we call in the strike."

"Before we lose the Light of Allah, let's extinguish him."

"Yes, Sir. The carrier battle group in position has already launched their fighters."

"Good. Execute Operation Lightning Strike."

"Yes, Mr. President."

"And on your way out, ask Kate to bring the Joint Chiefs in as soon as they arrive."

"Yes, Sir," William said, as he went out the door, but then leaned back in. "Sir, they're here, standing by, waiting for you."

"Excellent! Bring them in." The President picked up the phone and buzzed his secretary. "Kate, hold all calls unless it's my wife or children."

The military men entered the office as the President waited to speak.

"Earlier this week the USS Sheboygan successfully test-fired two dummy cruise missiles at an island off the California coast. Since that time we thought the ship was out of commission due to the EMP bomb. Hours ago, they fired another missile. From the satellite pictures it looks like it was one of the missing nuclear Tomahawks. Somehow it got off course and crash-landed in the Pacific. We discovered that the bosun on the ship may have been compromised and is helping the terrorists. Regrettably I must order an airstrike of the Sheboygan, even though we suspect our sailors and a few Marines are still on board. The ship hasn't responded to our communications, and we've seen satellite pictures that indicate the ship has been taken over by terrorists."

"That's impossible," the admiral exclaimed. "How can an American warship be pirated off our coast?"

"I don't know," the President admitted, shaking his head. "We'll have a full investigation once this crisis is averted. I've got to believe they're going to fire the next Tomahawk very soon, and I can't allow that."

"So you would sacrifice the lives of the sailors on my ship?" Admiral Stockton asked.

"Do I have a choice, Admiral? William, is another satellite in place?"

"No, Sir. We won't have another in position for an hour."

The President paused and then shook his head. "I can't take that chance. Admiral, have your birds seen anything?"

"Sir, I should hear something any moment now."

"Then unless I hear differently, my orders are to destroy the Sheboygan before it destroys an American city."

A Navy captain with a gold braid around his shoulder, indicating that he was an aide, knocked on the door. Admiral Stockton nodded to him, and he walked into the room and handed him a slip of paper. The Admiral read the paper and then raised his eyes to meet the President's. "Sir, our jets flew over and confirmed there was gunfire on the deck of Sheboygan. They also saw another small boat alongside the ship. I believe Sheboygan is fighting back."

"Will that guarantee the last missile won't be fired?"

"No, Sir," the admiral admitted, "but I have a suggestion."

"What is it?"

"We have a platoon from Seal Team Six ready for deployment. We could send them out by helicopter, fast-rope to the deck, and take back Sheboygan. Now that we know where the missiles might be, we could scramble more jets in the air, just in case there's another missile launch."

"Very well. How long till they're on the deck of Sheboygan?"

"One hour, Sir."

"I hope to God you're right, Admiral. If the other missiles are launched we're in trouble."

"Mr. President, I've got two Marine helicopters warming up on the deck in Camp Pendleton. With your permission, I want to send my team in with the Seals to bring my man back," the Marine general added.

"You know this man of yours?"

"I do, Sir. Five years ago he won the unofficial Marine Corps MCMAP championship. If anyone's alive, it's him. I don't want to leave any of my men behind without trying to get them."

The President knew what the general was up to. He could smell the smoke from the bombing run thirty years ago as he was lying in a rice paddy. He remembered being left behind as American jets ripped through the air and dropped their incendiary bombs. "All right, General, but the Seals have the lead."

"Wouldn't have it any other way, Sir. We'll pick them up in twenty minutes and head out to Sheboygan."

The President locked eyes with the general. "Semper Fi, Commandant."

The stocky general of the Marine Corps crisply snapped to attention, saluted the Commander-in-Chief, and left the room.

"Sir, I'll keep you up to date on all the events," the CNO said.

"Very well. Now I've got to go to a news brief." The President nodded in dismissal, then got up and walked out of his office.

⌐

Stevens watched his President leave, and then leaned over and whispered to the admiral, "I hope they get out there in a hurry."

"Do you think they'll fire the remaining missiles?"

"It's not that. Satellite photos show a fogbank with mist moving toward Sheboygan, and if it gets there before they do, that ship won't be easy to find."

"Don't worry. We'll use radar to locate it. It'll be like landing at night."

58

San Diego Harbor

Seal Team Six, reassigned to Developmental Group, had actually been formed to fight terrorists and were actively bolstering harbor security in San Diego. They had been getting ready to deploy to Iraq when San Diego was hit with the blackout. When the Marine Corps helicopters landed in Coronado they quickly loaded the two choppers with flash-bang grenades and Heckler and Koch nine millimeter MP-5's with silencers. Then a fire team of four Seals boarded the lead Marine helicopter, and they were off at over 200 miles an hour in search of the USS Sheboygan.

Using constant radio comms with the base, they got ready for the fast-rope assault of Sheboygan. After twenty minutes air time, the helos spotted the ship in their radar and went into silent mode. The last thing the strike team wanted to do was to give up their element of surprise. The helos slowed as they approached Sheboygan, hoping not to overshoot it in the fog. Using thermal imaging they spotted the ship's engine stacks one thousand yards away. AK-47's were punctuating the night, and they could see a force of four men, firing from the bridge deck.

"Alpha One, this is Blue Leader. I see the tangos, and they're on the boat deck, firing at the bridge. This ship is trying to defend itself," Commander Becker, OIC of the Seal team said into his mic. "Do they know we're coming?"

"Blue Leader, I don't think so. We haven't had comms with the ship since the EMP bomb went off two days ago. Do you think you can stop them from firing any missiles?" Major Westphal asked.

Becker looked through the infrared night vision and knew their assault would come under heavy fire, but there was no other way. Their only hope was that the ship's force was smart enough not to fire on them, as they fast-roped down from the helos. Even then it would be very risky, especially if the terrorists turned around while they were embarking to the flight deck.

"Alpha One, I see the missile launch pad, and it looks like they're getting ready to fire. We don't have a choice. Use a fast-angle deployment."

"Roger that, Blue Leader. Securing the Tomahawks is the most important objective. If they're fired, American cities will be nuked."

"I read you, Alpha One. Missile security is top priority." Becker gave the signal to the pilot to take them in. "Red Leader, this is Blue Leader. We're going in. If we take heavy fire on approach, strafe their main deck. The bridge appears to be held by ship's force."

"Blue Leader, I copy that. We'll deploy right after you, unless you're taking rounds. If we have to we'll strafe the ship to give you cover."

"Roger that, Red Leader. Let's go!"

The helicopters accelerated but were still very quiet. They burst through the fog and were upon Sheboygan before the terrorists had a chance to react. Gunfire erupted from the boat deck.

"Red Leader, begin strafing run. We're going in. The tangos are in the truck tunnel and around the crane and lifeboat davit. We'll do an angle approach and drop down. Do you copy?"

"Roger that, Blue Leader. Beginning strafing run."

"Go, go, go," Commander Becker ordered to his men, as his helicopter swooped down and toward the flight deck of the Sheboygan.

Red Leader's helicopter flew right over them, missing their blades by a few feet but giving them the cover they needed for their rapid assault. Becker was the first out of the helicopter and slid down the rope to the deck below. Bullets whistled by him as he hit the deck and rolled to his right, trying to get his bearings. Immediately he began returning fire, as three other Seals slipped down the rope and the helicopter banked to the left. Becker turned around to see if his men were okay. Just as he did, one of them caught a slug in the forehead and dropped to the deck. The other two rolled into firing positions flush with the deck, fired their weapons, and quickly ran to the side of the flight deck. They dropped to the ladders on both sides, taking up new firing positions behind some heavy steel.

"Red Leader, we're in position," Becker radioed. "In thirty seconds make your approach and drop. We'll provide cover for you, but this LZ is hot as hell itself. One of my men is down, so drop quickly."

"Roger that, Blue Leader. We'll be dropping in twenty seconds."

The second helo approached the ship, and the first one took off on a strafing run. With machine guns blazing the helicopter with the Red Team made its rapid-angle approach to Sheboygan.

"Abort, abort," Blue Team Leader screamed into his mic, as he saw a handheld RPG shouldered. The second team fast-roped to the deck as the pilot waited, hoping to get out, but it was too late. The first helicopter blew up in a mass of flames and plummeted to the ocean as the second team hit the flight deck. The explosion back-lit the Marines, but somehow they dodged bullets and scurried forward taking a position behind the port crane.

Becker motioned to his other two men to advance forward, but they were pinned under heavy gunfire.

59

The bridge of USS Sheboygan

"Elena, stay with Jim and your sister," Captain Davey said, as he returned to the bridge.

"Is Liz going to make it?"

The captain wished he could be more encouraging. Elena might have been working for the enemy, but Liz was still her sister. "I don't know," he admitted. "We've got to get down to the mess decks and get the doc. She doesn't look good. A gunshot to the stomach isn't easy to survive."

When the helicopter exploded, the captain turned to his bosun. "What's going on now?"

"I think reinforcements have arrived. I'll go out on deck and take a look," Boats replied, heading outside just minutes before automatic weapons sprayed the superstructure. Then a grenade went off. The bosun came running back into the pilot house, this time with Deek in tow and carrying a couple of guns.

"Captain, two squads of men dropped from the helicopters before they hit one of the choppers. I also saw a small boat along-side," Deek said, throwing him an M-16.

"What about the missiles?"

"I don't know, but there's a firefight on the boat deck," Deek answered.

"Let's give them some support and get to the mess decks."

"Roger that, Captain," Deek said as they ran aft on the 05 level and opened fire on the terrorists.

Bosun Browder looked down at the firefight and knew what had to be done. "I'm going back to the bridge wing to get the M-240 from its mount."

"Can you handle that thing? It's got some serious kick," Deek said as he and the captain ducked down while bullets whizzed through the air above their heads.

"Don't you worry. My strength is in my legs," Boats answered, then ran forward to get the heavy machine gun. Most men couldn't fire the gun accurately unless it was in its stand, but he was strong and in great shape.

"What now, Rambo?" Davey asked when Boats returned, proud of his bosun for taking the initiative.

"Got no choice, Sir. Whoever came aboard those helos is pinned down. I've got to go one deck lower and lay some cover fire down in hopes of distracting them. I saw a bunch of terrorists go down to the missile control room."

"Roger that; we'll cover you," Davey said. "Go!"

Boats dropped down to the next deck as they opened fire. Bullets flew all around them, but Boats made it to the edge of the 04 level and opened fire. The big gun blasted the terrorists off the boat deck.

ᔕ

Commander Becker watched, as the hail of gunfire from the bridge deck ripped through the night. "Go, go, go!" he yelled into his mic, and the two Seals from the other side of the ship ran forward and joined the Marines at the base of the crane. With silencers on their weapons they began to pick off the terrorists who were trying to shoot whoever held the M-240 machine gun. Suddenly the gunfire stopped, and Becker, checking the area for more tangos, hoped the brave soul with M-240 hadn't bought it.

One of his men on the other side of the ship fired his weapon, and Becker saw two tangos in the shadows of the trunk tunnel. He quickly fired his weapon and pointed for the Marines to advance forward. Deadly silence stilled the night on Sheboygan. Four terrorists lay unmoving on the steel decks, and Becker quickly checked to see if any of them were still breathing. Then he looked down at the missile launch station and saw someone pushing buttons.

Staring death in the eyes Becker led the Seals and Marines as they ran into the dark truck tunnel to the ramp that led to the welldeck. It was so dark he couldn't see ten feet in front of him, but he kept running, hoping he wouldn't get shot. He had memorized the layout of the ship from the drawings that were sent to him while they were flying out to Sheboygan.

Two more terrorists were outside the control booth, and they shot at him as soon as they saw him. Knocked down hard but thankful the body armor had done its job, Becker rolled to his stomach and emptied the clip of his Sig Sauer. Ejecting the empty clip, he slammed another one home as the other two Seals ran forward to the control booth. They crashed the door down, and Commander Becker followed them into the room. One man with his back to them was trying to fire the missile.

"Back away from the controls! Now!" Becker shouted.

Haviv turned around but kept his hands at his waist.

Becker didn't relax a moment. Focused, he waited for Haviv to make a move.

"It's too late anyway. Look," Haviv said, pointing to the missile. It was in the final launch sequence, and Becker knew that all Haviv needed was a second to push the second confirmation button on the computer.

Becker kept his eyes riveted on Haviv, and when the terrorist reached for the computer, Becker double-tapped him in the forehead with his Sig.

Haviv fell to the deck, and Becker looked at the control panel and saw that it was paused, awaiting confirmation.

Just then Boats approached the missile control. "I'm Bosun Browder, ship's bosun," he announced. "Who are you?"

"We're Seal Team Six. Where's the rest of the crew?"

"The mess decks, but they're being watched by guards who won't hesitate to kill the sailors."

"We've got to move quickly. Lead the way, Bosun. We've got flash-bangs to distract them, but we'd better get going before they blow themselves with your crew up."

"You mean, *my* crew," Captain Davey said, as he hobbled in, slowed by the bullet in his thigh. "I'll lead the way to the mess decks after I disable this launch sequence."

Quickly typing on the keyboard he completed the abort command. Davey limped up the well-deck ramp and through the watertight hatch to the inside of the ship. Becker followed the big man, noticing the bloodied CO's insignia on his chest.

"Captain, let me go first. I've got body armor and flash-bangs."

"Negative, snake-eater. This is my ship and my crew. I've got both barrels loaded. I'm headed straight to the mess decks, and I'll blow a hole in the first terrorist I see. Back me up. That's an order!"

Becker shook his head in disapproval. "Sir, with all due respect, we're highly trained in this and you're injured. We've also got silencers on our weapons. Strongly request you follow our lead and keep the element of surprise."

Captain Davey hesitated for a milli-second before agreeing. "All right, snake-eater, let's go!"

Becker nodded with pride at a ship's captain who would put himself in harm's way for the sake of his crew. They raced up the ladder-way and surprised the guard on the portside passageway.

Becker blew him away with a short burst. The second Seal in line quickly threw a couple of flash-bangs into the mess deck area. The Seals and Marines turned their heads then ran in after the explosion, firing at anyone with a weapon. The crew of the Sheboygan was rescued, but the officers were still tied up in the wardroom, the next compartment forward.

60

Oval Office, the White House

In the Oval Office the President had a television on, and when it showed the destruction to San Diego, he reached over and turned it up. "This late breaking news from San Diego. Electricians from all over the country have converged on our nation's sixth largest city and are busy running wiring throughout a ten-mile radius from the point of impact. Projected time for electricity to be restored is ten days. Housing electricity will take much longer, and it could be months before residents have power restored in their homes. In an effort reminiscent of New Orleans after Katrina, volunteers are pouring in from all over the nation," the talking head said on the nightly news, just as Director Stevens walked in.

"Mr. President," he said without waiting for formalities, "the strike in Sudan went off without a hitch. Our team was airlifted out after they went through the destruction. They found the command complex one hundred feet beneath the desert floor, and it's totally destroyed."

The Chief Executive's heart leapt with this positive report. "What about the Light of Allah? Was he there?"

"We have found remains of a man that matches his description, but we can't positively ID him. His fingerprints have been lazed, so we're not sure if this was a double."

"Keep your people on the alert for him. What has the Sudanese government said about the strike?"

309

"We've encouraged them to keep quiet. None of their people were at the complex, and they have enough problems in Darfur. Besides they need some financial aid."

The President smiled. It was a relief to hear some good news for a change. "Well done, William. What about the Seals and Marines on Sheboygan?"

"They've landed, Mr. President, but I haven't heard."

"I'm giving them twenty-two more minutes, and then we've got to take that ship out. We can't afford to have one of our cities destroyed."

"Yes, Sir, Mr. President. I'll let you know as soon as I hear anything."

61

USS Sheboygan

The Marines popped the door open to the officer's wardroom, dropped to the deck, and fired on the lone guard. With the help of the CO they released the officers, who quickly vacated the wardroom to report to their stations. The Seals joined the Marines in the wardroom.

"Commander, Major, I can't thank you and your men enough for coming out and saving my crew," Davey said to them, and then added sincerely, "I'm sorry about the loss of your man."

"I am too, but we had no time to set it up any better."

The captain nodded, understanding full well the gravity of the situation and the time pressure the rescue team had been under. "We're headed back to San Diego. If you want to stay aboard, I'd be honored. We're four hours away."

"I'd be proud to come in with you, Captain. You and your men handled yourselves quite well."

"If it wasn't for your team," the captain said, knowing every word he said was true, "we would have been toast."

Becker smiled. "I'm not so sure of that, Captain. You put up a good fight."

⌐

Deek, who knew Major Westphal, made his way to the Marine rescue team. "Semper fi" was all he said.

62

Balboa Naval Hospital

Elena wheeled Jim up a couple of floors in the hospital so they could check on Liz. When they entered her room, Boats was already there, sitting beside her bed and holding her hand. From what the doctors had told her, Elena knew her sister still had a long way to go before she was out of danger.

"Oh, Lizzy," Elena whispered, leaning down to kiss Liz on the cheek. Liz smiled weakly, even nodding briefly at Jim as he steered his chair to the opposite side of the bed, across from the bosun.

"Boats," Jim said proudly, "hero of Sheboygan."

Elena grinned when she saw Boats blush.

"Hey, it wasn't just me," he groused. "The captain, Deek, Jake, the Seals and Marines were there too."

"That's not what the President said," Jim countered.

"Well, strange as this may sound, she's the real hero," Boats said, turning his attention back to Liz, as he lovingly stroked her hand. "I just can't figure out why she didn't shoot me, so I came to ask her."

"Probably because you're so cute," Deek said, as he entered the room with flowers.

"Now you know *that's* not true," Boats replied with a big smile.

Liz opened her eyes and whispered, "I couldn't shoot the man who was willing to risk his life for me in that parking lot.

Abdullah would have killed you that night if it wasn't for your friend." Then she coughed and closed her eyes.

"Easy, Lizzy," Elena said. "Everything's going to be okay now. Jim told the Director of National Intelligence what we've done. They aren't pressing charges, especially because the missile landed in the ocean."

"I can't take the credit for all that," Jim said. "Captain Davey and Deek here put in a strong word for you."

"Boats, did NCIS ever figure out who put the money in your account?"

"Nope. They investigated, but couldn't connect the money with anyone. Good thing we were at sea when the transfer occurred."

"Did they confiscate the money?"

"Nope, they couldn't prove there was a crime, but I think someone was setting me up. I've never taken a bribe, so my guess is that it was all part of the plan to discredit me and get me in trouble."

Liz opened her eyes. "Thank you, all of you." She whispered and then looked at Boats. "Elena's right, Boyd. You are cute."

Elena saw Jim's eyes widen. "Boyd? Is that your first name?"

"Yes, Sir, it is," the bosun admitted. "But don't you ever call me that!"

"No problem, Boats."

A couple hours later Boats left the hospital and walked across the street. Before he got into his car he slowly looked up to the clouds and said, "I'll see you this Sunday morning bright and early."

Glossary

1 MC: The public address system on a ship.

Accommodation Ladder: A portable set of retractable steps on a ship's side for the accommodation of people boarding from small boats or the pier.

Aft: Toward, aft, or near the stern.

Astern: Going towards the stern or going backwards in the water.

Automatic Buss synchronizer: An electronic control that balances the frequency of incoming generators.

AWACS: Airborne Warning and Control System. Long-range radar capable of locating other aircraft.

Ballast: Any weight or weights used to keep the ship from becoming top-heavy. Sea water is pumped into tanks to lower the ship in the water, increasing the ship's draft. Some of the largest cannons in the navy were on hospital ships and kept in the bilge for ballast.

Boat deck: A deck on which lifeboats and the captain's gig are kept.

Bosun: Primary assistant to the First Lieutenant for the running of the ship's deck department.

Bow: The forward end of the vessel. (Usually the pointed end.)

Bridge: A compartment on the bridge deck from which the ship is navigated.

Brow: A gangway that reaches the pier from the ship and is used to embark and disembark people from the ship.

Bulkhead: A vertical partition corresponding to the wall of a room.

Cleat: A fitting having two arms or horns around which ropes may be made fast welded to the deck, usually double-horned.

CHENG: Chief engineer, a department head, in charge of maintaining the machinery plant onboard the ship.

CNO: Chief Of Naval Operations, in charge of the Navy.

CIC: Combat Information Center

Coaming: A piece of raised steel on the edge of a deck, a vertical boundary for a hatch or deck.

CO: Commanding Officer, Ship's Captain.

CAC: Common Access Card used by both military and civilians to identify them.

Comms: Communications with other entities.

Connex box: Usually a twenty-foot container that has been converted for various uses.

Corpsman: A Sailor trained to handle casualties until a doctor could be obtained.

Davit: Crane arm or devise used in handling small boats or lifeboats to launch them over the side of a ship.

Deck plates: Steel plates put down in the engine room to act as flooring over the bilge.

Elephant toes: Pointed toes on the bottom of the capstan located on the forecastle.

Engine order telegraph: A devise to send signals to the engine room to order up the speed of the ship.

Executive Officer: (XO) Second in command of the ship

First: Shortened form of the title, First Lieutenant, in charge of the deck department on the ship.

Forecastle: The forward upper portion of the hull. On sailing ships it was the forward fighting section of the ship equipped with cannons.

Forecastle recovery: This is a recovery initiated from the forward deck on the bow of a ship.

Forward: Near, at, or toward, the bow of the ship.

Gangway: A ladder or staged walkway for boarding a ship.

Gapped billet: When a replacement does not show up in time and the former sailor has left the ship to report to his next duty, the billet is gapped and someone steps up to fill the vacancy until the replacement arrives.

Go-fast boats: Cigarette boats used by drug runners.

Hawser: A large line used in towing or mooring.

Heaving line: A line that is tied to a hawser and thrown to the pier or tugboat so that the hawser can be passed to the securing device.

Hull: The body of the ship.

IC men: Sailors who handle all internal communications for the ship.

J-bar davit: A small piece of round steel bent to look like an upside down J and equipped with a rope and pulley. Used to load or unload small, but heavy items in remote locations.

Joint Chiefs: The military heads of each branch of military service.

Knee knockers: A piece of vertical steel that separates compartments on the ship. It is usually 12 to 18 inches in height.

Ladder: Inclined steps, used aboard the ship in place of "stairs."

Landing Craft Air Cushioned (LCAC): Large vessels with gas turbine engines that fly across the water on a cushion of air.

Landing Ship Dock (LSD): An amphibious ship capable of carrying Marines and their vehicles for a shore landing.

Lee Helmsmen: Receives and relays engine orders from the CONN to main control.

Liberty Chit: A permission slip to go ashore for an extended period of time.

MPA: Main Propulsion Assistant, the Chief Engineer's right hand man or woman.

Maintenance Figure of Merit (MFOM): an arbitary number assigned to a job that determines its importance.

MCMAP: Marine Corps Martial Arts Program

Messman: A sailor who works in the galley and serves the officers in the wardroom.

Monkey fist: A rope intricately tied together in the shape of a ball with bolts in the middle, used by sailors to heave a tag line in mooring the ship.

Mooring lines: Heavy lines used to tie the ship up to a pier or buoy.

NCIS: Naval Criminal Investigative Service

NAVSEA: Naval Sea System Command

NMCI: Navy Marine Corps Information System

Nixie winch: Used to launch and recover a device that gives off false signals to sonar.

OPS: Operations Officer

Paralleling control module: An electronic devise used to parallel to generators by getting them to rotate at the same speed.

Photovoltaic: Cells used to convert sunlight into electricity.

Port: The left hand of the ship looking forward to the bow.

RHIB: Rigid Hull Inflatable Boat—New lifeboats that are much faster and have replaced the old whaleboats.

Sampson Post: A heavy vertical post which supports cargo booms.

SDRMC: San Diego Regional Maintenance Center

SAR: Search and Rescue—Swimmers trained to rescue people in the water.

Sheilas: What women are referred to in Australia.

SWIS: Ship Wide Intelligence System

Shipview: A new concept that uses metrics to judge performance.

Stairway to heaven: The outside metal stairway that leads from the Boat deck to the Bridge deck of an LSD.

Starboard: The right hand of a ship, looking forward to the bow.

Stern: The after or back end of a vessel.

Tangos: Enemy targets.

Williamson Turn: A type of maneuver used during a man overboard recovery, intended to maneuver the ship to its position when the man fell overboard and used for his recovery.

Peter H. Zindler has worked for the Department of Defense for the last 22 years. During that time he has spent many days at sea on various naval vessels. He is a high school wrestling coach. He has trained as an Ultimate Fighting Championship fighter and won a national championship for body building.

His science fiction novel, *Spirit Warrior,* was the 2007 San Diego Christian Writers Guild runner-up for fiction book of the year. He has authored several plays, a children's book, and a devotional book. He lives with his family in Ramona, California.

Peter is available for speaking. Contact him through his web site, www.peterhzindler.com.